MW01260225

*Even fate needs a little help...*

# THE COINCIDENCE
# MAKERS

## MERADETH HOUSTON

COINCIDENCE MAKERS

by Meradeth Houston

Copyright ©2018 Meradeth Houston

All rights reserved.

Bleeding Ink Publishing

253 Bee Caves Cove

Cibolo, TX 78108

www.bleedinginkpublishing.com

info@bleedinginkpublishing.com

Quantity sales: Special discounts are available on quantity purchases by corporations,
associations, and others. For details, contact the publisher at the address above.

Printed in the United States of America.

Paperback ISBN: 978-1-948583-02-2

Ebook ISBN: 978-1-948583-21-3

# THE COINCIDENCE
# MAKERS

*There are no coincidences.*
*I should know. I make them happen.*

# CHAPTER

# 1

The car Luke rented looked like it had been in a demolition derby. I had to hand it to the rental place—keeping the bumper on with chicken wire was some kind of sorcery.

My head hit the window and jammed my earring back into my neck as we bounced over a crater in the Mexican toll road. I rubbed my forehead, giving Luke, my work partner, a pointed look.

He didn't notice. No surprise there—he'd ignored the last three questions I'd asked. Before I thought better of it, I reached over, chose an arm hair, and plucked it out by the root.

"Hey! What was that for?" Luke rubbed his arm while his thoughts seared into my mind. One of the bonuses of our position—telepathic link. It was great for communicating while invisible, but a serious liability when it came to privacy. Unfortunately, the switch that kept my thoughts to myself shorted out like wiring chewed by a rat.

I held up my hands with a grin and slipped into the non-visible realm. The air around me shifted, like I had walked into an air-conditioned room after being outside in scorching hot weather.

"Funny. You know I can still see you," Luke said with a little tilt to his lips.

Wasn't that the truth. Luke was the only person I couldn't hide from. Of course, whether or not he wanted to find me was a whole other matter.

"What's got you wound so tight?" I asked.

Luke shook his head, dark brown hair falling into his eyes. "You can't feel it yet? The next job?"

"Already?" I laughed. "We're not even home yet."

"Me either. Normally." This time his eyes squinted. "This is going to be a big one."

That was enough to sober me up quick.

"Like, how big?" A shiver raced up my spine. I liked the little jobs. The no lots-of-lives-in-danger ones. Getting people to meet. Helping people find their way. Putting lives back in order, even if just a little. The small coincidences, at least in our line of work. The kind that ended up helping someone out in ways that even I never saw coming. I mean, who knew that making sure someone made it to work on time meant they'd get the promotion they'd been hoping for? Or that finding another person's wallet would lead to meeting the love of their life? They were easy, simple, and every once in a great while, enjoyable. They didn't have massive ramifications if we messed something up.

That suited me fine.

But the big jobs? Some other workers described them as "a stitch that tightened down the fabric of time." Brought a whole lot of pieces all together to make sure everything worked the way it needed to.

I'd been part of one, once. It hadn't been easy or pretty, and it didn't have a happy ending either. But, the sacking of Rome had to happen.

2

I helped make sure it did. Several other partnerships, along with Luke and me, came together to coordinate massive amounts of small tidbits, gossip, and leaked information, devising a foolproof plot. Not that I was proud of what happened. Not that I liked to think of how many lives had been lost.

Still gives me nightmares, truth be told.

"I'm not sure yet. It just feels different. Urgent. Something big is going to happen. You sure you don't feel it?"

I shook my head, but after the doubtful look he cast me, I leaned back against the ratty seat and closed my eyes. New jobs always manifested the same way. A pressure that built against my sternum. Then the images. One by one, they told a story. A person, often, and a place. Where I had to lead them. Luke got the same ones, only tweaked to see what his end of the job was supposed to entail. And together we worked out what we had to do. At this point, we barely had to talk to do it.

I hated that.

The car hummed along the road, and I pressed my palms against my thighs and forced thoughts of the happy little job we'd just finished, to tumble out of my conscious mind. Then it hit. Like someone filled a balloon inside my chest. It ached like the memory of pain after the wound has healed. The fact I could feel it, now, when we'd only just finished our last job, made sweat gather on my brow, despite the cool air blasting from the vents.

"I'll take your expression as a 'yes,' then."

"What do you think it's going to be?" I chewed my lip, rubbing my hands against my khakis. "Another big war? I really don't want to be around that again." I didn't care what the ramifications might be, no way was I ever going near a death camp ever, ever, ever again.

Luke shook his head. "I don't think so. But I get the feeling it's going to be difficult."

"I hate it when you're right."

"I'm always right," Luke laughed, patting my shoulder.

That was a little too accurate, actually.

# CHAPTER
# 2

The first image filtered through my thoughts shortly after our plane home took off. The details were perfectly clear in a glossy way I associated with Photoshop these days—not something planted in my head by some unknown force.

The image sharpened.

Luke's giant hand gripped my wrist, so tight it almost hurt, his eyes shut when I whipped around to look at him.

"I told you this was a big one."

"Not the time for 'I told you so'," I muttered.

Bodies. Lots and lots of them. Lined up along the edge of a mass grave. Wrapped in stained white bags. Here and there a hand poked out, or hair; enough to identify each as a person.

Men in full-body white suits and respirators strapped to their backs slogged through mud as rain pelted down from a low-hanging sky. A tractor dug a trench.

Only on the most important jobs did Those Who Know Best give us images of what would happen if we failed. Luke said it was motivation. I said it was sick.

But whether it was motivation or sick, I had the image. I knew what we were up against. And our opponent made my palms sweat and my knees knock together. I gripped them with my hands and took a deep breath, pushing down the panic that bubbled up.

"What do you think it's going to be?" I rubbed the heels of my hands over my face. I still felt gritty from tramping through the Mexican jungle on our last job.

"Some kind of plague." Luke opened one dark eye and wrinkled his nose as if he could smell the corpses in the image. "Again."

Neither of us liked any of the plagues we'd lived through, clearly. The Black Death was a nice way of putting the horrors of the Middle Ages—the smell of those years had taken years to go away. Smallpox ravaging through Native American populations had resulted in the loss of so many lives and so much history. All of it was horrible and senseless. They often resulted in us attempting to put lives back together, or give some people hope, but for the most part it was just chilling. With lots and lots of death. I'd hoped we'd outlived that kind of thing.

"Well, that's just great." I crossed my arms and clunked my head against the headrest.

"It's probably terrorism." He peered around at the mostly empty seats around us like someone who lurked on the plane might be in on the plot. "Some kind of attack."

I brought the image back up, focusing on any details I could glean.

"The sign, in the background. Does that say Berkeley?"

My stomach lurched as I made out the white script against the green sign.

Luke replied with a low sound in the affirmative.

"Well, shit. Okay, and that one person in the suit, off to the left? Got to be a female from her shape. She's glowing." Which meant she was my mark. The person I had to watch.

Perfect.

"Mine's not here."

"Could be one of the dead bodies."

"Thanks, Ami, I really needed to think that," Luke said.

"Well, it could be." I turned to the window, staring out without really seeing anything. A plague. In the Bay Area, where Luke and I had lived for the last century. Which meant, what? We had to stop it, obviously, but how?

Drawing a deep, shaky breath, I reminded myself I didn't have all the pieces yet. There wasn't any sense in freaking out until I did. No job we'd ever worked came with everything at the start—that was what we had to do. Piece together all the little bits, find the pattern, and see what was supposed to happen. Then do it. Make the improbable probable. And once we knew more, we'd be able to figure out who was behind this mess and stop it. Hopefully.

So many body bags.

I stuffed my trembling hands between my legs. I didn't want this kind of pressure. I didn't want that many lives hanging over me. I didn't want to test how good a job I could do.

Luke pulled out his laptop and connected to the plane's Wi-Fi, searching for plagues and diseases. Tendrils of panic crept up the back of my throat when I caught sight of disfigured people and oozing sores. Just the pictures made me gag. I'd seen pretty much every kind of death imaginable but knowing how much the people had suffered didn't ever get easier. I closed my eyes tight and counted backward from a hundred.

Somewhere amidst attempting to read a book and staring at the horizon, I dozed off, drool and all, and didn't wake until we landed at SFO so I missed my favorite part of the landing, coming in over the bay.

Luke and I grabbed our minimal luggage and groggily joined the jostling crowd maneuvering to get off the plane. We herded like zombies through customs and out into the parking lot.

Already the gloomy fog threatened to drown any chance for a nice afternoon.

"Hey, see you later, okay?" I touched his arm to bring him back to reality. He hadn't said anything more than the 'yes' and 'no' to the customs agent in hours.

Luke managed a weak smile. "Yeah, of course." His gaze skittered off, distracted.

I pressed my lips together and shook my head, disappointment settling around me like the fog. "Later."

Stalking off toward my car, I tried not to stomp along like the asphalt had insulted me. I shouldn't have felt bothered by the situation. Luke and I may not have seen each other much, but he was never far away. He had every right to his privacy. Still, it wasn't like I had a lot of friends who understood what things were like for me, the strange way my job worked, and how my life flipped upside down every few weeks. Luke did understand and talking with him made it easier. Less of a burden and more like a crazy spy adventure. Plus, even when he was broody, he looked like a cologne ad.

So, yeah, maybe I was a little irked that he'd been so distant today.

And the last three times we'd seen each other after other jobs.

Not that I was counting. I hunted down my red vintage Mini Cooper. Stashing my stuff in the back seat, I got in and rested my head against the wheel for a moment.

I flashed on the image we had seen. A mass grave.

Another. An apartment building—a decent 4-plex in the residential part of the city. Off-white stucco walls, two bushes lined the entry to the main breezeway the four doors opened onto. One of the numbers carried the trademark glow of the woman I was supposed to track. A street sign in the corner showed the address.

It was a start. Sure as hell hoped she had a better idea how to stop the massive numbers of bodies piled up in my head.

Ice ran through my veins as I thought about what to do. I couldn't fail this one.

# CHAPTER
# 3

As I turned down my block, people with cameras and kites jockeyed for space in the fog. Tourists. I'd have picked a different part of the city if I'd known how crazy popular—and expensive—it would be after the 1906 earthquake. But deep down, I liked it. It was worth it to switch apartments every few years to avoid suspicion if it meant I got a view of the bay and grassy lawns by the water. Tourist season was in full swing as I turned onto my block, catching sight of people out with cameras and kites despite the foggy weather. My place was down by the water, just around the corner from Marina Boulevard that ran right by the bay. The view of the bay, and people out on the grassy lawns by the water, felt cheerful and comfortable after all these years. Even though staying in one spot meant renting an apartment every few years to trick my neighbors into not asking too many questions.

I hit the door opener so I could pull into my basement garage.

Having a guaranteed parking spot was the only thing that made having a car worth it in this city.

Gathering my bag, my head still lost in the new job we'd been given, and how I could get Luke to communicate about what to do, I trudged up my stairs and into the front portion of the house.

My place was pretty sparsely furnished. There had been times when moving a lot was part of the game and Luke and I hadn't kept permanent residences. So, I'd learned not to accumulate a whole lot of stuff. A few treasured little pieces from my adventures hung around over the years though: the Pueblo bowl from New Mexico, an arrow I'd mounted in a nice frame after "Robin Hood" tried to shoot me, a funny shaped stone I'd carted around since Luke and I watched the Parthenon being built. There were plenty more scattered around, though no one knew their significance, not even Luke. A small shell, rock, or bead, was all I allowed myself for mementos from the odd and too-long life I'd led.

After I dropped my bag in my bedroom, next to the oversized bed covered by an intricate quilt I'd made, a soft knock drew me to the back interior door.

Before I had a chance to touch the handle, it burst open and Melody scampered inside.

"You're back!" she crowed and threw her skinny arms around me like I'd been gone for months rather than just a few days.

"Just like always," I laughed.

"Hey, you can't blame me for worrying. I mean, who else is going to rent me an apartment for such an awesome price?" She trilled a laugh.

Melody had once been one of my marks. Which was probably an unfair screening process, but the coincidence Luke and I set up—to ensure her a position at the city library—had taught me a whole lot about the girl. I'd liked her instantly. And only sometimes regretted allowing her to rent the apartment I'd created on the top floor of my house.

"So, where did you go?" Melody turned on her platform heels and wandered into my kitchen. I followed, absently picking up the mail she'd collected for me and leafing through it. Bills and ads, how utterly exciting. I missed the days when people sent real mail—the kind with handwriting and stamps from distant places. Now I was lucky to get a newsletter from my dentist.

"Mexico, actually."

Melody, teapot in hand, paused at the sink.

"Mexico? Seriously?" Her brown eyes glinted with questions behind her too-big, and completely unnecessary, glasses.

Shit.

Normally I didn't tell Melody where I went on my 'work trips' so she didn't ask too many nosey questions. If I had to, I lied and said I went to dull places like Sacramento or Omaha. Normally, though, I wasn't quite so distracted by images of dead bodies hanging around in my head.

"You didn't bring back any drugs or anything, did you?" Melody tugged on the end of one of her long braids.

I laughed and settled into one of the stools at the breakfast bar. "No, definitely no drugs."

"Well, bummer." She returned to the teapot and plunked it on the stove. "Kidding!"

I rolled my eyes. "I know."

"So, what were you doing down there? Get time to go to the beach?"

For a moment I thought about telling her the truth. All the awesome ugliness of sitting in the back of a stranger's car, being invisible, all so some guy could meet his long-lost dad. But I'd learned long, long ago that telling a normal person about what I did usually resulted in bad things happening. Not such a fun lesson to learn.

"I did make it to the beach for an evening. Had a margarita. But other than that, it was mostly just meetings." Centuries of practice made me one helluva liar.

"Well, one night's better than nothing. Any hot men?" She leaned her elbows on the counter and rested her head on her palms.

"Yeah, right. It was definitely lacking in the men department." Except for Luke, but he didn't count. Especially since he made it clear that any kind of conversation these days was too much trouble. It hadn't always been that way. Right? Or was I just losing my mind after all these years?

"Double bummer!"

The teapot sang and Melody set about steeping the tea for us and we took it into my living room. I'd redone the place a couple of years before with an eye on how to make it the most comfortable room possible. Several deep leather couches with giant plush pillows sat in the big bay windows. The walls were painted a soft shade of grey that reminded me of the fog outside and Melody said was depressing. Too bad, I loved it. I closed the lower level of the shutters so the random family walking by in matching windbreakers wouldn't try to peer in.

Melody tucked herself into the giant beanbag chair I'd bought specifically with her in mind. She was one of those people who liked little nooks and comfy places where she could curl up.

I stretched out on the couch, sipping the tea. Today, I needed a few moments to collect myself. Knowing what was coming wasn't any consolation for the fear that settled into the marrow of my bones. Starting tomorrow I'd be facing a job unlike anything I'd ever seen before. For now, though, I was going to gather my strength.

Which, of course, was exactly when yet another image shot through my mind.

"Hey, are you okay?" Melody appeared at my side and I waved her off, spilling scalding tea, only half able to see her as the image settled behind my lids.

A wall with news clippings. I couldn't make out the titles, just bolded words that leapt out at me. Deception. Fraud. Angry. Deceit. Fruitless. Someone had carefully plastered the stories against a dark wall.

"What did you see?" I breathed at Luke, struggling from the blast of fear and unease.

"Ami, what's going on? Should I call someone?" Melody hovered over me, wringing her hands as I heaved in a deep breath and coughed.

"No, no, I'm good. I think I just inhaled some tea the wrong way. Took me by surprise. I swear I'm good." I choked out the words between spasms, smiling weakly at her anxious expression.

"You saw something? Another image?" Luke's reply was breathy, like he was distracted. What exactly had he seen?

"You didn't?" Panic crept into my words. How had he not? We always received these things in tandem.

"Ami? You're totally freaking me out," Melody said.

I forced my attention away from Luke's weirdness and back to my friend's freak-out. The last thing I needed was suspicions. "I'm good, really," I coughed once more for good measure and took a sip of tea. "Wanna know what I did do while I was in Mexico?"

Melody, her eyes narrowed in disbelief, must have convinced herself I was okay and went back to her chair. Ah, the art of distraction. She and I chatted until my eyelids got heavy, then she ushered my mug back to the kitchen and let herself out.

I never heard back from Luke.

# CHAPTER
# 4

I hated waiting for all the images to creep into my head to start a job. I especially hated it when they popped into my mental spotlight, waking me from a dead slumber. Not that I was totally surprised this time, a job like this called for some kind of urgency, something last night's image with Melody watching taught me. The new image included a cop writing something on a pad of paper, maybe a ticket, somewhere downtown, being screamed at by short woman with curly dirty-blonde hair, wearing an adorable sundress, with her hands on her hips.

She was also glowing.

Apparently, the woman I was supposed to be helping wasn't a police officer. Which narrowed things down exactly...not at all. I scoured the image for other clues while showering off yesterday's sweat and grit from hiking and flying. It kind of grossed me out that I'd waited so long to bathe, but at least I couldn't get sick from all the nasty germs on the plane—fringe benefit of my job.

While toweling off, Luke's voice shot through my thoughts.

I was infinitely glad he couldn't see me.

"I've got the cop."

"The cop?" I shook my head. "From the last image?"

"Yes. You have the female?"

"I have the woman there. And her address. Apartment 3 from before."

"I have apartment 4."

Pausing while wrapping my hair in my towel, I thought about that for a moment. "They're neighbors."

"Looks like it."

"And we know already that they're going to meet. Or really, they probably already know each other if they live so close."

"We must need to push them a little more."

"Good grief, you'd think they'd just come out and tell us what to do when it's something like this." It was a standard complaint. "It isn't like there are millions of lives on the line or anything."

Luke chuckled. "But where's the fun in that? Whoever *they* are."

"Yeah, tons of fun. Gods, I can't stop thinking about all those dead bodies. This one scares me." My inner voice got really quiet and wasn't sure Luke even heard me for a long moment.

"We can do this."

Before I could ask how, or launch into my rehearsed argument over why he'd dropped off the face of the planet last night, someone knocked on my front door.

I cursed. Still naked, I hopped into my bedroom and rummaged through my drawers to fling on the essentials.

"I've got company here. Talk later!"

Two minutes later, the person pounded a third time, rattling the front window. Clad in barely presentable jeans and plain dark t-shirt (without a bra), I pulled the door open and fixed the people standing on my stoop with my best 'what the fuck?' look.

"Can I help you?" There may have been a little added heat to my question, but seriously? Banging on my door? Use a cell phone or something.

"Amita?" The youngish woman who was standing there looked up at me like I was supposed to recognize her. The guy behind her, all tattoos and big black eyes, also wore a wide-eyed expression that said I should know him.

"That's me. And you are?" I was still out of breath from my costume change and, while something in her dark eyes and long blond hair seemed familiar, I couldn't place it. Even though I really wanted to tell her to screw off, I held my tongue, and waited to find out who she was.

"Lexi. We've met before." She held out a hand, her long fingers too warm for the chilly morning outside.

"Theo," the tattooed guy said, his handshake entirely engulfing mine.

"Lexi and Theo…I'm supposed to know you?" I frowned. If I knew them, the details must have been lost somewhere in my head.

"Call Luke over. I'm sure he'll remember us," Theo said. He leaned against the railing and crossed his arms over his thickset chest. Despite the leather jacket he wore, I could see the definition in his biceps. He reminded me of warriors from days long past—someone who knew their own strength and wasn't afraid to use it.

Melody would die of happiness if she met him.

"Um, let me go get my phone." I was backing into my house, planning on locking the door behind me, when I caught sight of Lexi's amused expression.

"What? Is the line down?" she asked, tapping her forehead. "Just talk to him."

"I don't know what you're talking about." My well-honed lying skills faltered as I stared at her. She couldn't possibly…well maybe she could know about my link with Luke.

"Just send him a mental message. We know you can." Theo tried to put on a kind smile, but it didn't reach his eyes.

"Luke! Where are you? Do you know some little blonde chick, and a muscular black guy?"

"Look, what do you want?" I asked the two, trying not to show the mental freak out I was having. How could they know about Luke and me? And why couldn't I remember them, at all, if they knew that kind of very personal detail about me?

"We're here to work the job. We've been instructed to help you two out. It's a biggie, it seems." Lexi grinned up at me, her black eyes still suspicious.

Luke cut in. "You don't remember them? Think Germany, about two centuries ago?" Something in his tone was tense, like he wasn't keen on bringing up the memory.

"He's going to try and remind you of Humboldt. In Germany. We weren't on the same job, but in the area. You got so drunk Luke had to carry you home."

Shame bloomed across my cheeks. Okay, that's why I didn't remember much. I did remember some seriously amazing German beer. We'd holed up at a little tavern for an evening so rare I couldn't believe I didn't think of it—Luke and I had gone out.

We'd met up with another partnership working in a nearby village... and I'd made a fool of myself. I must have blocked out what the other partnership looked like, enough that I didn't recognize them standing at my door all these years later.

"I'm certain you're going to want to crawl under a rock when you remember them."

"Thanks, yeah, figured that out."

"So, can we come in?" Lexi asked, motioning toward my open door.

"Yeah, yeah, sure."

"I'll be there shortly."

"Luke says he'll be here soon."

Lexi and Theo wandered inside, peering around my home. Which made me wish I'd picked up a bit more before I left last week. Newspapers sat in a pile in the living room and tea mugs occupied various horizontal surfaces.

Lexi picked up a small vase I'd acquired the last time I was in Japan, and examined it before setting it down. Theo wandered to the prints on my walls, nodding as he took in the Degas, the Picasso, and the recently purchased print by some random guy down by the Pier.

Bored with the room Lexi turned to me, her knobby elbows poking out as she rested her hands on her hips. "So, how are things going with Luke?" she asked.

I was totally not comfortable with the piercing look she gave me. I longed for these two to be gone so I could sit down and start looking up information on this next job, alone, like I always did.

But, considering what we were attempting here, I had to stifle my sarcasm. Another partnership getting involved meant that this was as serious as it looked. The confirmation of that fact left me twisty-stomached and I-want-to-puke nervous. I had to play nice. For now.

"Fine." I frowned at the woman. Why would she ask that?

Theo left the artwork and settled onto my couch, patting the cushion next to him. Lexi pranced over and settled in, her leg straddled between Theo's.

Whoa. Back the train up here. What was up with these two?

Before I had a chance to ask, Theo slid an arm around Lexi's petite waist and pulled her onto his lap.

Oh. Okay. Apparently yes.

Which was odd. I'd never seen another partnership, well, pairing up that way. Then again, I didn't really know many of them. I tried to keep my mouth from hanging open, but Lexi started to laugh and leaned back against Theo's broad chest.

Yet, I'll admit it. I was totally jealous. Not of Theo, but of the fact that they had each other. A little part of me crumbled inside. Luke had never so much as looked at me in any way that suggested we had a chance at something more than what we were obligated to by work. And here were Theo and Lexi, casually touching each other on my couch.

It wasn't helping me like them.

"I'm going to guess from the look on your face that you really don't remember much about that night."

I had opened my mouth to say something nasty when the front door opened.

Sputtering at the fact that someone barged into my home, I went to deal with the much more manageable issue.

Even though it was the first time he'd ever set foot in my house, Luke owned my doorway, his broad shoulders spanning the entry.

"Nice place," he said, closing the door behind him.

I'd never presumed to check out his home in all the years we'd worked together, and he'd never invited me. Or I him, for that matter. It just wasn't how we worked, for better or for worse. Mostly worse.

"Did you know these people were coming?" I asked, grateful to be out of sight from the other two.

He shook his head. A smidge of amusement curled his lips up. "I didn't have a clue."

"And why did they come here and not to your house?"

"Because my house isn't as nice."

"And they knew where I live, how?" I yanked on my hair, which was drying into a long and tangled mess. "I so don't like this."

Luke sighed. "I know, I'm sorry. I didn't know they would show up. I would have told you."

"And did you know they're a couple, couple? As in, more than just friends?" I wanted to see his expression before he caught the two canoodling on my couch. How would he react to knowing that at least one other partnership didn't spend most of their time pretending the other didn't exist?

Yeah. I was a tiny bit bitter.

Luke raised an eyebrow. "I did know that, actually. From the last time we met. You don't remember…" he chuckled. "That's right. You don't remember much of anything from that night."

"Thanks. Thanks so much. So happy to have made such an amazing impression on you all."

"In your defense, it was good beer, and you've always been a lightweight. But I'm sure they're wondering what's going on."

Luke and I went back to the living room where Lexi and Theo were having a silent battle of wills of their own, sitting inappropriately close on the couch. I wondered if I looked that ridiculous while mentally chatting with Luke—I liked to think I didn't make quite that many facial expressions.

"Nice to see you again Theo, Lexi." Luke extended a hand to the two. They shook it like Luke was some long-lost relative they were overjoyed to see again. At least Luke had made a good impression.

"We weren't informed we'd be receiving aid on this one, but we're happy to have you here." Luke scanned the room, then chose the armchair in the corner to tuck his lanky frame into.

That left me with Melody's beanbag contraption. "Speak for yourself," I shot at Luke, trying to look distinguished as I sat down, which was simply impossible. After squirming around a bit, I pulled my knees up and tucked them under my chin like I'd watched Melody do a hundred times. It was actually kind of comfortable, if I didn't have the mocking stare of Lexi to deal with.

These people already thought I was a moron. Fine. They could keep thinking that. There were bigger things to deal with.

"We started getting the signals about a day ago. We were just in Reno. So, we drove over right away. Do you two have your marks yet?"

Lexi asked.

I nodded. "We know who they are, but haven't found them. Looks like they're neighbors."

"Nice. That makes things a bit easier. We have a couple of people who work for the FBI. They're heading up an investigation into some lead here in the Bay. They're due to arrive in a couple of hours."

"Any idea exactly what it is we're supposed to stop?" Luke asked, glancing at each of us in turn.

Theo let out a low breath. "From the looks of it, some kind of pandemic. Doesn't look good."

"I'd put money on our task being getting someone to prevent it. Maybe some way to stop the perpetrator from releasing it?" Lexi piped in.

"Sounds about right. But, who? And why?" I shook my head. "Who would want to kill all those people?"

No one had an answer. Not that I expected one. It was too terrible of a situation. All of us had seen what horrific things humanity had to offer; it was impossible to understand why anyone would want to continue committing such atrocities.

"So, goal number one is to figure out who's going to get their hands on this weapon? Biological weapon, I guess?" I said.

"I'd say goal number one should be finding our marks," Lexi said with an eye roll she didn't try to hide. "But, after that, yeah," she amended once Theo elbowed her.

"Yeah, well, obviously we have to get to our people first," I said, glancing at Luke, who was wearing his patented blank expression. Thanks for the help, man.

"Are we sure this is some kind of bio weapon?" Theo asked.

"I did some research. Based on what they're wearing in our first image, it's consistent with that. There would be a whole lot of other gear if it were nuclear, and I can't think of anything else that would take down so many people. Unless you know something more?"

Luke and the internet to the rescue.

Theo and Lexi both just nodded in agreement and got to their feet. We did a cell number exchange and planned to meet up later after we'd done some investigating.

I ushered them out the door as politely as I could, plastering on a smile that couldn't have looked remotely authentic. All I really wanted was to slam the door and lock it behind them.

"You're staying?" I asked, turning back to Luke. Something about him leaning against the door jamb to my living room made my stomach flip. He may have been an integral part of my life, but having him in my home weirded me out.

Which must have shown on my face, because Luke made for the door.

"Hey! You don't have to go," I said, catching his arm as he brushed past me.

He paused, dark eyes searching mine. "Sure about that?"

"Yeah, yeah. I'm sure. Come on, I need some breakfast. You want some?"

"No thanks."

I led the way to the kitchen and rustled around in the fridge, wishing I'd stopped at the store on my way home.

I threw the last frozen breakfast sandwich in the microwave. While it nuked, I started some tea and tried to unobtrusively pick up some of my scattered mess. I found no less than five mugs tucked around the kitchen, and dropped them into the dishwasher.

"What do you think about those two?" Luke asked after a few minutes of silence.

He'd folded himself onto one of my kitchen stools and it was way too small for him—his knees were wedged under the counter. His hands were clasped before him and he watched me move around the kitchen with unveiled interest.

"I have a feeling you know perfectly well how I feel about them.

Well, Lexi at least." I raised an eyebrow and leaned back against the counter after slamming the dishwasher shut.

"She warmed up last time. Took a while, and a few beers, then she was alright."

"I'm so glad you have such a perfect recollection of when we met them before," I snapped. "Nothing like working with people who are convinced you're a total screw-up."

"I'm sure they don't think that. I know you're not."

My ears warmed. Luke didn't often give compliments. Thankfully, the teapot started to shrill. I prepared two mugs of tea, my back to Luke until I got a grip. I set a mug—the only clean one that wasn't chipped—before him, and he wrapped his fingers around it.

"You want to come with me over to see where the marks live?" I asked after devouring my breakfast.

"That's why I stayed. Figured it made sense to go together."

It made sense, but it was a little odd. We never did this kind of stuff together, which really, thinking about it now, was strange in and of itself. Why didn't we work together more? If Lexi and Theo managed it, what was it with Luke and me that left us the most intimate strangers?

# CHAPTER
# 5

Clown-car-ing himself into my Cooper, Luke glared at me over his knees.

"Serves you right for making me sit in the beanbag chair," I said, pulling out into the mid-morning traffic. "Where's your car?"

"I took the bus."

I laughed. "No, really, where did you park?"

"I always take the bus in the city. I hate parking here." He winced as I swerved around some dumb tourist going too slow along the embarcadero.

"Really?" I turned inland and cruised up the first set of hills, revving my zippy little car up to the steep crest and gunning it down the other side. I loved cutting through traffic and flying along, making the most of shortcuts and semi-secret alleys. Luke turned green and somehow got even quieter.

Twenty minutes later, we turned onto a road lined with homes all pressed up against one another, where we'd been shown our marks lived. Luke consulted his phone. "Should be just on the next block."

The houses came right to the sidewalk, bars on most of the lower windows. Bright flower boxes someone had hung from every window of a larger apartment building, each blooming precociously in the filmy sunshine.

I parked right in front of the building, its squat shape and unassuming appearance belying what was probably a huge rental price. At least there was parking this time of day.

"I have the chick on the top floor," I said, pointing to apartment #3.

"I have the cop in four."

"They're probably not here right now. How do you feel about a little B & E?"

Luke laughed. "You know it's not like that. Stop calling it that."

"Hey, you're the one who's going to break into a cop's apartment." I did my best to keep a straight face, but my giggle broke free.

It felt good to laugh. The pressure from this job, along with Lexi and Theo's visit, had left me weighed down, but the way Luke seemed to loosen up buoyed me like I'd tied a thousand helium balloons to my shoulders.

Still chuckling, Luke cloaked himself from the rest of the world, his clothes and anything he touched or had on his person all disappearing from mortal eyes. I still saw his glowing self as plainly as before, although the faint light around me told me he was invisible from everyone else. I was damn grateful that he couldn't hide from me—something told me that if Luke could become invisible from me, I might never see him.

Following his lead, I stepped out of the car and after a quick look around, also went unseen. It was always a little comforting to be undetectable by the rest of the world—it allowed me to dance in the streets or poke into places without worrying about anyone seeing or judging me. Except Luke. He seemed to regard our ability as just one more duty, and definitely not anything fun.

We did a little recon work, which mostly entailed the two of us canvassing the building to see if anyone was home. An old woman lived in the ground floor apartment on the other side of the breezeway. Absorbed in a soap opera, I doubted she would hear much of anything considering how high she had the volume up.

"Come with me." Luke grabbed my hand and tugged me to the cop's apartment door. His palms were the perfect mix of cool and dry— just a little rough so they felt like he'd been doing something manly with them. Perfect in a way that I couldn't even begin to explain.

Wait, what? Since when did we do this kind of thing? Luke never wanted my help. It took me a moment to reconcile his request, and his casual touch, once he dropped my hand to work the lock.

There were going to be strange things about this job, things I'd probably remember forever and ever—even if I didn't want to. That was already obvious. And working with Luke to pull off the biggest coincidence ever was probably not a bad thing. 'Two heads were better than one' and all that.

I just wasn't so sure about the way it wound my stomach up into funny knots.

Or how Luke short-circuited my brain.

That wasn't going to help things much. But there was no ignoring the way being close to him made me feel like I'd wandered into an electrical storm and expected to get hit any second.

"You know there's going to be an alarm." No chance of there not being one. Not with a cop.

Luke flashed me a grin over his shoulder. What was up with him? He was weirdly excited about committing yet another felony.

"Handled it already."

"How?" I always screwed up alarms. Always. Thank the gods I could go invisible, or I'd have been arrested about a billion times in the last couple of decades.

The apartment upstairs wasn't wired and I hadn't been worried, but if Luke had some kind of trick up his sleeve and hadn't shared, I would beat it out of him.

"Sloppy installation job. I hit the breaker in the back and unhooked the phone line." I raised a brow and he shrugged. "It's not that hard. A cop should know better."

"You will have to show me how you did that." The door clicked open after Luke's ministrations. "Once we get done here."

The apartment was about as cheerful as it could get, brightly colored curtains, an assortment of toys scattered across the room, the works. The cop was obviously married from the plethora of framed photos on the walls. He had a couple of cute kids, too.

"And this guy wins the nice guy of the year award," I said, picking up his son's soccer trophy. Another couple of awards nestled behind were for 'Best Coach.'

"Almost over the top." Luke curled his lip.

I laughed. "You're just jealous."

"Nope. Not at all. Trust me." Luke ghosted into the kitchen where I could hear drawers and cupboards opening.

"Jackpot," he said a minute later.

Joining him, he held up a list of phone numbers, the header on the laminate sheet noting it was for a babysitter. Luke took a photo of it with his phone before heading into the back bedroom.

I studied the drawings stuck to the fridge with big alphabet letters. A stick figure dressed in blue with an oversized badge held the hand of a blonde woman and an odd assortment of scribbles I could only guess had to be the daughter. A clutter of other crayon colored images filled nearly every available space, photo magnets holding everything precariously in place.

It was just so sweet. Luke and I never got to have lives like that. Sure, we'd dated people over the years, but with the strange way our lives ran, well, it wasn't something that would ever lead to anything long term. And kids? I was 100% certain that couldn't happen, since I had never had a 'monthly visitor.'

Most of the time I was okay with the strange pattern of our immortal lives—or whatever the hell we ought to call them. But sometimes, seeing stuff like this rubbed it in. I had no idea what led me to having the kind of life I led. It wasn't like I chose it; it chose me. That much I remembered quite well. Even if so many of the details had been lost to time. Hell, I didn't even know where our jobs came from. That was a particularly sore spot. All I knew was that when we did them, good things happened, if not, well lots of people died, or someone never met the love of their life. But the fact that we existed, period, said something about the universe.

"What's going on?" Luke shot from the bedroom.

"Sorry, sorry. Just ogling too cute kid drawings," I hurried down the short hallway.

"Jealous?" Luke asked. His eyes flashed concern when I stepped into the bedroom.

"A little." I shrugged. "Not much I can do about it, right?" My mouth tipped up in a smile I didn't feel.

"Yeah," Luke's eyes drifted to another family photo for a long moment before he shook his head and held up a computer mouse. "Doing a quick calendar check. She's far too busy and he works too much."

"Sounds about right." I leaned on the desk in the corner to look over his shoulder. The calendar system was color coded and looked like someone had tossed confetti at the screen.

Luke snapped more shots, frowning as he attempted to get a handle on when and where his mark would be on most days. He'd complained before that he really didn't care much for the snooping part of the job, but it was essential for getting people to do what we needed them to. If we were supposed to guide people to act in a certain way, we had to know what they were already doing.

Luke spent a while gathering more information while I leafed through files, careful to leave everything just as I'd found it. The last thing I wanted to do was freak them out by thinking someone had been in their home. There was good reason for being invisible.

It took about a half hour before we were done, then we slipped out the back door to the small fenced-in yard with a scraggly tree in the corner. Not many places in the city had open space, and even though this made me think of a prison yard, it was probably awesome for the kids.

"Ready for your turn?" Luke asked, motioning for me to go ahead up the stairs.

I nodded, shaking off the melancholy. I had to remember what we were here for, which wasn't hard: those body bags still flashed behind my lids every time I closed my eyes.

"Time to see what's going on with the random survivor." The image of the woman walking amidst the dead bodies curdled my stomach all over again.

At the top of the stairs, I kept lookout while Luke took point on opening the door.

"She's got some serious locks on this," he muttered, scooting forward and jiggling the handle like he wished it would just pop open.

"Well, that's just great." I leaned against the rough stucco exterior and watched him fiddle with the long delicate pieces of metal he fed into the lock, as invisible as he was while he held onto it. My brain tried to sort through what we were supposed to do, the million permutations of getting the two—no, four—people coordinated. Though, the more I thought about it, the more I realized there were just too many pieces missing. We knew who we were supposed to organize, but they already had to know each other. So, if it wasn't a matter of getting them to meet, what was supposed to happen? And getting Lexi and Theo's marks together with the cop certainly wasn't hard to do. It definitely didn't require getting another partnership involved.

I spent a short moment reveling in the thought of getting rid of the other partners. Theo seemed okay enough, but Lexi...

Oh, whatever. I was stuck with them so I just needed to chill.

The last lock clicked over and Luke swung the door open, a smug grin on his lips.

"Finally!"

"Those were serious! And I couldn't leave any marks behind, could I? Not with the cop downstairs." He was indignant until he looked at me and broke into a grin when he realized I'd been joking. He swatted my shoulder then held out an arm for me to enter the apartment.

I set foot inside and instantly wished I could turn around and run right back out.

"Oh, holy crap," Luke muttered aloud.

"Yeah, crap. Just crap."

The interior of the space had been decorated with a sense of au-de-devil. The wall next to the kitchen table had long neat rows of pictures, all of them depicting mass graves or other death-filled scenes. The windows had blackout curtains hung behind the regular window coverings so it was impossible to notice from them from the outside. And the whole place smelled like something strange had died and then burned to a crisp.

And the kitchen. I walked in there, avoiding the masses of boxes, small tables, and coolers that made an obstacle course. Every available counter top had equipment set out. I may not have had any idea what any of it did, but the vials of different colored liquids slowly rocking back and forth looked pretty intense. A low hum from several spinning gadgets left me with a pretty high confidence that it was all laboratory based.

Luke opened the fridge and whistled.

Inside were stacks and stacks of clear, round Petri dishes.

"What is she doing?" I asked.

Luke stood and shut the door to the fridge, his eyes huge. "It looks like she's making some kind of bacteria. Or something."

The fact that we couldn't get sick from whatever it was left me majorly grateful right then.

"She's going to be the one to release it?" I turned in a slow circle to take in the massive mess that was the room.

A pile of documents and a binder thick with papers sat off on one side. I carefully leafed through it, wary of being unable to put it back as I'd found it. Lists and lists of different attempts ran down the pages, each with careful notation of "variants" in the middle column.

"She hasn't gotten it to work yet." The latest entry from last night had a freshly inked 'failed' next to it.

"That's a small blessing."

Pulling my phone from my pocket, I took photos of everything in the book, the kitchen, the fridge, whatever might be helpful later.

Luke wandered back into the living room, pouring over the assembly in there like he actually understood it. I made my way into her bedroom, where things seemed a little less lab-like.

Not normal though. Not by a long shot.

The walls were painted a dark blue, almost black, and along the far wall, she'd cut out hundreds of newspaper clippings. After inspecting several of them, I realized the theme. Corruption: in the government, and in businesses. Mostly those based in the States, but also in other countries.

Dirty politicians. Corporations who committed terrible acts against their employees or the environment. Bribes. Dishonesty. Someone seemed to have consulted a thesaurus to write every headline she'd pinned up.

Exactly what I'd seen in my image last night. I stood frozen in front of the wall, my jaw hanging slack as I read the headlines over and over.

"I don't think she's all that happy with the way things are." Luke appeared behind me.

"You think?" I said. "I think she's gone a little nuts." I wanted to ask him about why he hadn't had an image of the cop last night, but somehow it just didn't seem important in light of seeing the wall in person.

I'd never had a mark that was the bad guy or gal before. We almost never worked with them, always going around them to make sure they got caught—that they left some clue or whatever that made it a coincidence the cops found them.

Apparently, all the rules were different for this job.

I snapped a few more photos. The bed was made and a small nightstand overflowed with books on politics and the Holocaust.

And a journal.

I always felt sick reading anything someone wrote in such a personal manner. It was wrong on so many levels.

"She's going to try and kill millions of people," Luke noted, catching my undoubtedly attractive expression of foreboding and surmising my reasoning.

"I know. It's just, it makes me feel all dirty." Still, I reached for the small leather-bound tome. A pen marked her spot.

Flipping open the pages, the bold words and harsh marks made my hands shake.

"They have to STOP! We can't keep on this way. WHY does NO ONE see this?"

A few more pages, dated to just a couple of weeks ago: "I am doing everything I can to CHANGE things. Why can't anyone see that? Why do I have to work ALONE?"

Luke read over my shoulder and let out a low whistle. "I would say she's a little upset about things."

"Yeah. Upset." I swallowed. Upset and deranged. I read a few more pages, getting a better sense of her feelings, searching for more on her plans. But there was nothing anywhere about when and how she intended on carrying out whatever it was she wanted to do. Just vague allusions to changes, to saving the world from itself.

Which was incredibly unhelpful.

I snapped two photos of the interior of the journal, then went for a hunt through the bathroom—nothing of note there—and searched for some kind of electronic device that might offer me more information. Judging from the plug in the wall she had a Mac, but apparently, she'd taken it with her.

"There's a paystub here from a biotech firm," Luke said, holding up the slip of paper from a drawer he'd rooted through.

"Well, that's a start," I took note of the company and the name of my mark: Laura. Not the name I would have associated with a future mass murderer.

A quick sweep to make sure we hadn't left anything out of place, though it was probably useless in the mess, and we locked the door behind us.

Back in the car, I dropped my head against the headrest and let out a long breath.

"This is going to be interesting, isn't it?" Luke asked, emerging from his invisibility and rubbing his forehead. "I don't even know where to start."

"Me neither."

"I did get an idea of what she's working on in there. I believe I saw it online. I'll look up more later. Though I don't know how much that'll help."

"Should we just call the cops?" I was worried that this was way out of our depth.

Luke shook his head. "I think we need a little more information.

It's not like they're going to be able to do much on an anonymous tip. They'll need more to pay attention to what we say. We need to figure out what she's doing."

I thought about the time I'd called the cops, about five years ago, when I'd found a drug lab during the course of a job. I'd called it in, but nothing had happened. Luke had a point, without some more information there wasn't much we could do. And I couldn't send the cops the photos on my phone. That was a quick way to get myself in a ton of trouble for breaking in.

I drove us back to my place on autopilot. I just couldn't get the apartment out of my head. Who lived like that?

Who would ever want to do what Laura planned on doing?

How could we possibly stop her?

We had to do something. But what?

I'd never felt so unsure about an assignment before. But Luke was right. We still needed to learn more. Maybe it would come clear.

Gods, I hoped it did.

# CHAPTER
# 6

After an hour of searching and hacking into information on SynthTech, the company where Laura worked, I threw my hands up and whooped, "Found it!"

Laura's boss was loaded. His grandfather had ties to an Iranian oil field from two generations back. And that meant the guy was swimming in cash. He now used the money to fund his own company.

"Everything good?" Luke asked, looking up from my laptop where he was working on a permanent crease between his brows.

"Yep! Well, sort of." I filled him in on what I'd managed to dig up so far. It didn't seem like much when I reported it, but Luke nodded appreciatively and went back to his research. Somehow his silence felt more normal now, even if he chilled on my couch like he'd been here a hundred times before, not just twice.

"What'cha got over there?" I asked, setting my tablet aside and stretching.

Luke motioned to the screen and I perched onto the armrest next to him to look at what he'd found.

"I think this is what she's trying to create."

I sucked in a quick breath and almost choked at what I saw on the screen. People with ulcers covering their skin. Swollen lymph nodes. Glassy eyes. Clearly in pain. The website headers listed several strains of the tularensis, a bacteria like Luke mentioned earlier.

"How much do you want to bet she got her hands on that stuff at work?" I asked.

"I wouldn't be surprised."

Luke walked me through more of the details of what the bacteria, *Francisella tularensis*, did once it was released. It wasn't pretty. And with how contagious it could be made to be with some genetic tweaking described on the web, it wouldn't take long for it to spread, first here in the Bay, then to the rest of the world.

"It's going to make the Spanish Influenza look like a cold." He closed the screen.

I swallowed back bile and leaned against the couch, trying not to imagine just what that meant. We'd been around for that horrible exercise in early pandemics. I didn't need to witness another iteration.

It was then that the next image for our ongoing puzzle lit up my mind like I'd been struck by lightning.

The sky was dark except for the huge blooms of colored light that reflected off the water below. In the background, the Golden Gate Bridge shone red, lit as bright as day. Along the waterline, rows and rows of people huddled, heads turned upward to watch the show.

"Fourth of July," I breathed, opening my eyes and turning to Luke. He watched me; his expression so carefully blank he had to of worked to keep it from betraying any emotion.

"Less than a week to figure this out," he said, the crease between his brows getting even deeper.

"Shit." I struggled to analyze the image in my head, searching for details or clues. But all I got were people down by the bay watching fireworks. None of the little blobs of silhouetted people looked like Laura or the cop and none of them glowed.

"She's going to release the stuff then?"

"I'd guess that's her plan. Though she's not quite ready," Luke said.

I thought about the extent of her workshop at home, her careful notes. She wouldn't release it on the holiday if she didn't think she'd be ready. There had to be something she was doing to make sure she was prepared.

"Less than a week." I dropped my head in my hands. "Why don't we just call your cop guy and tell him his upstairs neighbor needs something. He'll go up there and see all the lab stuff?"

Luke shook his head. "It's not illegal to have those things, so long as you're not making drugs. And he'd probably realize it's not drug stuff— it's too high tech for that. So, unless he realizes she's trying to make some kind of bio weapon, what would be able to do? Shut her down for not having the right permits? That could take weeks."

He was right. I kind of hated it. Pushing off from the couch, I went into the kitchen and dug through my cupboards for food. There wasn't much stashed away, but I emerged with a box of crackers and grabbed a handful before offering them to Luke.

"Sure you don't want to order some delivery?" he asked.

I raised an eyebrow, once again caught off guard by his willingness to hang out today. My heart gave me a good kick in the ribs. "Um, sure."

"Indian okay?"

I nodded, already eager for some naan and curry. The crackers were stale, but I shoved a few more in my mouth to ease the curl of hunger and nerves.

Luke wandered into the other room to order and I found myself staring out the kitchen window, which, unfortunately, only had a glimpse of the bay. Still, it was enough to see the joggers racing past and a few kites enjoying the afternoon wind.

How many of those people would die if Luke and I didn't do this right? If whatever coincidence we were supposed to make happen didn't go smoothly? And how were Lexi and Theo's people supposed to play a role in all of this?

This was so over my head. Even if Luke was right that calling the cops wouldn't help in time, I still wanted to. The pressure of making sure this happened settled in my abdomen with the force of a fist. I couldn't do this. I didn't want this kind of responsibility.

The last time, well, the last time had been enough. We'd done what we were supposed to. The pair of scientists, who Luke and I had been assigned to get to meet, had met, and they'd tried. Luke and I had watched, while the death toll mounted. But it still hadn't worked out. I still wondered, sometimes, when night didn't bring rest, if we'd done something wrong. If we'd been able to get the coincidence to happen sooner, or at a different place, anything, if it would have made a difference. I'd never breathed a word to Luke, and never would, but I wondered. And worried. And prayed this didn't end the same way.

Luke returned, set his phone on the counter, and crowded onto one of the stools. "Should be here in twenty. I got your favorite, the chicken tikka masala."

I barely even processed his words. "Great. Look, isn't there someone else we should call, other than the cops? Some hotline that we should tip off about what's going to happen? There are people out there who handle this kind of thing." My words ran together in their eagerness to find some kind of solution. Something that didn't involve Luke and me. Anything that would pull us away from this kind of major coincidence and back to our small jobs that wrapped up nice and neat and never involved the police, governments, or anything beyond a few little lives.

Luke shrugged. "Lexi and Theo have their marks, and they'll handle that. But the question is why were we shown this? There has to be a reason why we were given this job."

"It already seems like kind of a strange coincidence these two people live next door to one another." How could he remain so easy-going about this? He'd seen all those dead bodies, and Laura's apartment. Didn't he worry, too?

"They have to know each other, or of each other. The question is then, what else is there?"

"No idea." I slumped onto the stool next to Luke and tried to think through the situation. But nothing made sense. A coincidence needed to happen. But what kind of coincidence would possibly make all this work out?

We batted ideas back and forth for a while until Luke's logic evened out my heart rate. Somehow it always did, and I wondered why we didn't do it more often. The doorbell rang and Luke went to gather our meal. Was it strange that after just a couple of hours, I felt completely comfortable with him in my house, answering my door?

The fact that it didn't bother me at all was actually more of a concern.

We were in the process of chowing down, still discussing ideas, when the back door opened and Melody called out a cheerful, "Hello!"

I quickly swallowed my bite of the best spicy chicken and jumped to my feet. Luke's eyes went wide, leaving me unsure of what to do. How could I get her to leave without being totally obvious?

"Smells divine in here," Melody said, popping into the living room with a wide grin. Which melted right off when she saw Luke. "Oh! Sorry. Didn't know you had company. I'll, just, uh, talk to you later!" She unconsciously re-arranged her vintage dress and spun on her funky old-lady heels.

"You can join us," Luke broke in, stalling Melody's hurried retreat.

I glanced at Luke and he shrugged. It was his idea—not mine—if this went weird.

"Sure? I mean, I don't want to intrude." She poked her head back around the corner, one braid hanging from her ear.

I motioned toward her normal seat. "No worries. We were just talking about work and taking a break. Melody, this is Luke; Luke this is Melody."

"She rents my apartment. Remember, we helped her before? I don't think the two of you met though."

Luke got to his feet and shook Melody's hand. She looked like a pygmy next to his super tall frame and fluttered her overly long lashes up at him, unconsciously pressing her shoulders back to give a better view of her cleavage. At least it better have been unconscious.

I loaded her up with a plate featuring all the amazing dishes and she settled in to eat, arranging her legs for maximum effect.

"How were things at the library?" I asked. Better to distract her with easy conversation subjects than have to lie about what Luke and I had been up to.

Melody tittered and shook her head. "Oh, nothing interesting. What I really want to hear about is what you did in Mexico, Luke. Anything fun while Ami was all business?"

Holy shit! She was flirting with my partner.

Something hot and scratchy settled under my skin and it took a lot of effort to keep myself seated and silent. Luke, oblivious, ate up her attention, chatting and smiling a whole lot more than I'd ever seen him.

I ate on, only chiming in when I knew I could speak without spewing fire.

"Well, I'd better get going," Luke said an hour later, standing and gathering his plate and several of the empty containers.

"Aw, you don't have to go!" Melody chirped, looking genuinely sad.

"I'm afraid I do, actually. I have a few things to check on tonight. It was a pleasure meeting you though," he said, heading into the kitchen.

I followed him with the rest of the trash.

"You need a hand with whatever you've got going on?" I didn't dare meet his eyes as I dumped everything in the bin.

"That's okay. Thanks though. Just a few things back at my place. I'll see you at tonight's meeting." Something in the way he said that, like he was grateful we'd be seeing each other later, made me jerk my head up.

All I caught sight of was his back. He leaned over the sink, rinsing the dishes.

Imagining things. I had to be imagining things.

I was so not imagining Melody's behavior, though. I could practically smell her attraction.

Five minutes after Luke left, Melody grabbed my arm and tugged me around to look at her.

"Who was that?" She dropped her voice to a low conspiratorial tone. "Seriously?"

"That was seriously Luke. The guy I work with. My partner." I wanted to tack on that he was off limits, but that wasn't the truth. Luke could do whatever he damn well pleased, and since he hadn't ever made a move with me, if he was into Melody there wasn't much I could do. Made me wonder if I could turn green from jealousy though.

"Damn. If that was my partner, I'd be happy going to Omaha any time."

The laugh that burst out was so forceful I snorted and laughed even harder. "It is not like that!" Even if I wished it was.

Melody cocked one perfectly sculpted brow at me. "Sure about that? Because I was sensing some major chemistry there." She was still fishing. It was a play I'd used enough times that it was like a neon sign lit up above her words. She wanted to see what I'd confess about my feelings for Luke. But no way was I going to say anything. Because, no matter how I felt, it didn't matter; not when he didn't reciprocate.

Doing my best to keep from totally losing my shit, I pinched my lips together and shook my head. "Swear it's. Not. Like. That. At all." Not that I hadn't once, long, loooong ago hoped that it might be. But Luke never showed any signs otherwise and I'd all but given up every last bit of hope. Well, maybe not all of it, considering how badly I'd wanted to freaking mark my territory to keep Melody away.

"So, does that mean I could, like, give him a call?" Mischief lit her eyes.

The suggestion was like a blow to the head. "Um, yeah, sure. I don't see why not."

Melody narrowed her lids. "You don't like that, do you?"

I worked my jaw for a moment, attempting to come up with the best response. Nothing sounded right. Yeah, it was weird to think about, but logically there wasn't anything I could complain about. "It's fine. Really. Just seems a little strange. I guess I don't think of him like that much."

"Liar." Melody echoed the little voice in the back of my head.

"Hey, if you're interested, I'll give you his number. He's a really good guy. I'd be happy if you two went out." Those lying skills came in handy more often than not.

If only I could strangle that little voice. Luke. Was. Not. Interested. In. Me. And I sure as hell didn't want things to be even weirder between us if he knew how much I'd really enjoy seeing him naked.

"Okay, well, great. I just wanted to be sure." She winked at me, thanked me for dinner, and pranced out of the apartment after I texted her his contact info.

Well, just awesome. Luke and Melody. On top of saving the world from a plague, I got to watch my two closest friends fall all over each other. Just what I'd always wanted.

# CHAPTER
# 7

T he four of us agreed to meet at an all-night diner in the heart of the city. It wouldn't be busy at this hour and would allow us to talk relatively freely about our plans. Plus, it wasn't my place, or Luke's, and hopefully neutral territory would help ensure I didn't strangle Lexi. Or at least make me less likely to slap her.

I pulled into a parking spot two minutes late and rushed inside. Three faces turned to greet me and I slumped into the booth next to Luke, flashing him a tight grin. The cracked vinyl seat dug through my leggings and pinched, but I didn't dare complain.

Luke pushed a mug of coffee to me, along with a slice of pumpkin pie. "I ordered it for you. It was the last one."

I raised my brows. "Thanks."

Luke shrugged like it was no biggie and turned back to Theo.

Taking a quick bite, my mind couldn't help going back to Melody's earlier words. He'd gotten me my favorite kind of pie. And my favorite Indian dish. Did that mean something?

For crying out loud, *it's pie*, I chastised myself.

"What's pie?" Luke's voice cut through my thoughts and my fork paused in midair, loaded with another bite.

"Nothing. Nothing at all," I replied, taking a bite and keeping my eyes glued to the scarred, beige Formica tabletop.

Note to self: stop broadcasting to Luke at random times. How long had I had that ability under control? Way, way too long to start screwing it up now. Especially when I couldn't stop the niggle of thoughts about what was going on with this job and its impact on 'us.'

I ate and drank in silence while Lexi filled us in on their coincidence marks.

"It's strange. They're partners already, you know? It's not like we have to get them to meet, and I don't get why we weren't just given one of them if we needed them for something. They follow each other around already."

"Not that I'm complaining," Theo cut in with a look at Lexi that was full of all kinds of innuendo that made me blush.

"They spent some time in the main office downtown. We tailed them, which turned out to be a whole lot more difficult than we would have wanted. But, basically, they're working a lead that something's going to happen here. Soon."

"If they already know," I shook my head, "that makes no sense. Why are we working this?"

"Well, Luke did tell us about your mark. She sounds like a real piece of work," Lexi noted.

That ticked me off. Laura freaked me out all on her own, but some part of me felt a need to protect her. She was my mark after all. Only I got to say how incredibly scary she was.

"There's something more we're missing here. What are these

partners looking for exactly?" That was the question Luke had asked before and it had rattled around in my head while I tracked Laura online.

Theo played with his coffee mug. "They don't really know. They've just had a couple of strange tip-offs of odd emails and other red flags popping up in the system. They're here to investigate. Security alerts are always a little more ramped up around the Fourth and all."

"Do we nudge them with information on Laura? Give them some solid evidence to work on? Get her stopped?" I hated to say it. Again, with the strange protectiveness. It wasn't like I wanted her killing millions of people...but the afternoon of reading about her and all her suspicious activities online left me feeling like we were missing something massive that would give us a complete picture of this job.

"I guess. It does seem far too simple. Like something's off." Lexi pulled a face as if agreeing with me tasted terrible.

"Tomorrow we're tailing my mark, the cop. Maybe that will give us a few more clues. Then we work on nudging your marks to take down Laura," Luke said.

It took a second for that to sink in. "Wait, what?"

"Something's not adding up, like you said. Tomorrow, we're tailing my mark. It'll be fine." Luke spoke like this was some foregone conclusion that we'd be hanging out again tomorrow.

Without anything to say to that, I tried not to appear as stunned as I felt. Hadn't seen that coming. What was it with this job?

"We're going to see what else the agents know. We have about a week. If it's just a simple nudge, it won't be hard to manage," Lexi said.

With that, the conversation turned to more trivial things. The hotel where Theo and Lexi were staying, some of the jobs they'd had over the last few years. Favorite places they'd been. I longed to ask them about their relationship. When Theo placed his hand oh so casually over Lexi's, like it was nothing, my heart totally melted. I'd dated a lot, but that casual touch never materialized. The look that said so much more than words. I'd never had any of that. And really, that kind of pissed me off. What the hell was the whole point of this immortality shit if I didn't get to have that?

I caught myself before I launched into a mental rant, frightened that Luke might catch bits of it.

We left, the four of us bundling up against the summer chill and stepped out into the thickening fog. San Francisco at night is a mess of damp and lights reflecting off every surface. The city always got so quiet—a contrast to the daytime that never failed to amaze me. I loved it.

Theo and Lexi waved goodbye, he wrapped her in close to his side, and they set off to their hotel a couple of blocks away.

"Hey, want a ride?" I asked Luke, motioning to my car. It was only then that I saw I'd parked crooked, not even remotely in a designated space, and felt a wave of shame heat my cheeks.

Luke hesitated a moment, then bobbed his head in agreement, settling his tall frame into my car with a resigned expression. His knees almost reached his chin in my little Cooper.

I pulled into the street then paused at the realization I had no idea where to go. "So, you're going to have to give me directions." I'd rather have driven into the bay than ask, but I kind of needed his address.

Luke chuckled. "You never looked me up? We've been in this city longer than anywhere."

I could only shrug and sneak a glance at him through my mirror. "I wanted to respect your privacy."

"It wasn't like I was trying to pry when I found your place," he said, hunching his shoulders.

Ugh. I hadn't been trying to be snide. "I know. It's no biggie. I really didn't mind that you knew. I mean, it's kind of strange that I don't know. That we've never really done much together outside of our jobs."

Luke fixed me with a funny look, one I felt creep over my skin and only saw out of the corner of my eye. When I had to stop at a light, I scooted around to get a better view of him.

"Did you give Melody my number?" His voice was low, a little rough around the edges. It took me a moment to place it. Hurt. He sounded hurt.

"Sorry. She was asking about you. She's a great girl. I thought, well, maybe..." I trailed off, wanting to bonk my head on the steering wheel.

Luke shrugged, the pain I'd thought I'd read in his features sliding away and covered by a pleasant smile. "Yeah. She did seem nice. We're doing dinner tomorrow."

"Oh." My jaw worked as I attempted to come up with a response. "That's...cool." I wasn't sure if my tone conveyed the pleasantness I stove for, especially when I was mentally screeching, *Whaaaaaat?*

I really hoped I managed to keep that from broadcasting.

From the look Luke gave me, I wasn't 100% positive it had been limited to my own head.

The rest of the ride was uncomfortably quiet. I should have asked where he was taking Melody. Something polite and cheerful. Supportive. But I just couldn't do it. Instead, I followed his one-word directions around the city to the Mission District, and a small older house nestled into the recently reclaimed area of the city.

"Wait, you lived here in the 80's?" I asked, my nose wrinkling. While there were cute pastry shops and interior design places everywhere now, this area hadn't been anywhere near as nice in the past.

Luke shrugged. "It's home. And I put out a serious badass vibe then. No one messed with me."

I burst out laughing. Luke playing a role like that reminded me of a kid dressed up like Superman and pretending to fly. Luke didn't have a badass bone in his body.

"It's not that funny, Ami," he noted in a dry tone.

"Oh, yes it is!"

Luke rolled his eyes and extricated himself from my car. "I'll pick you up tomorrow at seven. His shift starts at seven thirty."

"Sounds good!" I saluted, earning a sigh and headshake.

He walked up the little path to his front door. I spent a moment staring at the careful garden he'd cultivated in the tiny yard. While it didn't surprise me how immaculate it was, it did surprise me that he had one to begin with. I guess that explained what he did with his hands that gave them the appealing hint of roughness.

The memory of him taking my hand that morning brought a flood of heat through my veins. I took a deep breath and forced the feeling away. It was a distraction I didn't need, and it wouldn't do any good to keep thinking about it.

Light spilled out from his living room and I watched his silhouette cross behind the blinds. As I pulled away from the curb, I wondered if I would ever actually see the inside of his place.

Maybe after we saved the world.

# CHAPTER
# 8

I woke feeling pretty damn horrible for the way I reacted to Luke's news about Melody. I should have been happy for them. Luke had dated before. A whole helluva lot. Which considering his dark good looks, was only natural. And Melody deserved a good time. If things didn't work out, well, the nature of Luke's and my relationship wouldn't be screwed up. Really, there wasn't much of a problem. And I'd acted like a total idiot.

I'd just finished applying mascara when the doorbell rang. I glared at my reflection. "Just be nice!" I ordered myself. Though, really, my tongue had way too close of a connection to the snarky side of my brain.

I grabbed two mugs of tea, my bag, and went to the door. Luke leaned against the railing on the stoop, arms crossed, staring out at the swirl of fog that masked the bay at the end of my street.

"Ready?" I asked, unnerved he didn't move when I stopped next to him.

"Why don't we ever do anything together outside of our jobs?" Luke still stared off down the street.

Some part of me tightened, hard, in my chest. Swallowing, I shuffled my feet. "I don't know. I guess I always kind of thought you didn't want to." Maybe not the nicest thing to say, but it was the truth. He had to know I'd always wished there were more but I'd wanted to respect his wishes to keep his distance. So I stayed away. He had to know that. Right?

"Funny. I always thought the same thing."

Thus commenced a horribly long, pregnant pause in which I swapped the hot mugs of tea from hand to hand. "Well, um, have you wanted to do something? I mean, outside of work?"

Luke finally, finally met my eyes. The dark rings under his told me he hadn't gotten much sleep the night before either. "Of course."

Huh. Okay, that was something. "Well, in that case, if we get this thing stopped in time, want to go see the fireworks with me?" He knew I had an unabashed love for fireworks. Hopefully it would be safe to go by then, if we'd managed to stop Laura. Perfect plan, right? And bonus, I'd get some Luke-time.

Luke nodded with a small grin. "Sounds good."

"Here." I handed him his mug of tea and took a deep sip of mine. Mainly because I had to hide the ridiculously giant grin trying to take over my face.

Luke accepted and handed over a white paper bag. "This will taste a whole lot better than the nasty frozen kind."

Laughing, I took the proffered food and followed him to the curb. A sleek black Mercedes, complete with tinted windows and silver trim, waited for us.

"Wait, are we picking someone up from the airport? Or are you going to be in a Jason Statham movie?" I laughed, getting into the fancy ride.

My damn tongue-brain connection needed to be severed.

Luke slid into the leather driver's seat and pulled on a pair of shades, despite the overcast day. "We've been around long before invented the car. What I can do behind the wheel would put anyone to shame." He tipped the glasses down enough to look at me over the rims. "Hold on!"

Giggling like an idiot, I grabbed the Oh Shit handle as we sped around the corner, right into standstill traffic.

"Well, we're definitely going to get there in time," I noted, biting my lip to keep from laughing. I opened up the bag and dug into the amazingly greasy, cheesy egg sandwich.

"Hey, don't doubt me," Luke said, his tone still mocking and light.

I shouldn't have. He managed to make a turn at the next corner and zoomed us through backstreets and alleys I didn't even know existed. And I thought I had a great grasp of the best ways to get across town. We arrived at the station with time to spare.

Luke pulled into the loading zone outside of the precinct building and we both stared out the window, attempting to locate the cop.

"What's his name again?" I asked.

"Mike Nowak. His car is parked in the lot, so he's got to be here."

All we could see was the stream of people going through the doors—those in uniform and the general public. Mike could have been anywhere in the mix.

"Want me to stay with the car while you go in and find him?" I offered.

"I'm not letting you drive my car, Ami. Sorry." The look he gave me made it clear that wasn't up for debate.

"I'm a good driver," I said under my breath, craning around to see if I could spot any familiar faces.

"Why don't you go in?" he said.

Reminding myself I probably wouldn't want him behind the wheel of my Cooper, I got out, ducked around the corner, and cloaked myself. Then it was a simple matter of following a beefy guy through the door into the building. Well 'simple' if you've had a few centuries of experience. Otherwise, it was easy to get too close to someone and creep them out. Or get stepped on. Invisibility would be a ton easier if we could just walk through walls, but it wasn't like anyone had asked me.

Several harried looking officers stood behind the counter, trying to deal with the growing line of people waiting to file complaints and deal with other issues. After figuring out how the building was laid out, I edged around people as best I could, avoiding toes and treacherous purse straps. I did bump into a large woman in a floral muumuu, but she just gave the skinny guy behind her a dirty glance.

Breathing out slowly, I worked my way over to the door that led into the officer's area behind the counter. I had to wait a couple of minutes, watching as two men nearly came to blows over the last seat in the waiting area, before another officer came through the door and allowed me to gain entry.

The back area was busy, but far easier to get around in. I searched to find Mike's familiar face in the sea of blue and black uniforms. This early in the morning, most of them were drinking from mugs and the air was heavy with the scent of coffee.

And there were donuts. With sprinkles. A whole lot of them in a big pink box along one wall. Some stereotypes just don't die.

I wandered around, peering into offices, even the bathroom (not that I looked all that close there—if I ever wanted to check out men, the police station wasn't the place to do it. A club downtown on the other hand…well, that was a lot more fun). Finally, I found my way into the back of the building where a small conference went on in a meeting room.

"I don't care if this isn't our jurisdiction, I want at least a couple of my guys on your team to make sure I know what's going on!" Someone thundered as I stepped inside.

A huddle of men stood at the front of the room. But that wasn't what caught my attention. Off to one side, Theo and Lexi were cloaked and shimmery, watching the proceedings with interest.

"Holy crap, guess who's here?" I thought at Luke.

"The saccharine couple?" Luke responded.

"Wait, that's what we're calling them? Why didn't I get a say in it?" I demanded.

"Do you have any other ideas?" I could almost see the smile he wore.

I paused, holding up a hand to wave at the two. They smiled and waved me over to join them. "No, not really. Nothing nice, at least. That works."

"So, they're there?"

"Yeah, looks like a meeting's going on with some boss here and their duo. And guess who else?"

"Mike."

"Bingo!" I said, turning my full attention to the meeting.

Mike and another cop stood off to one side while a man and woman, dressed in business suits and looking a whole lot like Mulder and Scully from the X-Files, faced off with each other.

"Look, we didn't have to tell you we were here on a case. We just wanted you to be alerted to that fact. So, if you don't mind, I think we're just going to be leaving now. Alone." The woman, her dark hair perfectly coiffed in an A-line bob, spun on her comfort heels and made for the door.

"Fine! But I'm calling your superior! He's going to know that you're flaunting local jurisdiction," the man in a too-small suit hollered after her. He had to be the boss, or captain, or whatever it was here, with his potbelly and the sprinkles that clung to his tie.

"Looks like we're off to see what's up," Theo whispered to me. "Call us with your plans, okay?"

I nodded, waving as they hurried after their marks.

"Look, I want you two tailing them. If there's something going on in this city I want to know, and soon. I am not letting something that dragged in two out of town FBI hot shots get ignored just because their heads are too big to accept local help."

Mike and a Latino guy with enough muscle definition to leave me gaping, nodded. With a wave from their boss, they hurried after the FBI agents.

"Pick me up around back, where the patrol cars are," I called to Luke, following the guys out the door.

A dark blue sedan peeled out of the lot while Mike and the other guy, who had to be his partner, made their way to an unmarked police car and revved out of the lot.

I raced down the cracked cement toward Luke, grateful I'd been smart enough to put on flats today. No way could I navigate the pothole-riddled area with any kind of heels.

"Follow that car!" I pointed as the car in question turned into the main body of traffic. I flung myself into the seat and slapped the dash, urging Luke on.

Luke raised an eyebrow and gunned it.

"I've always wanted to say that. Clearly I've watched way too many cop movies."

Luke's laughter was warm and I joined him.

With Luke driving, it wasn't hard to follow the cops and the FBI agents. I grabbed Luke's phone and texted the other pair, filling them in on where we were and what we were up to.

A minute later, Theo texted back. "The agents are headed toward some lab they want to check out. SynthLab."

I read the text to Luke, my palms beginning to sweat.

"That's where Laura works, isn't it?"

"That's it."

Well, that was going to make for fun times. Everyone was going to meet, and we hadn't had to do anything. Obviously, we had a bigger coincidence than that to pull off. If only we had some kind of idea what it was.

I closed my eyes and hoped that something would clue us in on what we were supposed to be doing at the lab.

# CHAPTER
# 9

N ow that we knew where we were headed it wasn't as hard to tail the other cars. Luke flipped on the radio. Classic rock filtered through the impressive sound system, filling the cab with enough sound that I felt like I was at a live concert.

"Still listening to this stuff?" I asked, unsure of whether I should change the station or start singing along.

"It kind of grew on me. The seventies were a fun few years."

I shrugged, bobbing my head. "I liked the twenties better. Better clothes."

Luke laughed. "Remember that red flapper dress you wore? With the little black hat and heels?"

"Wow, impressive memory for something you only saw me in once." I didn't know if I should be embarrassed or happy he remembered.

"It made an impression."

I didn't know if I should ask if it was a good or bad impression, but was spared the necessity by the swerve of the car exiting the freeway.

The street we found ourselves on was a long stretch of one office building after another. They all looked a little dull, a little tired, and despite the big names plastered to the sides, they might put you to sleep the instant you walked inside. As much as my job sometimes sucked, at least I'd been spared working here.

Keeping a healthy distance, we watched as the FBI agents parked, the cops hanging back on the street. We circled around back to the shared garage and jogged up to the building, cloaked and curious.

Please let there be some answers here.

"We are headed inside," Theo texted. "Third floor."

Luke and I made our way into the entry area. A man sat behind the reception desk; his eyes glazed over as he stared at a computer screen.

"I think he's a robot," Luke noted, pointing to the guy.

My skin prickled as I realized I'd had that very thought.

"I didn't broadcast that, did I?" If I had, I was seriously going to need to work on guarding my thoughts.

"Nope. Just great minds, thinking alike."

We both snickered as we made our way down the hall and to the stairwell.

"Laura works on the third floor." I was grateful I'd done my homework. "What do you think the agents are looking for?"

Luke shrugged. "No idea."

We eased out of the stairwell and were greeted by the answer.

"What the hell does it look like we're working on? We have all our permits. Everything is in order. Explain to me again why you're here?" A man's voice carried down the hallway.

"Well, this'll be interesting," I said to Luke.

We made our way down the hallway, careful to keep out of the way of employees trying to gather near the doorway to hear the ruckus.

"Sir, we're just here to check on a few things. If everything is in order, we will be out of your way shortly and you can continue your work." I recognized the voice of the male agent from back at the station.

"After you've disrupted a day's worth of work. Do you know how much that costs me? It's already impossible to compete with the big companies, you know, the ones with all the government grants and subsidies. I need every hour here!" The fight had left his words though and it was clear he was about to give in.

We managed to edge around a woman who had about five pencils knotted into her hair, and made our way into the lab.

Black topped counters formed several rows down the middle of the room, with towering cabinets above them. Litters of small tubes, beakers, and small scraps of paper were everywhere, along with other tools my online research hadn't explained. It looked like both a huge mess and incredibly high tech.

A tall man with a shock of dark hair graying at the temples faced down the two officers against the far wall. Next to them, a bank of sterile looking boxes hummed with a small panel of LED lights flashing along the side.

The officers continued with their placating speech, while the boss ran his fingers through his hair and finally threw up his hands. "Fine! Do what you want. It's not like I can stop you!" He glowered at the two agents, settling his arms across his chest in a classic 'screw you' position.

"Thank you, sir. We'll be as quick as possible."

The female agent picked up a sleek metal briefcase and went to a counter to open it. She snapped on some blue gloves and retrieved a set of swabs.

"I'm going to find Laura," I thought at Luke.

He nodded, waving me off as he made his way to Lexi and Theo, who watched from off to one side.

I'd let Luke handle those two. I much preferred to find my mass-murderess.

I navigated my way on tiptoe around a large man taking up most of the opening, my breath catching as I accidentally brushed against his girth. He absently rubbed a hand across his belly, his attention still on the scene unfolding with his boss. I sighed and kept moving, cursing silently as a tower of binders and paperwork behind the man started to shift at my passage. I swear, sometimes I attracted stuff like some kind of magnet, just to make being invisible more of an obstacle course. Steadying the pile of papers, I edged my way toward the back of the room. Sunshine poured in the windows, while something almost physical tugged me in that direction—a need to see this woman, know what I was up against. And, answer the questions lurking in my mind.

I rubbed my sweaty hands against my pants as I came around the corner and caught sight of her. Her dirty-blonde hair was pulled into a knot at her neck. A white coat unbuttoned over a t-shirt and jeans. She perched on a stool, chewing on a pencil loud enough that I could hear the wood crunch between her teeth.

How could she look so normal? It felt so unnatural to see someone I wouldn't think twice about saying hello to on the street sitting there when I knew what she planned on doing. Creepy, really.

Sweat gathered at her hairline and she glanced down the aisle, her body leaning like she wanted to run for it before she settled back on her stool.

In front of her, two neon colored plastic squares with small holes along the top held a tiny set of tubes. Some kind of sample, I guessed. An orderly arrangement of sharpies and sticky notes, along with several sheaves of paper completed her work nest.

Could she look more guilty? I couldn't help the urge to uncloak and go back down the aisle, running and calling for the FBI guys to come and check out her workspace. There had to be something incriminating there. Or on Laura's hands. Maybe their swabs would pick up something, like the check they sometimes did on laptops in the airport.

But I hung back. I didn't have an explanation for why. A hunch, maybe? A feeling this job wasn't over yet. That there was something bigger at play. There had to be a reason why all four of us had been called in, more than just to avoid the massive loss of lives. I never spent too much time wondering about what guided us around, because there was no explanation and no one to ask, and, it kinda hurt my brain after a while. But this, this had something bigger stamped all over it.

Leaning over Laura's shoulder, I tried to make sense of what was written on the papers, but it might as well have been written in another language. A series of numbers and short words scrawled next to dates—lab code for something I couldn't begin to decipher.

The agents came down the aisles and Laura's brow grew shinier and there was a distinct green tinge to her skin. The agents carefully selected certain equipment, took samples in labeled baggies, swabbed things, and took careful stock of everything in the room. The majority of the employees watched this parade in silence, hesitant glances exchanged as the employees kept out of the way.

"So, why is Laura different? Why isn't she over talking with the rest of her coworkers?" I asked Luke as he came around the corner, Lexi and Theo in tow.

He shrugged. "I have no idea. What's she doing?"

Laura was moving small amounts of clear liquid from one tube into another, in some kind of order, but without any reason apparent to me. "Science." I shrugged.

The FBI agents were now around the other side of the lab bench. Laura, her hands shaking, shut the tiny caps on the row of tubes in front of her and slipped them into her lab coat pocket.

"What did she do that for?" Luke asked, confusion scrunched brow into furrows.

"No clue."

"We've got to let the agents know. They should probably see and test those tubes."

I caught Luke's arm as he strode away. I knew what he'd do—some kind of clue to tip them off: a tube hanging from someone's lab coat, something dropped into the agent's own pockets, anything that would draw their attention.

It would work, too. They'd launch into a more intensive examination of everyone's clothing.

But I couldn't let him do it. "Stop! Look, something's off about this. Don't tip them off, okay?" I caught his arm to hold him back.

"But, Ami, this could potentially halt the whole situation, and it would be so simple."

I shook my head. "There's something going on here. I don't know what, but something. This, this isn't right. Just let it go. She's my mark. And this isn't something we should get involved in." How could I explain how I knew this? I didn't know myself. But I did know it. We couldn't interfere yet, no matter how much we wanted to.

Luke let out a long breath. "Seriously?"

I nodded, suddenly resolute, the last of my doubts forced from my mind. "I don't know why, but this is supposed to happen this way. We've got to leave it alone."

Luke's eyes widened before he pulled away and crossed his arms. Finding a free spot against the bench, he leaned back to watch the proceedings through narrowed eyes.

I turned back to watch the agents politely ask Laura to move as they worked over her space. No one even thought to look in her pockets, even though she kept her fists dug deep within them.

"How are they not going to detect whatever is in her pocket?" Luke asked.

"How should I know?" But as I said it, something clicked into place. "It's normal for it to be here. It's got to be related to what her job is.

She's using some of whatever they're working on in this lab to further her own stuff."

Luke cocked his head to the side, discernibly surprised I'd come to that conclusion. But the glimmer of admiration in his eyes told me he believed it.

"Point for me," I said.

He cracked a grin and I tried to brush off the happy little sparks in my chest. Because, really, that was just ridiculous right now, when we were trying to figure out how to stop so many deaths.

Gah, those damn body bags!

Theo and Lexi waved us over a few minutes later when the agents headed into another room to continue their sample collection.

We met in the stairwell, blocking the door so no one would come in to catch four invisible people talking. Luke and I had had that happen once, in London, about a century ago. The poor guy ended up in an asylum for a year and ever since I'd really tried to keep that from happening again.

"Okay, what's going on?" I asked.

Theo and Lexi exchanged a glance. "Our marks got an anonymous call that this lab was doing something illegal. At first they thought it was a disgruntled employee. But, they checked up on it again. And the things going on here are, well, strange. They are working on some diseases that are pretty scary. They think they've managed to weaponize a strain of tularemia. Make it contagious." Theo's explanation was accompanied by a wary glance at the door to the lab.

"Yeah, from everything I've read, if you know what you're doing, it's not too hard to weaponize a bunch of different bacteria, and if they got a hold of the stuff the government's already made antibiotic resistant, it could be bad," I noted. It was also scary as hell, but that went without saying.

Luke did a quick rundown of what we'd learned and done, and the syrupy couple about went into apoplexy when he told them that I hadn't tipped off the agents to the contents of Laura's pocket.

"Are you out of your fucking mind? That was completely irresponsible!" Lexi screeched. "What if they were supposed to find it?"

There was a brief second when I really wanted to shove Lexi down the flight of stairs behind her. It wouldn't kill her, but at least I wouldn't have to face her scrutiny.

"Look, she's my mark. And something was wrong about the whole thing. There's something not right about tipping your guys off right now. I don't know what it is, but it's wrong." Now that the moment had passed, a wave of uncertainty crashed over me. What if I had been supposed to nudge the agents to find that? What if that was our job? What if all those people were going to die because I'd been so stupid in letting the moment pass, all for some random feeling? I did my best to keep a straight face, but the zing of concern pinged around in my chest.

Lexi looked like she might launch at me, but Theo grabbed her around the waist to hold her off. Not that the look he gave me was any kinder.

"If this job fails, I will be laying all those deaths at your feet."

Gulping, I held my ground. It would have been so much easier if I could come up with a logical explanation for what I did, but it just felt wrong. But no way was I changing my mind, especially not now. Not for these two. If I'd screwed up, hopefully there'd be something else we could do.

A commotion in the hallway alerted us to the agents heading toward the stairwell. I peeked through the tiny window in the door to catch the annoyed looking boss-guy flipping them off once they had their backs turned.

"We'll talk about this more tonight. The agents are going back to the lab to run the samples." Theo turned and had to nearly carry Lexi down the stairs to follow their marks.

"They took that well," I muttered, slumping down onto the top step. Luke hesitated a moment before settling next to me, close enough that his leg pressed against mine.

"We've all gotten that feeling when we aren't supposed to step in yet. Lexi's just a little high strung. She was talking last night about how much this job bothers her. She can't get that first image out of her head."

"Yeah, well, that makes two of us." I didn't want to say how many times my thoughts turned to that image, all those dead bodies piled up. It wasn't exactly something I wanted imprinted in my brain.

Luke patted my arm and we sat in silence for a long minute.

"I'm going to go check on Laura again. Want to grab the car and we'll tail your cop for a little longer?" I asked.

Luke nodded, then stood and extended a hand to help me up.

As I slipped back into the lab, I fought against the strange melancholy that welled up within me. So what if Lexi and Theo were pissed at me? They'd made it clear they didn't like me. Still, this felt strange. Off. And I wasn't sure what to do.

Making my way through the huddled groups of employees, I found Laura back on her stool, absorbed in her work. The sunlight lit her from behind, and now that she didn't look like she might throw up from nerves, it was possible to get a better feel for her.

There was a sharpness in way she analyzed the samples in front of her, care in every movement she made, which spoke to her sincerity as a scientist. The intensity of her gaze reminded me of photos of past great men and women who had furthered their chosen fields.

What might she have done for the world if she hadn't decided to bring it to its knees?

I could see the row of tiny tubes in her pocket, and thought about stealing them. But again, the feeling of wrongness filtered through me, accompanied by a bitterness worse than sucking on a lemon. From so many years of doing this, I knew it had to do with our job here, but I couldn't get my head and heart (or really, taste buds) to agree.

I hoped I'd figure out what that was before it was too late.

# CHAPTER
## 10

"We're going to have a hard time following that cop car," Luke said as I slid across his leather seat and settled back into the visible realm. He ran his hand around the steering wheel then gripped it with both hands, his foot tapping on the gas even before he'd turned the key.

I laughed. "I know you can catch up to them. And I know you're going to enjoy it."

Luke revved the engine twice, tossed me a devil-may-care grin that almost stopped my heart, and set off for the freeway.

"You know what I wish we could do? Make the car we're in invisible," he said, weaving through traffic like a madman. I'd put serious money on him having a secret collection of movies with every great San Francisco car chase.

"Yeah, that would be great. Until someone merged into you." My eye-roll was implied.

"That could be avoided." He suddenly downshifted and wove through a pair of cars, about two inches and my gasp the only thing separating us from them. "I wouldn't have to worry about cops."

"You do see the irony in the fact that we're chasing cops right now, don't you?"

Luke laughed and tapped the brakes before whipping across two lanes of traffic. We weren't in any real danger, but that didn't keep me from letting out a little squeak and hanging onto the Oh Shit handle for dear life.

Once Luke stopped laughing, I asked the question that had been lurking in the back of my mind all day. "So, where are you taking Melody tonight?"

Luke's hands tightened on the wheel and his eyes locked onto the road ahead of him. I half expected to see icicles hanging from the rearview mirror from the chill that invaded the cab.

I silently cursed myself, wanting to sink through the seat and out of the car. Oncoming traffic sounded much more friendly than the pissed off look Luke now sported.

"We're going to Greens. That vegetarian place?" I could feel the tension in his tone in my marrow.

"That's cool. I've heard it's good. And Melody will love it."

"Yeah, I figured she would."

Hesitating with my tongue on my teeth, I almost dropped the topic, but his mood swing was way too severe to be ignored. "Okay, seriously, is it so bad that I asked? She's my friend, too."

Luke's heavy silence continued for a few more beats, his speed increasing until the ugly sedan of his mark appeared up ahead.

"I don't know why it bothered me. It shouldn't have. I just...I don't know. I'm not used to sharing my private life."

Nodding, I tried not to let on how much that annoyed me. "I get that. We don't share a whole lot. Which to be honest, I'd be pretty happy to change. I mean, you're literally the only person alive that I've known my whole life."

Luke loosened his death-grip on the wheel and glanced over at me. "That's true. Does Melody know anything about how long that's actually been?"

Smooth way to change the topic, Luke, smooth. But I ran with it. I mean, what else was I supposed to do?

"Gah! No. At least, I hope not. She thinks I'm some twenty-something heiress with a job that makes me travel to boring places all the time. Which, I guess you should probably know I classify as Sacramento and Omaha. We go there a lot for work."

Luke merged in a few cars behind the cop. "Good to know, before I keep telling her about my fabulous adventures in Mexico."

"I pretty much told her I did nothing in Mexico, only one trip down to the beach." I wracked my brain, trying to think of what else I needed to fill Luke in on the cover story I'd been playing with Melody for years now. "I really hope that's it."

"Yeah, me too." His tone was cold enough to make me shiver.

I thought about asking Luke what he thought of Melody, of what he hoped might happen with her, but I couldn't come up with anything. I didn't want to piss him off again and apparently it was 'too personal' a topic to broach.

Seriously? Too personal? After this morning's little heart-to-heart about how we never spend any time together, it made no sense. I pulled my knees up and stared out my window, desperately wishing I was in my own car and not having to deal with the ache in my chest. He had no idea—none at all—how I felt, nor how long I'd felt that way. I'd made my peace with he and I never being an item, but it sure as shit didn't make watching an up-close and personal view of a new relationship any more fun.

I let myself have a two minute pity party before I set my jaw and got back to the really important thing right now: our job. And, what I'd done with Laura back at the lab. Had I really completely screwed things up? I knew my hunches were usually right, but with something this big, I couldn't afford to be wrong. The thought squeezed my lungs and I had to fight to draw breath.

We tailed the cops off the freeway to the FBI offices, where they sat for a good half hour. Not that we could see anything from the street—the entrance below was in a fortified garage, which left us staring at the random people filtering through the front doors. I watched Mike, Luke's mark, talk on his car radio before he and his partner finally gave up on waiting for the FBI agents and left.

"What now?" I asked, glad to break the silence. I'd been twitching for what felt like years, unable to stop dwelling on Laura's nervous actions with the agents earlier. The seats made awful squeaky noises every time I shifted my weight, which meant that I had to do so every thirty seconds.

Luke didn't fall into traffic right after them, but frowned when they turned left at the light ahead. "They're not heading back to the station. We should see what's going on."

Without waiting for my response, he set off to follow them. We sat in silence as they seemed to meander aimlessly through the city, though the other car must have had a destination in mind.

Eventually they pulled over next to the fence that lined the yard of a preschool. At least a hundred kids ran screaming and racing around on the other side of the chain-link, intent on enjoying the warm afternoon.

They were only paused for a moment, just long enough for a small boy to pause in his ball game to glance at the idling unmarked sedan at sidewalk and giggle. A quick wave and the blond kid was back at his game while the car pulled back into traffic. My heart tugged at this little stolen moment—no one would have ever known the boy's police officer dad had made the stop, but it was clear that the kid had loved it.

"Ever wonder how we ended up being the ones who got this 'awesome' end of the stick?" I asked, my voice catching on the words. I didn't want him to take things the wrong way, but I always wondered what he thought of our roles here. Again, it struck me as strange we never talked about these things. That I'd spent millennia wondering about them alone.

"All the time."

"Any hypotheses?" I asked.

"I sometimes think that I must have done something pretty shitty to end up here like this forever. But there's a big flaw in that logic."

After waiting a beat for him to continue, I twisted around to look at him. "Which is?"

"You." He said it like the reason was so obvious that I shouldn't have had to ask.

His comment knocked the air from my lungs. But what was it supposed to mean? What kind of reaction was I supposed to have? After his little pissy-fest earlier, I didn't feel like I could ask for an explanation. Which left my old standby: flippant.

"Well, then maybe we shouldn't discount your idea if that's all you've got to argue against it."

Luke didn't respond, just looked back at the road to tail the cop again.

What did he mean? The question hung on my tongue, but I couldn't get it past my lips.

# CHAPTER
# 11

"**A**mi? You're home, right? I need help!" Melody called from the back door to my place. I'd put the chain on when I arrived, hoping for a few hours of quiet, but yet again that was not in the cards.

Setting aside my laptop, I hurried to find Melody with her nose pushed through the crack in the door. "Melody, if you've forgotten your keys again…I swear!" I tried to keep my tone light to hide my irritation. She had locked herself out ten times in the last couple of months and I was about to go ahead and install one of those keypads on her door instead of attempting to keep a spare around.

"I didn't lock myself out. I need your sartorial help."

Convinced by her tone that she was at least not in bodily harm, I unfastened the chain and Melody burst through, an armful of clothes clutched to her chest. Without a second glance she went down the hallway to my bedroom and dumped them across my bed.

"These are my options for tonight. But I'm stuck. Help!"

I pursed my lips and groaned, pinching the bridge of my nose. "Seriously?"

"Look, Luke seems actually decent. Like, not a crazy freakazoid like that last guy I went out with. Remember him? The one that thought I was the reincarnation of his great Aunt? So, please, I beg of you, help me make a decent impression tonight!"

I did want the two of them to hit it off. They could do so well together. But did I want to watch them date? The two people I cared about most? Yeah, not so much. It just felt...lonely. And I hated admitting that.

But Melody had the dating track record of an Olympian when it came to finding crazies. They scented her out like ants scent sugar. Even if they first seemed completely normal, it only took about an hour before she was calling me from the bathroom, begging me to make up some excuse so she could leave early.

Considering she was about to go out with my partner, who was who-knew-how-old and received messages from the Great Beyond about how to make coincidences happen, could go invisible, and was psychically linked to me, well, it was a step up.

Maybe.

"Maybe, what?" Luke's voice filtered back instantly.

Shit. "Nothing, sorry, just a slip." Damn rat-gnawed neurons.

Shaking my head, I went to see the outfits she arranged on the bed, scrutinizing the second-hand dresses and weighing the options with a running commentary.

After Melody stripped and tried on a couple of things, we went with a red and black dress (hadn't Luke said he remembered my red dress?) with a lacy black cardigan. I was pretty sure Melody owned more cardigans than Mr. Rogers. Really, I'd never seen her without one.

She looked amazing. I loaned her some great little heeled booties then settled her in front of my makeup mirror to braid her long hair.

"What would I do without you?" Melody breathed, her eyes closed as I ran my fingers through her waves. I crafted a low side-braid that gathered in a loose bun behind her ear.

My hands kept moving, but I watched her reflection more. She was cute. Sweet. Smart. Luke would be lucky to spend some time with her. I knew I counted myself fortunate.

We were all adults. It was her choice, but a small part of me niggled at the thought of what she'd do if she knew the truth about Luke and me. It wasn't like she could have any kind of long-term thing with Luke. He wasn't aging any and was unlikely to do so any time soon. As far as we knew, none of the other partnerships we'd met ever managed to escape their immortality without dying—and not for lack of trying everything short of suicide. And the only reason I didn't know about that last one was because I only knew of about five other partnerships and that made for a small sample.

Was it unfair to let her get involved in our lives, such as they were? I didn't think being her friend was too terrible, but maybe I was biased. But a potential relationship? That seemed like a huge difference.

But both Luke and I had dated before. He wasn't an idiot, and Melody could have some fun for a while and then move on. Right? I was just going to have to keep telling myself that. As far as I knew, I hadn't royally screwed up any previous boyfriend I'd had.

Or maybe I was just making a whole lot of excuses to make myself feel better.

I so wasn't going to dwell on that.

I fastened in a bobby pin and took a breath. It was just a date. There was a good chance they wouldn't even hit it off. But if they did, it wasn't my problem to think about their choices. Luke could figure it out for himself.

So long as he didn't hurt her, because then I'd have to kill him. Or try at least find a way to do so.

Finished, I stood back to admire my handiwork. Melody twisted and turned in front of the mirrors, giggling, her hands clasped together in front of her. "It's perfect! Thank you!" She stood, now almost as tall as me with my shoes on, and wrapped me in a giant hug.

I hugged her back, the weight in my chest lightening just a smidge.

"Have fun tonight! And you'd better report later. And don't do anything I wouldn't do." I held out a finger in mock reprimand.

Melody tipped her head back in laughter. "Yeah, I'll try to remember that. Especially since I'm going out with your partner who's been totally relegated to the friend zone for however long you've worked together."

Ouch. I bent to gather an armload of her clothes to hide the spasm of pain that rocked through me.

The worst part—she was right. Not that it was my fault. I'd tried to start something, once, a few thousand years ago. We'd been working in Egypt at the time; it had been incredible chaos to wander those city streets. I still dreamed about the heat and the flies and the push of the crowds—and the spices and exotic goods and amazing craftsmanship that made almost anything I could imagine. The only better thing about today was having google and a cell phone, otherwise I would give my eye-teeth for an afternoon at the bazaar. Even then, Luke and I hadn't been very close—there'd been a guarded distance between us. Mine was because I couldn't help the crush I had on the tan and tall man whom I shared some weird part of my existence with, and talking with him still sometimes made me giggle and lose my train of thought. Thankfully that sort of stupidity was something I no longer suffered from.

After completing one of our coincidences, we'd been walking home and gods only knew what came over me, but his hand brushed mine in what I thought was some kind of invitation. I reacted before I had thought, well, anything and tugged him into an alley and kissed him for all I was worth. He didn't protest. I bunched the rough linen he wore in my fists and could feel the heat of the day trapped in the wall behind him. His lips were an amazingly soft contrast to the rough of his stubble. It was like everything poured out of me—all the feelings that I'd locked down for so long, even then, and for some stupid reason I thought that maybe Luke would understand them. Reciprocate.

Luke put up with my advances for exactly fifteen seconds. Well, my estimate may be off, but it wasn't long. I still am certain he enjoyed them, because that kiss was *not* one-sided. But then he pushed me away, wiping his mouth, staring at me with wide, horrified eyes.

"What in the hell, Ami?" He shook his head and edged toward the opening that would grant him freedom from my presence. Which is when I saw the truth of how he really felt about me, written all over his features: disgust. Revulsion. Total and complete horror at what I'd done.

It seared some part of me, burning back any tendrils of hope that maybe, just maybe, Luke reciprocated my crush. That burn had been strong enough, and Luke had maintained his aloof nature all these years since, that I felt pretty damn confident that he didn't have one iota of feelings for me.

I was honestly deeply ashamed of having put myself out there, made an effort, but I wasn't going to think about it. Nope. Luke and Melody would be good together. And I was going to keep my ass in the friend zone. Luke certainly was comfortable with keeping me there.

Stupid Lexi and Theo in all their happy couple-ness. They didn't need to put those kinds of thoughts in my head. I was plenty happy with the way things were.

Plenty happy.

Ugh, that sounded really horrible. I helped lug everything back to Melody's apartment, wished her a good time once more, and headed back to my place. Settling on my couch, I tried to get back into the research I'd been doing online, reading up on the stuff Laura did at her job, but who was I kidding? I was listening for Luke to arrive. Every creak in the house caught my attention.

I must have peeked out the windows a dozen times.

Right on time (of course), he pulled into the driveway and I watched him get out of his car—which had been freshly washed—and go to the outside door leading to Melody's place. Not that I cared, but he'd dressed in nice jeans and a button-up that definitely looked appealing.

Hidden behind almost-closed shutters, I spied on him as he made his way up the side path that led to Melody's outside door. He paused a moment, glancing up at my front door, and for an instant I thought he might come knock. I took one step in the direction of the door, wanting nothing more than to let him in and just smell him, but ended up punching a throw pillow instead. Luke's expression, half in shadow, collapsed. His eyes closed and his mouth tugged down like he'd just buried his best friend. Not that he could know I spied on him, but it still hurt to see him shake his head, run a hand through his hair, and continue his march to Melody's.

What had that all been about? Had I pissed him off, or worse, disappointed him so much I made him sad? I turned away from the window, wishing I'd just left it well enough alone.

I listened at the back door as Melody greeted him and the two of them chattered about dinner on their way back outside.

They both sounded happy and comfortable, which was exactly as it should be. Even if it bothered me. Just a bit.

# CHAPTER
## 12

I must have fallen asleep because my phone buzzed to wake me ten minutes before I was supposed to meet everyone at the diner.

Groaning, I rolled to my feet. A spoon and empty ice cream carton clattered to the floor. When had I polished that off? I barely managed to drag my fingers through my hair and grab a sweater before I raced out the door. The whole theme of unkempt and late was going to rule these meetings for me. Whatever. Like I cared.

I checked my texts at the stoplights as I hurried across town. There was no hope of being on time so I didn't push it. All of them already thought I was a screw-up, and I was beyond caring.

"Hey, I'm exhausted, but I had a fab time tonight with Luke! I'll fill you in on the deets later!" Melody wrote, adding several winky emojis.

Winks? Really? What did that mean?

Just one face turned to greet me at the diner. Luke. Still looking dapper in his date clothes, although they were a little mussed now. Too mussed. Like they'd been rolled around in.

I really wished I hadn't noticed that.

"Where are the others?" I asked, hesitating at the end of the booth, unsure where I should sit. Next to him? Or across? Not that either meant anything, but if I was being honest, I didn't really want to sit in either spot.

"Late?" Luke asked, clearly not buying his own excuse.

He patted the seat next to him and I slid in, careful of the torn vinyl this time, and dumped my bag between us to act as a barrier.

"They don't strike me as the type to be late," I stated the obvious, peering around to see if they could be anywhere else. But the only other patron was a wizened old man eating a sundae at the counter.

Luke shrugged. "Maybe something came up with their marks?"

"Maybe." But neither of us had received a text of any kind. Which meant it was pretty unlikely.

"Have you tried calling?" I asked, unease settling in my stomach like a coiled snake. "Something seems really off."

I met Luke's dark eyes and was a little gratified to see he was just as concerned.

"Texted, called, both of them. Their lines have been cut off. Not even accepting calls."

My mouth fell open. "Seriously?"

Luke nodded and stirred his coffee until a small whirlpool formed. "I have no idea what that means."

I flopped back against the seat, the vinyl squeaking in protest. Shit. What did that mean? Nothing good.

"What do we do?"

"We wait for a little longer and hope they show up."

I let out a long breath, chasing my hair away from my face. "Yeah. And when they don't?"

"We go to their hotel. And hope nothing bad has happened."

Bad, how? I wanted to ask, but didn't dare. Were they hurt? Possibly. We got hurt just like anyone else. Though it took a whole lot of effort to kill one of us.

Could someone have captured them? But whom? And how could something like that happen? We were able to turn invisible. That had to make it trickier to track us down, or hold us.

"What if the agents have infra-red? They'd be able to see them, even if they were cloaked," Luke said, still playing with his coffee.

I hadn't even thought of that, but since Luke was the tech-y one, I would put money on him having tested it. "We just have to hope they don't."

Luke shrugged, his shoulder brushing against mine briefly.

I got up and moved to the other side of the booth, earning a confused look from my partner.

"Sorry, just wanted to spread out a bit." An utter lie. I just couldn't handle being close to him. Especially since he smelled like Melody's perfume.

To prove my point, I turned sideways and let my feet dangle off the far end of the seat.

Luke narrowed his eyes. Not for one second did he buy it. But it wasn't like he was going to ask, so he could stew over it all he wanted.

"How was your date?" I asked, really not caring if it pissed him off. Or maybe some petulant part of me hoped it did. Which was totally pathetic. I knew it. And couldn't seem to shove a sock in it.

"It was fine. We had a good time."

I raised an eyebrow, daring him to continue. He heaved a sigh. "She liked my library."

"Oh, so she got to see inside your place?" I asked, raising my brows and lifting my chin.

"You're welcome any time. You know that."

Yeah, I'm sure, especially with the stiff formalness to his tone.

I plunked my elbow on the table and rested my chin on my hand, staring at the assembly of empty tables and the long-worn counter with red-topped stools spaced along it.

He must have gathered how annoyed I was as we lapsed into silence. With everything going on, I had no right to make an issue of this. It was inconsequential and petty. But damn it if it didn't piss me off. How could he have asked me why we never share anything just this morning? Then get all upset when I asked about Melody? I really did not need that kind of shit.

I eventually ordered some coffee, and after two refills, Luke cleared his throat. "I think we should go by their hotel."

Nodding, I gathered my things and dropped money and a tip on the table. Outside in the fog, we walked down the street, trees dripping water around us, neither one of us saying anything.

In my head, I couldn't help imagining myself as a string pulled too tight, fraying in the middle, about to come apart. Somehow it was the only way I could explain how I felt. But I remembered all too well what happened the last time I snapped—the look in Luke's eyes back in Egypt was enough to make me swallow back the questions I wanted to scream, the frustration that filled my chest.

It took us five minutes to make it to the adorable old-fashioned hotel Theo and Lexi said they rented a room in. The lobby lights were down low, so I couldn't see anyone behind the desk.

Luke cloaked himself first and I followed suit. He opened the heavy glass door as little as possible and wedged himself through, holding it for me.

Inside, a hush settled over the room, chilling me more than the fog outside.

"I'm going to go check the log," Luke thought at me and I waved him off, going to explore a bit.

The place had been decorated like a ritzy sitting room from the nineteenth century. Thick Persian carpets. Stuffed velvet chairs that looked less than comfortable. Mirrors and portraits along the wood paneled walls.

Before Luke and I moved here, we'd lived in the south of England. For a while I'd rented a room in a place that looked kind of like this. Somehow, while peering into the dark corners, the past seemed to steal over me. Like I could walk into it from here, return to the person I'd been then. All it would take was a little push. Maybe then I'd be the person who didn't worry about friend-zones and losing their only connection to the one and only person who knew their history—even if he didn't know my darkest secrets.

Luke's hand dropped onto my shoulder and I yelped aloud, spinning to face him.

"You scared me!" I accused.

"I can see that." Luke tried to hold in a grin but failed. "Sorry. I really didn't mean to."

I took a deep shaky breath. Something about the way he smiled relaxed me. "It's fine. I'm just jumpy. What did you find?" I brushed my hair out of my face, wishing I could not seem like an idiot for just a few hours. That really wasn't too much to ask, was it?

"That this hotel doesn't get enough customers—only two other guests. Lexi and Theo were staying in room 709. But they've checked out."

"Checked out?" I shook my head. "What?"

"That's what I thought."

"Well, are we going to go look?"

Luke held out a hand and motioned to the stairs. "After you."

"I'm taking the elevator."

Luke chuckled outright. "They're going to think the place is haunted."

"Last I heard, that's kind of good for business," I retorted, heading toward the modern contraption in the corner.

It dinged open as soon as I hit the button and once the doors closed behind us, Luke turned to me. "If I'd known it would upset you that I had Melody over, I wouldn't have done it."

Heaving a sigh over having to deal with my stupid snit, I managed a polite nod. "You shouldn't worry about stuff like that. I don't know why it pissed me off. It shouldn't have." Liar, liar, pants on fire.

"I guess we're both having moments today?" he asked, his thoughts tinged with laughter even though his expression remained completely blank.

"Yeah, seems to be that kind of day."

Luke squeezed my arm. "If you'd like to come over and check out my library before the fireworks, I'll even show you the backyard. Melody hasn't gotten to see that."

I laughed and hung my head. "Yeah, that sounds fun. You like to garden?"

"A little." He gave a modest shrug. "Helps pass the time."

"Looks like you're good at it. At least from what I could see in the dark."

Luke laughed and nudged me out of the elevator once it opened.

The hallway was quiet and freaky. Mirrors at either end reflected one another, and not us, making my head hurt as we padded down to 709.

The door was locked, of course, with one of the modern credit card-like readers that made Luke grumble. I stood guard while he messed with it, getting the thing to hiss, beep green, and allow us to open the door.

"What did you do to it?" A small trail of smoke wafted from the card-reader slot.

Luke gave it a hard look, like the thing had offended him. "Let's just say it's gone to door lock heaven."

We shut the door behind us and flicked on the lights.

Any good humor I'd allowed myself on the trip up here, any hope that whatever happened to Theo and Lexi was just a misunderstanding, dissipated right along with the smoke from the door.

"This can't be good."

"Yeah. I was going to say 'oh shit' but that works, too," I said.

The room looked like a tiny tornado had gone through it, kicking up furniture, chairs, and pretty much everything else in its path.

The mattresses, stuffing hanging out like guts, were tilted against the windows. Curtains were slashed and half ripped off. All of the glass in the bathroom had been shattered. The TV hung by its cords from the wall mount.

The reality of the situation crashed down around me. Someone, or something, had gotten to Theo and Lexi. We had no idea where they were, if they were even okay, and now we didn't have anyone to help us with this job. As if it hadn't felt impossible enough already.

My knees went weak and I leaned against the wall. Luke grabbed me before I slid to the floor, supporting my weight against him.

"What do we do?" I whispered, moisture gathering in my eyes. I may not have seen eye to eye with the other partnership, but I didn't want anything to happen to them.

Luke, his arms wrapped around me, shook his head. "I honestly don't have a clue."

# CHAPTER
# 13

I t wasn't until we got back to the diner, standing next to my car, that I broke the silence. "Should we go to the cops?" We both knew the answer, but I had to say something, anything, to keep the soul-eating silence away.

Luke's brow furrowed. "Maybe? But what are we going to tell them?"

"Oh, hey, you know the immortals, the ones who can go invisible and make coincidences happen? I don't know! That our friends are missing? That there may have been foul play?"

"We can't explain how we were in their hotel room." His words weren't meant to be as infuriating as they hit me.

I took a deep breath and pressed my palms against my thighs until I was sure I wouldn't strangle him. "I know. It's just—" I met his eyes as a heavy weight seemed to settle on my shoulders. "I'm scared. We've lived through some strange times, but this scares me." Part of me wanted to run, hide, forget all that was supposed to happen. But that wouldn't help anyone, least of all me.

Luke pressed his lips together. "You're not the only one."

That didn't make me feel any better.

"This is my fault, isn't it?" I said, breathing a long white cloud into the night air.

Luke shook his head. "What?"

"If I hadn't stopped the agents from finding that stuff Laura had, Theo and Lexi probably would be long gone. Not...not whatever happened." I dug my shoe into the cement. I hated my words, but they were the truth. I'd followed my gut earlier, and it had been so, so wrong. Not only were we no closer to figuring out how to stop the attack, but we'd lost our help to do it.

We were quiet for a long moment while I struggled to fight back the tightness in my throat, the burning in my eyes. Luke stepped closer and settled a hand on my upper arm. I looked up in surprise, catching sight of the warmth in his dark eyes. Some errant little neuron piped up to note that his expression was one I'd hoped to see all those years ago after I'd kissed him.

"It's not your fault. Whatever happened, happened. You can't blame yourself."

Everything in me wanted to argue, but I just nodded. He wasn't right, but it didn't matter. We just had to fix all of this. Somehow.

Luke's hand slid away, once again leaving a gulf of space between us. "I know you're not going to like this much, but I don't think either of us ought to be alone right now. At least until we figure this out. Do you want to stay at my place?" He didn't dare look at me, directing his speech to his shoes.

I tried to hide my shock. I really did. But when Luke chuckled, I knew it was hopeless. "I have a guest room. And you have Melody, who I'd prefer we didn't drag her into whatever might be going on."

Melody. Of course. He should be worried about her. I should have been grateful that he was. But really, all I wanted to do was get in my car and make him eat my dust.

Heaving a dramatic sigh because I couldn't wrap my head around all of this, I swallowed the quip ready to launch from my tongue. "I need to get my stuff."

"We can go in the morning, okay?"

"Fine. Whatever." He was right, of course. It would be better to stick together, and honestly, I was about to fall over from exhaustion. But I didn't have to like it.

I tailed Luke across the city, grateful he wasn't driving like he was auditioning for a video game. When we reached his place, he opened his garage and guided my car into the space next to his sports car.

He led the way through the darkness—the shadows bothering me more than I wanted to admit—to the back door. It swung open and he flicked on the lights, illuminating a small mudroom where he kicked off his nice black shoes.

I unzipped my boots and left them askew, just to be annoying.

We went into the kitchen, Luke turning on lights as we went. His house was exactly what I imagined. Yet, so completely not. Despite its small size, there was an open, airy feeling. The colors were muted in shades of grey and tan. There was a distinctive maleness in the chrome counters and black fixtures, but it didn't scream 'I'm a man, and this is my space!'

And, it smelled clean, like he'd sprayed everything down with Windex and Febreeze. Of course, he'd planned on bringing Melody here earlier, so that explained that.

"Did you hear me?" Luke waved a hand in front of my face.

I started, taking a step back as I returned to reality from a brief foray into what Melody and Luke had done here earlier. "Sorry, sorry, I'm just tired. What did you say?"

If Luke was frustrated by my spacing out he didn't let on. "Just that the bathroom's the door across the hall. The guest room is this one." He led us down the short hallway and pushed open one of the doors. Inside, the room was tastefully decorated in navy, with a plush bed and an armchair in the corner.

"Looks great. Thanks. You have a nice place." I pushed a smile onto my face, trying to gloss over my earlier lapse from reality.

"Thank you." Luke frowned at me. I smiled and nodded while he explained the toothbrushes and towels situation, but my attention wandered like I'd had a triple shot espresso and then had to sit through one of Melody's artsy films at the library—the kind lacking in shirtless men.

"Great, great. That's perfect." I must have repeated myself twenty times. Extra blankets? "Great, great. That's perfect." How to turn on the nightlight? "Great, great. That's perfect." How to change the thermostat? "Great, great. That's perfect." How to take his shirt off? I wish. Finally, he made his way up the stairs to his room.

With a deep breath, I looked around. Someone else might have said snooped, but really, I just practiced my research skills and pictured Luke doing everyday things there, like folding his underwear and making the bed. The whole place felt distinctly comfortable. Lived in, and very much like Luke, which probably explained why I wanted to touch everything.

I used the little bathroom, longing for my own giant countertop and toothbrush. The chances of a blow-dryer for the morning had to be slim.

On my way back to the guest room, Luke appeared carrying a pile of clothing and got my attention—boxers and a loose shirt. Must. Not. Stare. Well, too much.

I bit the inside of cheek to stop remembering the time I saw Luke naked. Okay, to be honest, I've seen Luke naked twice for a few moments before I could turn and run. It was bound to happen at some point, what with spending centuries together and seeing every fashion trend come and go, or so I told myself. His nice blue boxers weren't anything special. It's not like they were a loincloth. Or a Speedo. Or...my cheeks heated to a roasting red.

Good grief, how could I even think about that, now of all times, when so much uncertainty surrounded everything? I felt like a jerk, but there was no controlling my errant thoughts; I just hoped they stayed in my own head.

"I tried to find something smaller that might work for sleeping in. Maybe if you roll the pants up?" He handed over a pair of sweatpants and a grey t-shirt that looked practically new.

"Great, great. That's perfect." I rolled my eyes at myself. Idiot.

Luke smiled and escaped around the corner like the room was on fire. Carefully securing the door, I peeled off my clothes and yanked on Luke's things. The shirt hung almost to my knees. The pants were so long nothing was saving them and I ended up folding them back up and leaving them on the dresser, but not before inhaling his scent.

Once I turned out the light, the backyard came into view. The silver moonlight illuminated several tall garden boxes and foliage creeping along trellises that were impossible to identify at night. All I could tell was that it was careful, meticulous, and probably perfect.

I cracked the window, letting in the sound of faint traffic and several crickets seeking mates.

Somewhere Lexi and Theo were in trouble. And somewhere, Laura plotted to kill millions. Both thoughts left me shivering and I shut the drapes, wishing I could shut off the rumble of my thoughts as easily.

Sleep felt like the last thing I'd manage, but as I slid under the rich covers, heavy exhaustion waved over me, lulling me into the dark waters of unconsciousness.

Ж

Why did he have to smell so good? I nuzzled in closer to his neck, sighing as I drew in his scent. His arms tightened around me and I lifted my head just a bit, seeking Luke's lips and the kiss I knew waited for me.

Except, instead of lips, all I found was empty air. And the sound of someone knocking on the door like they were in desperate need of a bathroom.

"Ami! Seriously, you sleep like the dead!" The door creaked open and I managed to haul one eyelid open.

Luke's jaw hung open from where he'd poked his head around the door. It took a long moment, but a chill creeping up my leg made me realize I'd managed to bunch the covers into a body pillow shape and was wrapped around them with Luke's shirt bunched up to my armpits. Showing off my fabulous panties.

Our eyes met for just a second before his gaze drifted south, taking in every last bit of exposed skin. My dream still felt close enough to touch, and a little voice in the back of my brain screamed at me to say something, do anything, to get that kiss I'd expected.

Or more. My skin burned at the thought of more.

Instead, the door rattled closed and I groaned. Perfect way to start the day.

Taking a moment to get my bearings, I stared at the ceiling, thinking over everything that had happened yesterday. The lab. The cop and his son. Luke's date. And Lexi and Theo going missing.

Where were we even going to start today?

I got to my feet, threw on my dirty clothes, and made the bed in record time. After splashing water on my face, I padded barefoot into the kitchen.

"Sorry about that," Luke said in a low voice from where he brewed tea at the kitchen counter.

I shook my head. "We're just going to pretend it didn't happen, m'k?"

Luke nodded solemnly and handed me a mug. I sunk into one of the white chairs at his little table and inhaled.

"This smells familiar." I took a test sip. "Where did you get this?"

Luke grinned, raising a brow and settling in across from me. "I know you don't like to think about it, but after a few beers, you tend to get chatty. Especially about your secret tea concoction."

"I do not!" I wasn't totally sure if I should be indignant or humiliated. The latter was winning, and another award-worthy blush began to creep up my chest to my face.

Luke held up his hands, palms to me. "I've only been around you a couple of times like that, so maybe not always, but it has been a bit of a trend." He chuckled, eyes glinting with humor as he took another sip.

My jaw worked for a moment, trying to come up with some kind of response, but I just gave in. "So, same time as when we met Lexi and Theo? Or is there some other incident that I don't remember?"

Luke shrugged. "Maybe. But I got this out of you then. I'd been asking you for it for ages."

I did remember that much at least. I made a mean combination tea mix, something I'd perfected over the years, and Luke had tried getting the recipe out of me since at least the French Revolution. I guess I finally gave it up.

"Anything else I should know about this mysterious night?" I asked, staring down into my yellow mug and watching a few stray leaves swirl in the current.

"Nothing other than you professing your undying love." Luke shrugged.

I glanced at him, confused. He winked.

"Funny. Really, really funny."

He shrugged. "I thought so."

Rolling my eyes, I decided it was time for a topic change. We really shouldn't have been joking around with so much at stake, even if it did loosen the noose of tension around my neck. "So, today. What are we going to do about Lexi and Theo?"

"I was thinking we should track down their agents. See what we can find out about them. Maybe that will give us some kind of clue."

"Or get us captured."

"Do you think it was them who did this?"

I frowned. "I don't know. I mean, it's just so random. But something feels off and that's the only thing I can think of that kind of makes sense. Maybe the agents caught on to them somehow and decided to track them down?"

Luke wrinkled his nose, "As possible as that is, I hope you're wrong."

"Yeah, me too."

"So, we follow the agents. And I think maybe if that doesn't give us any information, we speak with the cops. We don't have to give too many details, only that they were staying at the hotel. Who knows, maybe it'll help."

I nodded. "Sounds like a plan." I prayed it was one that would work. Because every minute we spent looking for the other partnership was time spent away from Laura. It was a necessary compromise, but not one that settled well with me. For now, though, I ignored the tug of wrongness in my chest. After what happened with Laura yesterday, and Theo's dire statement on the fate of all those potential dead, I decided that listening to my head was the wiser course of action.

No matter what, lives hung in the balance.

# CHAPTER
## 14

**F**irst stop after a detour by my place: FBI headquarters. It was in the towering government building downtown, right on the edge of the skeezy area I hated walking through even in the middle of the day. The building itself sat on a full city block with what would have been a nice courtyard if there hadn't been several bums sunning themselves. Otherwise, there wasn't much of note about the building, other than the flag clanging against the pole out front.

When most people thought about becoming invisible, I swear their first thought was getting to see people naked. At least, over the years, this is what I'd heard countless times. Honestly, I didn't understand the desire.

But, there were other perks to being able to cloak myself. Like, the fact that Luke and I parked a few blocks away from the building and walked right past the security guards.

Metal detectors? No problem. Just go around them. We hopped

the low wall that separated the inner lobby from the public one we'd entered through. While invisible, it was also important to be sure not to knock into one of the guards. They looked very freaked out when anything hit them by accident, such as an overly large shoulder bag.

"Sheesh, you'd think I just slammed him with a baseball bat or something," I thought at Luke as we hurried away.

"What do you have in your bag?" Luke poked my slightly oversized purse I had flung crosswise over my body, the close proximity of the material and way I wore it keeping the thing invisible even if it flapped out and smacked someone.

"Flashlight, a first aid kit, makeup, and some food in case I get stuck somewhere for a while and need to eat something." There were a few other essentials in there I'd found handy to have on hand over the years.

"Kitchen sink?" Luke asked as we scanned the department listings near the elevators.

"Just wet-naps."

I elbowed him hard when he laughed.

"Any idea where we're going to start?" I asked, returning my focus to what we were supposed to be doing.

Luke read through the list and we both shrugged. "The labs first? They might have more information."

Riding in elevators while invisible and you're not the only ones in there? Very hard. I ended up smooshed against the back wall with a very round man right in front of me, taking up all possible breathing room. When everyone else had emptied out, I thought he'd move. No dice. Instead, he farted. Right in my direction. I thought Luke might die from holding his laughter in.

Thankfully we got out on the next floor, and I smacked Luke's arm good for his antics. That only left him doubled over with mirth.

The hallway was long, white, and very dull. At the end, yet another lab opened up, and I silently prayed that whatever Laura was up to today, it wasn't too horrible, because as soon as we found Theo and Lexi, we were going to stop her.

The lab was nearly empty, with very expensive looking machines moving around or flashing lights, reminding me a bit of the videos on how cars were assembled, only these were working with tiny tubes and not engines.

Luke pointed to a logbook near the door and began leafing through the pages while I searched for whoever was working in the lab.

"I've got a number and a name," Luke said.

"Great. Can you track it?" I edged around another of the black-topped lab benches and found a balding man hunched over a computer, busily typing away at something. A woman was situated just past him, dressed in a lab coat adorned with a mess of doodles, doing something that looked similar to what Laura had done, involving a pipette and some kind of liquid.

I'd hoped that the computer might be free so I could poke around and find some information, but that wasn't going to happen. Instead, I returned to Luke, who was busily attempting some magic on his phone.

In the last couple of years Luke had taken a keen interest in new technology. While we both were fine with computers and the web, some things still overwhelmed me. Luke, on the other hand, embraced it all. He'd gotten quite excited when he figured out how to triangulate a cell phone back to its current location. Considering we spent a lot of time hunting people down, it helped. A ton.

A beep and his screen flashed. "They're here. In the building, I think." Luke sighed. "But where exactly isn't as clear."

"Well, it's a start." We headed back toward the elevators when one of the doors off to our left opened and a man hurried out, rushing down the hall toward the lab we'd exited.

His door swung shut, giving me enough time to glimpse his desk piled high with paperwork. And a phone.

"You have a name for those guys?" I caught the door before it latched.

Luke held up his hand where he'd scrawled the names and number of the agents from yesterday.

"I've got an idea."

Careful not to make it incredibly obvious the door was opening of its own volition, we went inside the office and left the door cracked behind us.

"Keep an eye out in case he comes back."

Luke nodded, sticking close to the door while I went to the phone and hit zero. Did they still have operators in these buildings? Or was it all automated? Someone, somewhere here had to handle this kind of thing, right?

The creepy dead-sounding automated woman came over the line, asking me which extension I wanted. I kept hitting zero until an actual person picked up.

"Hello, how might I direct your call?"

Score.

"Hello, I'm looking to speak with Agent Ramirez, visiting from D.C. I don't have an extension for where they've been set up while they're here."

The woman on the other end breathed static into the line. "Fine, hold up a second."

I bounced on my toes, urging her to hurry. The hold music was torture—some kind of muzak that made me wish that they'd stuck with classical.

"Okay, I found it. Extension 2509. I'll connect you."

I took a deep breath when the line started to ring. It only did so twice before someone snatched the phone, snapping a harsh "Hello."

"Hello, Agent Ramirez. It's the lab calling. We have a few of the preliminary results from the samples you brought in yesterday. I think you should take a look at them."

"Perfect. I'll be right up."

"We don't encourage too many people in the lab. I'll bring them to you."

The agent muttered something. "Sure. We're on the sixth floor. Office 603. Desks at the back."

"I'll be right down, sir."

I set the phone back in the cradle, grinning like a crazy person.

"Get it?" Luke asked.

"Yep! Let's kick it out of here before that guy gets back."

Luke edged the door open, allowing it to swing freely about a foot so we could sneak around it back into the hallway.

We called the elevator without really worrying about it. Elevators opened and closed without anyone in them all the time—someone pushed a wrong button, or just a glitch in the system. No one suspected, well, us in big buildings like this one.

Our ride down was almost empty, and I leaned back against the cool stainless-steel railing and went back to pondering what the agents might know. Or not know. Really, I wasn't quite sure which was more frightening at this point.

"We'll figure it out, you know that, right?" Luke noted, glancing at me around a woman who dug through her giant purse like her life depended on it.

"Yeah....Yeah," I sighed, wishing I felt even remotely more confident.

We escaped the elevator and wandered through the winding hallway toward their office. People drifted through the windowless space with paperwork in reams and otherwise looking efficiently busy.

Were Theo and Lexi here somewhere? Caught in some kind of trap?

Office 603 was not much more than a door that led to small sea of cubicles, some long open tables, and an otherwise dull space. I wasn't surprised Agent Ramirez wanted to get out of there.

The two agents we sought were at the back of the room, huddled over a joined set of desks, sorting through stacks of manila files.

The sound of the other agents moving, talking, and typing hid our footsteps.

"How are we going to get them away from the desk?" Luke asked as we neared the duo.

They looked just as colorless as they had yesterday, especially in the buzzing fluorescent lights. Someone needed to tell the woman, Agent Connic, that lipstick was not the enemy.

I edged around Ramirez to peer over his shoulder at what he was pouring over. It looked like documents from SynthLab, where Laura worked. A quick check of his computer screen confirmed my suspicions. I'd managed to hack into most of this stuff online, but the government seemed to have more extensive access. Not that that surprised me. But it did make my stomach clench, knowing that I'd stopped them from finding Laura's work yesterday. Had I royally screwed up? Would this whole mess have sorted itself out if I'd nudged them to look in her pockets?

Would Theo and Lexi not be missing? The agents would have been too busy with Laura to focus on the other partnership, more than likely. How much of their trouble was my fault?

I shook off the barrage of doubts. Nothing I could do about it now, except fix the whole mess.

"What's she got?" I looked up at Luke.

He frowned and shook his head. "It looks like purchase orders. For lab equipment?"

"Probably stuff from the lab. They've ordered a ton of stuff lately. Most of it seemed legit, from what I could google, but who knows."

"She's underlining a few of the chemicals."

"Make a list, would you? I'll look it up later."

Luke jotted stuff down on his phone, while I went back to wishing I could get into Ramirez's computer.

"That kid should be here with the lab stuff by now," Ramirez noted about twenty minutes later, looking across the desks at his partner.

She merely nodded, lost in whatever she was up to.

"I'm going to go up and check. Coming?"

"Perfect!" I thought as I clasped my hands together, excited that my plan had worked.

The agents gathered notebooks and pens and left their mess behind.

"How obvious is it going to be if we look through this?" I narrowed my eyes as I scanned Ramirez's desk. I debated about what to move first.

Luke didn't respond and I glanced at him. All the color had drained from his features, settling painfully in my gut.

"What is it?"

Luke just pointed at the spot vacated by the agent's shuffled paperwork.

Edging around the desks to get a better view, my heart rate spiked, thundering in my ears.

A photo lay exposed on the top of the pile of folders, showing two people walking down the sidewalk. I recognized both of them. Theo and Lexi, wearing the same outfits they'd had on yesterday.

Oh hell. I'd gotten them captured.

# CHAPTER
# 15

"What does this mean?" I couldn't quite get enough air into my lungs.

Luke slowly shook his head. Glancing around to ensure no one was looking, he grabbed the picture and pulled it close so that his cloaking covered it.

"It looks like yesterday morning. Before we saw them at the lab."

My mouth went dry and I tried to get a better view over Luke's shoulder, though he was much too tall for me.

"Is there anything else?" I asked, turning back to the desk to see if I could come up with some other tidbit, some kind of information on where they might be—what happened in the hotel room.

Anything.

"This is all my fault."

Luke cast me a hard look, but didn't voice his disagreement. How could he?

I forced the pile to tilt and fall like it had merely toppled over due to poor stacking. I waited for a young guy in a crooked tie seated a few cubicles over to go back to work before leafing through the files. Screw leaving it neat behind me. If the agents or anyone knew about us, about what we did, there were much more serious repercussions.

Like jail, experiments, and torture. At the very least, we'd be lucky if they didn't try some kind of enforced servitude.

As I hunted through the files and Luke tackled the computer, my mind went to the horror stories I'd heard during World War II. The Nazis had captured a partnership of our kind, another set like Luke and me, or Theo and Lexi. How they managed that, and how the two didn't escape, was beyond me. I'd never met them, but there were informal chains of connection between us, ways that we communicated that had grown easier as technology facilitated them. Not that we did so often, but still, it didn't take more than a decade before everyone heard about this other pair.

It hadn't ended well for the partners and ripples of their story were still discussed during the rare contact we had with one another. There isn't much that can kill us—it takes a whole lot of effort. But apparently, they'd found a way. It left me distinctly ill just thinking about it.

"Anything?" Luke asked, leaving the one computer and heading around to check the other.

"Nothing yet. But why do they have that photo?"

Luke just gave me a wide-eyed 'I have no clue' look.

Connic's desk was no better. Just lots of information on the company Laura worked for. I took my time searching, scanning documents while trying to see what else I could learn.

There wasn't much.

Just the photo. A shiver traveled up my spine. All my fault.

It was a whisper that tipped me off. "She's on the left."

I glanced at Luke, who was still absorbed in the computer. Whipping around, I yelped aloud and reached out for him, managing to grab his arm.

"What?" He asked, following my gaze.

"I believe the intruders have been alerted to our presence," the same guy whispered.

Did he think I couldn't hear him?

There were only two of them, dressed in bulletproof vests with guns trained on us. One of them wore military-type goggles.

Infra-red. Shit. "How did they know?"

"Someone tipped them off," Luke thought in a calm voice. "I'll bet it was Ramirez and Connic." Shit. The agents. Of course.

The guy with the goggles edged forward, hesitant, as he made his way through the cubicles. His gun never wavered. The other one, blind to our presence, tailed the first while his weapon wandering every which way.

We had two options: de-cloak and surrender in hopes of learning more, or run like hell.

"I say run," Luke noted.

Yet again, I'd broadcasted.

Luke wrapped his hand around mine. "Take the outside aisle. Away from the men. We have the benefit of them not being able to hear us communicate."

"He's going to shoot as soon as we start moving!" I panicked, my throat tight with the threat of tears.

"Get low and head for crowded areas. He's not going to fire into a group of his coworkers."

"Sure about that?" I looked around at the people concentrated in small huddles near the blue walls of the cubicles and dull metal desks, all of them watching this unfold with looks that wavered between disbelief and fear.

"You're staying with me, right?" I tightened my grip on Luke's hand.

"Right behind you. Now go!" Luke gave me a little push and I stumbled to get my feet working. My heart in my throat, I managed to move in a sort of crouch run, getting to the wall and racing down the side opening that led to the door we'd come in through.

"Block the door! They're headed that way!" the guy with the goggles cried from behind us.

"Shit, shit, shit, shit," Luke muttered, his hand beginning to sweat in mine as we kept going.

A group of people had gathered at the end of the row, a roadblock. From my vantage all I could see were knee length skirts and slacks, nervously moving around as the guy with the gun gained on us.

"Glen, get away from us!" One of the women screeched and scrambled back as the goggle-faced man appeared next to me.

He didn't have his gun up, more intent on keeping us in sight. His mistake. I stood, staring at the man for a split second. His blue button-up was stained with sweat around the vest, and his goggles made him look a little too much like a bug. I longed to rip those goggles off, but Luke pressed a hand into my shoulder to urge me on.

I ignored my partner and stepped closer to Glen. He sucked in a harsh breath, frozen. If he thought he was scared now, he didn't know a thing about fear.

In one swift move, I brought my knee up with as much force as I could. Tender tissue crunched under the impact and Glen's gun clattered to the floor as he bent double with a moan.

"Glen! Glen? What's going on, man?" The shrieking woman came to his side as I backed away.

"Ami, you are seriously certifiable," Luke said. He grabbed my hand again, racing down the hallway. The door loomed up; thankfully most everyone who'd thought to obey Glen's blocking orders had taken more concern in his wellbeing.

"Stop, or I'll shoot! Stop!"

I glanced over my shoulder. The other guy who had tailed Glen before now donned the glasses and had his gun trained on us.

"Don't listen to him!" Luke screamed in my head. He propelled me through the door and into the hallway.

A single shot slammed into the wall as we slid out of the doorway, creating a crater that rained dust and chunks to the ground.

"Elevator or stairs?" Luke asked.

The elevator dinged at the other end of the winding hallway, answering the question for us. Running full speed, my feet slapping on the linoleum, we raced toward the sound. Behind us, someone gave chase.

Please don't shoot anyone accidentally. I begged the guy, my whole body waiting for the next fire of the gun.

The elevator door was just about to close when Luke shoved his arm through to force it open again.

The young woman inside, carrying a load of files, stared around with wide eyes, as the re-opened doors admitted two invisible heavy-breathers.

The shooter rounded the corner just as the doors slid shut. His weapon trained on the elevator, goggles barely hanging onto his face. I resisted the urge to wave goodbye.

Luke slumped against the wall, his breath rasping in and out. The woman glanced in our direction, eyes roaming over the empty space. Her fingers blanched as she hit the button for the next floor.

The door closed behind her, her footsteps clattering into a run as she raced away from the 'haunted' elevator.

"Wonder how long she'll be taking the stairs?" I mused.

"A while, I'd guess."

"Do you think we're going to make it out of here?" I slumped down next to him as we rode to the ground level.

His eyes slid shut. "I have no idea."

The doors sounded and we stepped out into the lobby. We peered around in every direction before ducking low and making our way to the back of the building that let out on the street side.

Two men, wearing the same military-esk goggles, emerged ahead of us before we got two feet. Luke caught my arm and ushered us off to the side, into a small marble alcove where we could watch.

Luke looked me up and down, and then uncloaked himself. "We're never going to make it out if we stay hidden," he said.

Wrinkling my nose, I nodded and allowed my cloak to fall away. The lights hurt my eyes and every sound seemed like an imaginary masked man about to take us down.

"You go first. I'll meet you at the car in a few minutes," Luke said.

I wanted to protest. There were so many things that were just not cool about this idea, the biggest of which was leaving him behind.

Luke just shook his head. "It'll be fine. Trust me. Ten minutes."

Swallowing, I stepped out into the open of the lobby, light streaming in from the windows on either side. Smoothing back my hair and adjusting my clothes so I looked more presentable, I made my way toward the metal detectors and doors, head high, doing my best to put a no-nonsense air into my steps.

"Stop!" One of the men with goggles called out. I whirled around, hand to my heart, playing my part as best I could.

"What's going on?" I let a little of my real fear color my words. Considering I had two barrels pointed at me, that wasn't hard. My stomach was crawling up my esophagus.

One of the men stood. He was dressed in what looked like swat gear, the goggles giving him a predatory look more than anything insect-like.

"Where's your ID?" he demanded.

I glanced down, inspecting my pockets like I expected it to be there. Sunlight heated my back and I wanted desperately to just give it up and run for the doors. But that was the quickest way to say 'you're looking for me.'

"I'm sorry boys, I must have left it at my desk."

The second guy, still kneeling on the white tile floor, pulled back his goggles, peeking out at me.

"Sir, she's visible in the normal range. I don't think she's who we're looking for."

The other agent, the one I'd spoken with, lifted one of his lenses, careful to keep his gun still aimed at me.

"Visible in the normal range? What are you talking about?" I raised an eyebrow. "Is there something I should be made aware of?"

The standing agent shook his head. "No, nothing like that. Sorry to bother you. You may go. Just don't forget your ID next time." His tone was brusque and I lost no time in getting out the door. They must not have known what to look for, if they weren't screening too heavily. How long was that going to last? Long enough for Luke to get out?

Also, they didn't know what we looked like in the 'visible spectrum.' I'd seen movies with images from the infrared glasses, where everything turned into shades of red, yellow, orange, and blue. How hard would it be to come up with images? Some kind of likeness? It was hard to say.

That Glen guy had certainly gotten a good look at the both of us.

I kept my head down as I hurried along, pretending to do something on my phone so that most people ignored me.

Not that that kept my heart from pummeling my ribcage, the blood in my ears too loud to hear the passing people or the traffic.

Luke's car was up ahead. I shoved my hands into my pockets— front, back, nothing. Luke still had the keys.

"Keys? Where are the keys?" I mentally tossed in his direction.

No response.

"Luke?" I said again, stopping dead in my tracks, much to the annoyance of the woman behind me who glared as she wound around me.

I flipped her off behind her back.

Glancing around, I noticed a coffee shop just ahead of where Luke had parked. Better to be off the street. I stepped inside, my stomach churning.

It wasn't busy mid-morning and the guy behind the counter, playing with his lip ring, gave me a welcoming smile.

"Um, an iced coffee, please." My voice cracked.

He went to work, and I paid the woman at the register, my thoughts a million miles away.

"Luke! For the love of all things holy, answer me!" I screamed.

My hands shook as I took my drink, the ice rattling in the cup.

"Sure you need more caffeine?" the guy asked.

I forced a smile and shrugged. "Haven't had any yet, actually."

After adding three packets of sugar, I perched at the counter by the window, staring at Luke's car in the lot across the street.

I'd lost Luke once before, back on one of our first jobs together. It had to have been a couple of millennia ago, at least. I still remembered the feeling, the loneliness in my head. He'd been captured by a household patrol while sneaking some kind of necessary information out so that my mark could find the best way to abduct his fiancé. I hadn't heard from Luke for three days, his end of our line completely silent. All I remember about that time was the panic that seared through me, much too similar to what now jangled my hands and shortened my breath. I couldn't handle that again, couldn't lose him.

"Luke?" I couldn't have spoken aloud without sobbing.

"I'm almost there." Luke sounded strange, even in his thoughts.

I nearly collapsed across the counter, relief flooding me.

"You scared me to death! Seriously, you shit-head, why didn't you respond to me?"

Nothing.

Okay. So that was different.

I took my drink and nodded politely to the two behind the counter. They watched me like they expected me to strip naked and do a jig.

Honestly, this was San Francisco. They should be used to weird things happening.

Outside, I scanned the sidewalk up on my toes, peering around everyone until finally I noticed Luke's dark head slumped forward, stumbling toward me.

My feet took off before my mind managed to catch up. All I knew was I had to get to him.

# CHAPTER
# 16

"**D**on't draw attention. Take the keys in my pocket and get me to the car." Luke's thoughts were strained, like he was doing his best to keep from screaming, yelling, or otherwise admitting he was in pain.

I reached into his jacket pocket and found his keys. The clicker unlocked the passenger door and Luke slumped inside, his eyes fluttering closed as he rested against the seat.

I hurried around the other side, doing a quick glance around the sidewalk to make sure no one paid us any attention. Not that I'd really know if they were. I didn't doubt they would be completely capable of hiding in plain sight.

Chucking my purse over the seat and settling my coffee into the cup holder, I fumbled with the seat adjustments so I could reach the pedals.

"No food in the car, Ami." Luke glared down at my coffee.

"Seriously? You're over there, dying, and we've apparently tipped off the FBI, and you're going to give me shit about my drink?" I asked, unable to hold in a laugh.

If he was going to grumble about coffee, then he couldn't be hurt that badly.

I got the seat settled with about twenty adjustments of the little buttons on the door panel. Then I ripped out into traffic, loving the way the car handled a little too much. Apparently, there was good reason for Luke's NASCAR driving.

"See that little number '2' button on the consul?" Luke said when we stopped at the next light.

I pointed to the knob next to the seat adjusters and he nodded. "Hit 'set' and then hold it down until it beeps."

Following directions, I asked, "What's it for?"

"It'll save your seat settings. Next time you can just hit that, and it'll not take ten minutes to get driving." He gave me a wry grin.

I resisted the urge to ask him the probability of me ever getting to drive his car again. There were just too many other things to think about. "So, are you going to tell me what happened back there?" I asked, taking a long sip of coffee, hoping it would settle my nerves.

He groaned and shifted in his seat, clutching his side. "I thought I was going to get out of there no problem. A group of guys came down the stairs to leave, and I joined in at the back. But those uniformed morons stopped us and looked at everyone's badges. I couldn't convince them I had forgotten mine. The taller one decided I was a threat and tried to take me down. I managed to get away before the rest of security jumped in, but not before I caught a few good hits."

My brows must have been lost in my hairline. "Holy shit. So they saw you? Your face? Everything? Why didn't they chase after you?"

Luke's face went grim. "I didn't exactly leave them conscious."

The light turned green and we inched forward. I was a little grateful to have something else to focus on, because, well, that was incredibly terrifying.

"Wish I could have seen it," I managed to get out. It wasn't exactly true, but I couldn't come up with the right sentiment to portray the rattle of fear in my mind.

"I'm glad you weren't there." He heaved a sigh.

I kept driving, making my way to the freeway, which for some reason felt like the place to go. I needed to get the car moving; the stop-and-go of the city traffic was too much like the tangled mess of my thoughts.

I caught the Bay Bridge out of the city, riding on the darkened lower level for the first half before it opened out onto the new bridge, and resisted the urge to speed like a mad-woman.

"What now?" I breathed, a lump of panic in my throat.

"I think we'd better lay low. I don't know what they're doing with Theo and Lexi, but joining them isn't high on my priority list."

Oh hell. Theo and Lexi. What had I done to get them into this much trouble?

I should have just let Laura get caught.

"Do you think they'll be able to trace you?" Unspoken in my question was whether they'd be able to do the same to me.

"I have no idea. The only document I have in my name is my house. But, it's the government. Who knows what they could find out?" He breathed out heavily, shifting in his seat again.

"My house is in my fake great aunt's name." We'd both learned long ago how to cover our tracks. Getting caught somewhere without the right documents or access to money wasn't as bad today, but even a couple hundred years ago it could have led to some nasty business.

"Looks like you may have a houseguest," Luke said.

Perfect. Just what I wanted—him and Melody together in my house. "Should we go back?"

Luke shook his head. "Do a loop around the bay. If anyone noticed my car, we're going to have to try and confuse them. I doubt you'd be able to lose a tail, but we'll try."

"I could lose a tail!" I said, trying to lighten the mood. Really, I had no idea how I would actually manage that, but it never looked that hard in the movies.

Luke raised an eyebrow and smirked. "Yeah, I'm sure you could. Get off in Berkeley and I'll give you directions."

Luke apparently knew his way around the entire Bay Area, directing me down streets and around neighborhoods. We took a long break for some sandwiches, eating them at a park down by the water. Luke managed to get out of the car and lean against the hood next to me. I tried to forget reality for a moment, and pretend we were on some kind of lunch date, but my mind refused to go for it.

"I'll be fine in a day or so," he noted at one point, one of the few times he spoke.

"Sure about that? We could go see a doc," I said.

Luke shook his head. "I've had worse. Remember that time I got hit by that arrow?"

I wrinkled my nose. "Yes. Scared me to death. And you were all 'oh, it's just a scratch'." He'd been trying to be all macho back then, which only testified to how much he hurt now.

"Maybe I'm getting old."

We both chuckled at that, until Luke winced.

"Sure, old. I'll remember that." 'Old' was such a strange term for us. I couldn't remember how old I really was. It didn't matter; not anymore. We'd spent so many years existing, doing our job, and keeping busy. Immortality was all about keeping your head down. Busy hands meant not dwelling on the passing years, the loss of friends, the changes in the world around us. Lately that had become easier. There was always a movie, a TV show, a book, someplace to go where I didn't have to dwell on my past. Or on the fact that I'd spend eternity alone.

Every now and again, reality did seep into the cracks. How could it not? Our reality was something that defied description. And that could be damn depressing if I spent too much time on it.

At some point, Luke fell asleep and I headed back toward my place. I kept the music low and tried to hash through the best possible plan for what to do next.

Luke moaned and twisted in his seat. I shut up, worried I'd woken him. Then he reached over, his fingers slipping through my hair, down my neck, and settling on my thigh.

His eyes never opened. He was still fast asleep, breathing even and deep.

I stared at his hand, his heat seeping through my jeans. Gah, why did it have to feel good?

He probably thought I was Melody. Or someone else who he'd dated over the years. I knew it wasn't me. Which was fine.

Really.

It was like having a big brother who only stuck around to make sure I was okay, then disappeared. That was how we worked together. Allowing each other the space we needed. But, I didn't know what I'd do if he wasn't there for me.

Today, when he hadn't answered me, I'd remembered my panic from before, and it lingered fresh and terrifying in a part of my brain, like something pointy that was just wrong. I doubted it would go away any time soon. And the result was a fierce need to make sure he was okay. And that—that would never happen again. Because I couldn't lose him. Not now, not ever.

I reached down and wrapped his hand in mine, twining my fingers loosely through his.

I didn't let go until we were nearly back to my place, when I needed both hands to navigate traffic. He didn't budge.

Squeezing his car into my spot, I cursed the fact I'd left mine in his garage.

Luke woke enough to accept my help up the stairs. I settled him on my couch, got him some tea, and left him snoozing.

After a few minutes of breathing deeply to try and calm my still-racing brain, I called a cab to drop me around the corner from Luke's.

There were plenty of people out enjoying the early evening, couples holding hands and lines for ice cream. The whole place felt light and airy, completely at odds with my sentiments. I craved dark places and sleep, my brain more than a little fried.

A quick trip around the block and I felt confident no one was surveying Luke's place. At least, not yet. How long before they figured out who he was? That I'd been with him? It couldn't take long.

I let myself in the back door. A quick sweep of the house revealed nothing that linked to me. Upstairs in Luke's room, I went over my mental list of things to grab, mostly essentials until we got our lives sorted out.

It took one trip to dump a bag of his things, my stuff, and a few extra pairs of shoes in my mini before I went back inside to sweep for anything else. I grabbed his laptop, tablet, and a few other things left out on his desk, along with his passport and important looking documents in his desk drawer, still left unfiled from our recent Mexico trip.

I took care to wipe down every surface I touched, paranoid the FBI might have my fingerprints. It may not have been logical—I'd never been printed before—but I didn't doubt it was possible.

Taking one last trip through his bedroom, I noticed a photo propped up on his nightstand. I picked it up, turning it toward the light to see the image there, a cheerful Luke grinning with a woman tucked under his arm. From the clothes and her hair, it had to be from the 80's. I didn't remember her from any of our jobs, and a fist settled in my gut as I realized she must have been someone Luke dated.

I knew he'd dated. I had, too. But damn if it didn't make me want to rip the photo into a million little pieces and flush it down the toiled. Knowing that was totally insane, I set the photo back where I'd found it, wondering if it would collect dust there for another forty years or so.

Once in my Cooper, I slammed my palms against the steering wheel and then dropped my forehead against it.

What on earth was wrong with me?

Luke had been a friend for forever. Like, literally. So why was I suddenly pissed about the fact that he'd dated another woman? Especially if he looked so happy and relaxed? I did want him to be happy. I really, really did.

"Ami, you are such a moron." I grumbled to my speedometer.

I wasn't an idiot. I knew full well what I was feeling. And I knew how much I shouldn't have. Hell, I didn't really want to feel that way. But my emotions were going to bubble to the surface no matter what, apparently. Dealing with them was the only way to move forward.

The whole crush I'd felt so many years ago hadn't ever really gone anywhere.

I was totally in love with Luke.

"I need a lobotomy," I muttered to myself, backing out of Luke's garage and leaving his house, and the photo by his bedside, behind.

# CHAPTER
# 17

Once I pushed open my door at my place, the sound of Melody's laughter filtered out to greet me.

Ah, great, the lovebirds were going to take over my place. Perfect.

"Hey, need a hand with all that?" Melody asked. She skipped out from the living room and took the duffle of Luke's things from me, swinging it over her shoulder. "Luke told me about the repairs at his place. Sucks that he's not feeling well. Where are you going to put him?" Her eyes were shining and she bounced with way too much extra energy.

"The guest room?" I shrugged. It may not have been her fault about Luke but it sure as hell bugged me. Taking a breath, I forced a smile. "I have no idea what else to do with him."

"Well, it's nice of you to offer to put him up. I mean, I'd offer, but that would be weird." She laughed and shook her head. "I'll go dump this stuff in there."

She took the other handful of items from my hands and disappeared down the hallway to the back bedroom I never used. I went back to the car and brought up everything else.

"Are you sure you want him to stay in here?" she asked as I entered the room.

Glancing around, I had to laugh. I'd forgotten I'd left this room in a disaster state while packing a couple of jobs ago. It had been the middle of winter and Luke and I had to go to Costa Rica. I'd had a hard time coming up with proper beachwear.

"Yeah, I mean, where else? I'll just drag all this into my room." I dropped Luke's things on the plush chair in the corner and gathered up an armful of dresses I'd scattered over the bed.

"Nice," Melody said, holding up a little swimsuit definitely on the revealing end of the spectrum.

Heat rushed to my ears. "Hey, it looks pretty amazing on."

Melody giggled and helped me gather the rest of the mess and dump it in my room.

"So, are you going to dish, or am I going to have to beat it out of you?" I closed my bedroom door to ensure Luke couldn't hear us.

Melody settled herself on a bare spot on my bed, an evil little grin tilting up her lips. "No beating required. I've been waiting for you to get home so we could talk."

Pretend it's a date with someone else, not Luke. It helped that it was Melody. Even if I couldn't stop the small ember of annoyance smoldering inside, I didn't want to burn her happiness—she deserved to find someone nice. Even if it was the man who I was totally head-over-heels for.

The man who didn't reciprocate my feelings, either. Who had flat out shut me down and made sure I felt awkward about it for centuries afterward.

I went about grabbing articles of clothing and hanging them up in my closet, images of Luke's far too organized bedroom spurring me into action. Melody slumped back against my pillows, watching as she talked.

"We went to Greens. Have you been there? It's the nice vegetarian place, down by the water? So nice! And expensive. Crap. I'd never be able to afford to go there. Well, maybe if I just got an appetizer, and definitely not the bottle of wine he ordered." She laughed to herself, looking through a couple of the beach cover-ups sitting near her and holding one up to herself before giving it a critical lip-curl.

"Anyhow, we had a great time. He's just easy to talk to, you know? Like, I didn't even have to try. And I'll admit I kept waiting for him to let on to something really weird. I know you said he's normal, but with my track record, well, I was waiting for a taxidermy habit or something gross. I mean, why else haven't you tapped that?"

She gave me a long look like she expected an answer. I just grinned, a horrible tightness cinching around my chest. I desperately wanted to cry that I wanted to, before she'd ever been born, if he'd given one single little sign he was interested. But, yeah, I just kept my mouth shut and let her keep going.

"So, we sat around talking until late. Then, we walked for a little out there by the water. The lights were pretty and I was so glad I had my sweater."

She kept talking for a while longer but I had a hard time listening. It was next to impossible to keep myself from thinking about her and Luke going for a cute little romantic walk, nothing job related whatsoever, and not feel a jolt of jealousy. I managed to nod and laugh at all the right spots but it hurt too much to pay close attention.

That is, until she said that they went back to his place. "Wait! On the first date?" I couldn't help it. My jaw dropped. I mean, I already figured they'd done that, but still. It twisted in my chest.

"Ami! Damn, what do you take me for?" Melody threw a pillow at me, her cheeks turning a cute shade of pink. "No, nothing like that. We just had some tea—which by the way, apparently, he has your recipe, and I still don't? But, we sat around talking for a while longer. And he kissed me goodnight when he dropped me off. That's it. I swear."

She caught my look of disbelief I couldn't hide and crossed her arms. "I swear, that's it. He did say he wants to go out again, and who knows what'll happen, but really, we didn't do a thing."

"Okaaaay." I shook my head, wanting nothing more than to believe her.

Luke was a gentleman. I had a hard time thinking he'd sleep with someone on a first date, but then again, it was none of my business, as much as I wanted it to be.

"So, anyhow, he texted me early this morning, asking if I want to go out tomorrow night. I don't know if he'll be up for it—he kind of looks like death in there, but I think the offer's a good sign."

"Yeah, definitely a good sign."

She must have caught on to the forced nature of my tone because her eyes narrowed and her lips pursed in an unattractive expression. "Seriously, Ami, what's going on? I thought you'd be happy."

"I am happy for you. Both of you!" I shook my head, wishing I could find some better way to convince her. As it stood, part me of wanted to march out to Luke and poke him in his broken ribs.

Melody shook her head. "You're jealous. Damn it, Ami, I asked you if it was okay! You said it wasn't like that between you two!"

I held up my hands, dropping the little bikini to the floor. "I swear it's not! Really, really swear. Nothing is going on with us. Nothing ever will. I'm happy for you."

"Why don't I believe you?" Melody demanded, glaring at me. "It almost seems like you're trying to convince yourself."

Ugh. Why did she have to be so damn observant? "Look, if you're sensing anything, it's just that I'm happy for you, and I wish I had someone, too. Luke's great, but it's not like that between us. Never has been, never will be. We work together and that's it. Not that that means I don't wish I were dishing to you about some hot man I'd met, okay?"

Melody took a long minute to judge whether she bought my blatant lie. Okay, maybe not a total lie. There wasn't anything going on with me and Luke.

Finally, she threw up her hands, "If you're lying, so help me, I'm going to be seriously pissed. But I'd get over it. You could tell me."

"Totally not lying. I just want you two to be happy."

"Well, I am. Luke's great. Really great. And we had fun."

I went to her side and wrapped her in a hug. "Trust me, I'm glad. Really." And I was. That wasn't a lie. Even if I wanted to take up poaching.

Melody hugged me back before settling against my headboard, chatting about aimless things as I finished cleaning up.

Then she glanced at my clock and grumbled about an evening meeting before scrambling out of the house.

"Have a good girl chat?" Luke asked from his position on the couch as I wandered in.

"How much of that could you hear?" I asked, saliva flooding my mouth. This was going to be tricky one to get out of.

Luke just shook his head, hands up. "Nothing. I could only make out that you two were talking. I wouldn't eavesdrop like that."

Pressing my lips together, I tried to judge how much I believed him. Not that I had much of a choice. "Okay. Yeah, it was a good chat. She's over here a lot."

"I figured that."

"You going to be okay?"

He shifted and winced. "I'll be fine by tomorrow, I'm sure. Those boots were aimed a little too well."

Patting his head, I left him to his reading and went to grab my computer. I dropped onto the beanbag chair, wiggling to make a nice spot in the stuffing for my rear.

Stalking marks online always made me nervous. How easy was it to track my own computer? After today, looking up the stuff I did probably made me as much a suspect as Laura and the lab she worked for. I could just imagine all the little red flags going up at the FBI, CIA and Homeland Security offices every time I searched for 'deadly bacteria creation' and the other random stuff I typed into Google.

"So, tomorrow, what's the plan?" I asked some time later, idly going through Laura's photos I'd hacked into on Facebook.

"We can't go back to the FBI and I don't have any ideas on where to start looking for Theo and Lexi. At this point, I think we need to resolve everything with Laura and Mike. Then we can track down the other two."

Neither of us had to say it, but we were freaked at the thought of what happened to the partnership. It hit way too close to home. And there wasn't a thing we could do, no one to turn to, and no information on what we needed to do. Something about that made me feel very alone, like there was no one in the universe who cared to step in and help if I needed it. Except Luke.

"So, do we get Laura to go to Mike? Is he the one who's supposed to stop her?"

Luke shrugged. "I have no idea. But I think we need to get them together. If you're up for an early morning, I say we start at her place before she leaves."

I nodded, already going through possibilities on how we could convince Laura to go to Mike. There were plenty of options. But would she go through with it? Was there any hope that she'd give up her plans to kill so many?

I should have just let the agents apprehend her. What was wrong with me that I hadn't?

# CHAPTER
# 18

I set my alarm for five but woke far earlier. I stared up at my ceiling and tried to fit together all the miscellaneous pieces of my life. Melody. Luke. Theo and Lexi. Laura and Mike. The possibility the government had captured another partnership. And the image of all those dead bodies.

I rolled over and buried my face in my pillow. Luke and I had to succeed at this job. There was no other choice. But hell if I knew what we were supposed to do. Normally things were simple—get two people to meet. Make sure a lost object was found. Make an event happen. There were plenty of different types of coincidences. This felt different. Harder. And the stakes way too high for anything I wanted to be involved in.

Not that I had a choice. And, after all I'd done to screw it up, I had to do something to fix it now. The alternative was too horrific.

"Ami, stop being a damn wimp," I grumbled at myself, rolling out of bed.

Because of Luke, I pulled on a big sweater over my PJ's to avoid a repeat of yesterday's panty reveal.

I tiptoed into the kitchen and set the kettle on and went about grabbing supplies for tea. If I was going to go without sleep, I'd need it to face this morning. Before the teapot could start screaming, I yanked it off and set my drink to steep. I found a couple of stale cookies in the cupboard and munched on those, staring out my kitchen window.

The sky was a dense grey and it was too early for anyone to be out and about. The fog swirled at the end of the street, a misty white with a mind of its own. I drew my sweater tighter around me and pulled the collar up to my mouth.

Footsteps behind me and I whirled around. Luke shuffled past, hair a disheveled mess. Shirtless.

I almost dropped my tea.

"You're up early." He crossed his arms and leaned against the kitchen doorway.

I think my mouth flopped open and closed a few times. I couldn't really be sure. "Couldn't sleep." I shrugged and blew on my tea to cool it then took a sip despite it being too hot. At least that would give me an excuse for why my cheeks flamed bright red.

How had I never noticed how nice his stomach was? It was the kind of thing any human would have ogled.

There was still bruising, along his left side around his ribs. The vibrant purples and reds marked where the boots had hit. And, while it was obviously not bothering him as much today, it made my heart hurt and distracted a little from his otherwise perfect abs and that odd V dip that somehow boys manage.

Shaking my head and hoping that he didn't notice my long look at his muscles, I spoke, "Why are you up?"

"Bathroom." He shrugged like that was obvious.

"Want some tea?" I offered, motioning to the kettle.

He nodded before heading down the hallway, bare feet swishing against the wood floor. I made another mug and plopped myself onto a stool before he rejoined me. Still shirtless, which at this point was more than a little distracting. I mean, I'd seen him that way before but now it felt different. Definitely got a whole different reaction going down south, too.

Luke cupped the mug in his hands. "I'm going to need to go shopping. No sleeping shirts." He didn't need to read my mind to see where my thoughts were. Guess my staring hadn't been discreet enough.

"Oh. Sorry. I didn't know what to grab." Like, perhaps the photo by the side of his bed? Maybe I should have tossed that in.

"You did fine. They are the only thing I need." He smiled and I had to look away and focus on the safe scene out the window again.

We sat in silence for a good while, drinking and trying not to peek at one another. Well, at least that was what I was doing. Definitely not looking.

More than a few times.

At least.

When he finished, he leaned over the sink and rinsed out my blue and white mug. Which was when I saw it—the small tattoo. His sleep pants rode lower than any other pants I'd ever seen on him. And there, on the back of his right hip, was a small mark, not much larger than a quarter.

I blinked. And blinked again. An ornate 'A' inside a circle.

But, why did it look so familiar?

My brain felt like it was trying to hint at something but I couldn't get the points to meet. I would have never pegged Luke to have a tattoo, and yet, I knew I'd seen it at some point.

Touched it even.

Wait, touched it? How the hell was that even possible?

"You," I had to clear my throat to get the words out, "you have a tattoo?"

Luke stood up too fast, his wet fingers touching the spot before he pulled his pants up to make sure it was covered. "I got that a very long time ago."

"What's it mean?" I couldn't help asking. Something about it had to make sense. There was an answer there, something I needed to know.

Damn it, brain, work!

He shrugged and picked up a towel to wipe the now-clean mug and replace it in my cabinet. "It doesn't have a meaning."

I raised a brow. "No meaning? An 'A' in a circle, and it's just for fun? You're lying to me." I added a 'Fess up' as a silent challenge.

Some little part of my heart all but exploded at the thought that it could stand for my name. That somehow, Luke felt the same way I did. But I clobbered that part of me back into silence, praying that Luke wouldn't pick up on any errant thoughts in that direction.

He fixed a simple grin and an attempt at a wide-eyed innocent look. "It's nothing. Something dumb I did a few centuries ago."

"You've had that thing that long and you've never told me?" I crossed my arms, indignant for no good reason.

"There are plenty of things about my life that I've never told you, Ami. But I will tell you this, I'm calling dibs on the shower first." He raced from the kitchen, me in hot pursuit.

"Don't use all the hot water!" I yelled through the door and rattled the handle for extra measure.

Luke just laughed before turning on the tap.

I skulked back to my room to gather my clothes and supplies for the day, attempting to school my thoughts on what we should do. But, really all I could think about was the stupid mark. He hid something when he told me it meant nothing. It did. No way he'd ever mark his skin, when it was permanent for eternity, without a very good reason.

And for some reason, somewhere in my head was an explanation that refused to come clear. Like when you walk into another room and can't for the life of you remember what brought you there—I knew I had the information somewhere in my brain.

Giving my reflection a harsh look in the mirror, I placed both hands on my makeup desk, "Come on, brain, work!"

Not that it helped. Still, worth a shot.

Luke tracked wet footprints back to the spare room, a towel wrapped around his waist. "Shower's free," he called as he shut his door.

"There better be hot water!" I knew from experience my hot water tank was super small and I'd never gotten around to replacing the stupid thing. If Luke was around for any length of time that would be the first thing I fixed.

Soaping up my torso in the warm water, my brain managed to tie the points together in one blinding instant of clarity.

A wave of information rolled over me, a mix of a thousand images, sensations, and words that nearly drowned me with their intensity

I dropped the soap. And nearly fell over on the slippery tile.

Oh. Holy. Hell.

# CHAPTER
## 19

**M**aybe it would have been better not to remember. I pressed a soapy hand to my mouth, stifling the cry that wanted to escape. I had seen the tattoo before. Luke told me all about it. Once. In Germany. On a night when we'd both had way, way too much to drink.

I stumbled out of the shower, some part of my brain managing to shut off the water, even though soap coated my left arm and leg.

I grabbed a beach towel and wrapped it around myself so nothing showed, then followed Luke's footprints down the hall.

No plan on what I could even say came to mind. Not much of anything went through my brain. All I knew was I had to look him in the eye and see if I'd remembered right. And apologize. Because, holy crap, did I need to say I was sorry.

He must have heard me coming because he opened the door and poked his head out as I drew nearer.

"What's going on?" He stared at me like I'd completely lost it.

Right then, I really had. Drips splattered like rain on the floor, puddling around my toes.

"I just remembered where I saw it before." Very coherent. Suave.

Thankfully, Luke managed to piece together what I meant. He closed his eyes and stood ramrod straight. "I see."

"I'm so sorry. I didn't remember anything. Didn't even think about it. I mean, I could hardly even remember the night Theo and Lexi were talking about when they mentioned it. Much less what happened…after."

Pain pinched the skin around Luke's eyes. "I know. I figured that out rather quickly the following morning." The cadence and accent of his words changed, sounding much more like I remembered him from our time in England. He always started speaking in old-fashioned lingo when he got nervous.

"I'm so sorry. I-I don't even know what to say. How did you even look at me all this time?" I swallowed hard. Diving into the puddle at my feet sounded like an awesome alternative right then. But I had to get this out in the open. No way could I live with remembering it and not saying something.

Luke shrugged and tugged on his shirt, eyes fixed on the floor. "It wasn't hard to pretend like things hadn't changed. I'd gotten quite comfortable in your 'friend-zone.'"

"But it wasn't the same. What you said. And what…we did." I slumped back against the wall behind me, pushing my soapy hair out of my face. My fingers felt like ice.

"We'd both had way too much to drink. It should have never happened. I still feel sick about that." Luke's dark gaze flashed to mine. "I've hated myself for it ever since."

"You shouldn't. I don't remember much but," I gulped, "I do seem to remember me initiating. A lot." Images flashed through my mind. Luke suggesting we stop. Me kissing him until he gave in. That had been some seriously powerful drink. And a whole lot of undress.

Oh, gods.

What he'd said. How had that never surfaced? What the hell was wrong with my mind that that hadn't come back to me? And waiting until now of all possible times to think of it?

I wanted a lobotomy.

Luke took a deep breath. "It should have never happened. I'm sorry not to have said anything. I didn't know if I ought to remind you of something you didn't want to remember, or let you forget the whole thing. Especially after how I reacted in Egypt all that time ago."

Realization swept over me, filling my chest with a deep ache. "What you told me, what you said, do you still feel...?" I trailed off, unable to finish the sentence. Or even look at him.

His answer, either way, just might kill me.

Another sigh that sounded like it ripped him up inside. "We need to get back to work. Laura still has to be stopped and we have to locate Theo and Lexi. And I've got to find out what to do about my house." He shook his head, running a hand through his hair. "This isn't something I want to talk about now."

My stomach twisted. Okay, so he may have had a point, but no way was I going to work with him all day, and for years to come, with this between us. I didn't do that kind of thing. Couldn't do that kind of thing.

"Luke, just answer the question," I whispered.

His dark eyes narrowed and he stepped forward, invading my personal space. I held my breath as he ducked down, his nose nearly touching mine.

"What do you think?" His voice was so low it was almost a growl.

"I-I don't know. I never know when it comes to you." I couldn't get my tongue to work. My mind flashed to that look up downright horror after I'd kissed him so many years ago.

He raised an eyebrow. "What I think is that it doesn't matter. You

don't feel the same. You never have. And I think we have work to do."
He spun around and made his way back into his room.

My mind spluttered but made sense of one thing. "How do you know I don't? You've never asked. You're just ass-uming." Bonus to me for the pun.

Luke turned in slow motion to face me. The fire in his eyes made me shrink back. "You would have remembered if you felt the same. You were only interested in a fling. Which is fine. But if you felt the same, after I told you how I felt, you would have remembered."

"Yeah, well…well, you're just wrong! About everything." I set my jaw and crossed my arms over my chest. So much for winning any points. I couldn't believe I just did that.

Luke's lips parted to say something, but I could practically see his brain process what I'd just said. "Wait. What? I'm wrong that you wouldn't actually remember, or that you don't—"

"Have feelings for you. You're wrong about that. Okay? Yeah, I'm a little backward at talking to you about it, but, well, yeah. I just always thought you didn't." I clenched my fists and closed my eyes, trying to get my mind to give me something better to say. But…nothing.

Luke's phone beeped.

I opened my eyes and he just stood there, staring at me. Jaw hanging open a little. Frozen.

Which is obviously what you want a guy to do when you tell them that you have feelings for them. And have for ages. And have spent way too many years denying it because you thought the guy couldn't feel the same. Good grief was I a moron.

"Aren't you going to check it?" I motioned to his phone.

He blinked and seemed to come back to himself. "It's Melody," he said, reading her message.

Melody. Shit. Melody.

What the hell was I doing?

# CHAPTER
## 20

I had to get out of there. Just had to. I ran to the bathroom, slipped twice, and locked the door behind me. My heart felt like it might pound its way out my bellybutton.

"Just get dressed. Get back in the shower. One step. Just one step at a time," I told myself, desperate to keep it together.

Because, who was I kidding? I wanted to crawl under something and die.

I flipped the tap on, too hot, and scoured off the rest of the soap. Shaved. Got out. Dried my hair. My thoughts looped in the same horrific circle: I'd confessed to Luke. Luke was interested in Melody. Melody was my best friend. And I'd just royally fucked everything up.

Just like I fucked everything up. Millions of people were going to die because I'd fucked up this job. And Theo and Lexi, whatever had happened to them, was because I'd fucked them over too.

"There's going to be a way to fix this," I said, braiding my hair back in front of the mirror. Today required pep talks. If only I believed what I said.

Wrapping myself up again, I scurried from bathroom to bedroom, not without noticing that Luke had cleaned up the wet hallway.

It took far too little time to get dressed and ready. I wanted to procrastinate for a while longer but it was already time to go. And if anything, Luke was right in that this had to take a back seat to our coincidence.

Grabbing my keys and bag, I found Luke waiting by my car downstairs in the garage. He curled himself into my passenger seat without a word.

Oh, this was going to be gloriously awkward. At least in Egypt I hadn't had to see him for a few weeks after that fiasco.

Hyper aware of every move, I tossed my stuff into the back and wished I had something funny to say, something that would erase the last hour. Damn it, why couldn't we time travel?

Luke played on his phone, keeping his head down as we drove. That is, until we stopped at the first red light.

"Read this." He thrust his phone into my hands. I frowned at him but he shook his head. "I'll tell you when the light changes."

My fingers shook as I glanced at the string of texts between him and Melody. "This is private. I really shouldn't."

"Please. Read it. Okay?" He thought at me, eyes trained out the window.

It was already set at the top of the chain of messages. The first was from Melody, dated a few days back. "Hi! Melody here, Ami's friend. You met me at her place earlier. Remember? Now, look, I know this is going to come across as really forward, but I'm going to ask anyhow. How long have you been in love with her?"

"Wait, what?" I nearly dropped the phone, fumbling with it before I managed to catch hold.

"Keep reading."

The time-stamp was several hours later before Luke responded to her text. "It was a pleasure to meet you today. Ami speaks of you often. In terms of what you're asking, I don't mean to be rude when I say that that is none of your business."

Melody replied instantly. "Oh, I know it isn't any of my business. But I also know Ami feels the same way, but is never going to do anything about it. I just thought it might be fun to get her to confess her feelings. But if you're not interested, I'll butt out."

The light turned and Luke took the phone from me. "I am going to get to read the rest, right?"

"Not while you're driving," he said.

Cursing California driving laws, I hit every green light for the next fifteen minutes.

Finally, stuck in a line of traffic, Luke handed back the phone.

"I really don't think it's either of our place to try and get Ami to think or feel anything. She can do that very well on her own." Luke's response to Melody was perfectly polite.

Melody's felt a little more brisk. "Fine. But if you decide that you ever want something to work out for you two, I can help."

Luke didn't reply until much later. "What are your thoughts?"

The light changed again and I gave him a nasty look. "I can't believe you two did this."

He shrugged. "How else were we going to get you to act?"

"Oh, I don't know, talk to me?" I snapped. "You could have said something instead of fucking with my head."

Luke nodded. "And I'm sure you would have listened. And have actually spoken with me about it. Instead of assuming I felt nothing toward you. For centuries." He leaned in close to emphasize his point, his dark eyes glittering.

Ugh. I hated that he was right. Not that I was going to tell him that, but it was true. I would have probably thought it was funny if he'd told me how he felt. Maybe thought he was trying to trick me. Never in a million years would I have allowed myself to wonder if it could be the truth.

I was just one of those people who would always need a little extra push. Which it looked like he and Melody had effectively managed. The thought of how far they might have taken all of this crossed my mind and I cringed. Had they even considered what would have happened if their little mind-games blew up in their faces? Or would they have just laughed it off and left me feeling like shit?

Before I could grill Luke about any of my questions, my phone buzzed and I pulled into a parking spot a block away from Laura and Mike's. I fished it out, revealing a note from Melody.

"Happy for you two. Finally. Sheesh, you're thick-headed. Do you know how much effort went into getting you to realize this? Sheesh. Enjoy it."

"Thanks, Melody." I wrote back, rolling my eyes in real life as well as with several emojis.

"She's really not upset?" I asked, giving Luke a hard look.

"Not that I can tell."

I pursed my lips and chucked my phone back into my bag. "Well, you two are quite the dynamic duo."

He shrugged, his expression wary. "I didn't want to upset you."

Was I upset? I didn't know. My head felt like it had been flipped inside out. Nothing made sense any more. And I didn't know what to make of it all. But, upset? I had no idea. My head hurt and my heart ached with the weird and sudden flip everything had taken, and I wasn't quite sure what to make of what lengths they'd gone to in order to manipulate me.

"No, just trying to get used to…things. I don't know what to make of all of this." It was as honest as I could get.

Luke nodded. "Me either."

We fell silent and I stared out the windshield, though I could feel Luke's eyes on me.

"I think, for starters, I would very much like to take you out. So," he cleared his throat and twisted his fingers together. "Would you go see the fireworks with me? As a date?"

"Yeah." Delighted laughter bubbled up inside of me but I swallowed it back. Funny how that prospect seemed to outweigh all the rest of my frustrations. "I'd definitely like that." I reached over and touched his hands, tracing his fingers with my own. I couldn't say what made me so bold, but I had to touch him—maybe just to make sure he was real. That I hadn't somehow imagined all of this.

"I don't want to interfere with our friendship. But after seeing Theo and Lexi again, and how well they work together," he grinned at me, "I couldn't risk the alternative."

A lump settled in my throat, and before I could stop myself, I leaned over and pressed my lips to his. Warm, soft, a quick peck. I started to back away, heat rushing to my cheeks; I'd way overstepped my bounds. Again.

But the look in Luke's eyes stopped me. It was the kind of look I'd hoped for, all those years ago. The only word that came to mind to describe it was hungry. He slid a hand around the back of my neck, fingers tangling in my hair. Leaning in, he closed the distance between us. And this time, the kiss was far from chaste. He tasted like toothpaste and tea, and the warmth of his hands lit fires under my skin.

Somehow, I ended up balanced on the center console, entirely entangled in his seatbelt in the far too tiny space.

Managing to wrangle control over myself, I pushed my hands against his chest so I could look at him. His eyes were filled with laughter and more than a little lust.

"We were supposed to be doing something this morning, weren't we?" I wanted nothing more than to drive us back to my place as fast as my little car could go. Or just put the seats down and enjoy the perks of going invisible.

"Something about stopping the end of the world. I think." Luke groaned, attempting to disentangle his strap that had somehow become knotted around his upper arm.

I managed to scoot back into my seat, wishing my heart rate would slow a little. After everything this morning, I was going to have a freaking heart attack.

"Hey," Luke said, touching my shoulder.

Chagrin forced me to duck my chin. "Yeah?"

"The car is a handicap. At least this miniature one is. Can you not consider this our first kiss and wait until we are somewhere I'm not wedged against the dash? Or trying to not get strangled by this?" He held up the seatbelt.

I burst out laughing. "Uh, nope. Sorry. That counts."

Luke narrowed his eyes, though he couldn't keep from grinning. "You'll change your mind. Later."

# CHAPTER
## 21

"**C**oncentrate," I muttered to myself, finally out of my car and hurrying up the block. Luke tugged me along by my hand.

We'd cloaked ourselves as we dashed down the street. All my mind wanted to do was return to this morning. To Luke's kiss. To where I wanted to drag him—mostly my bedroom. Or the shower. Or back to my car. I wasn't terribly picky.

But there were other pressing things right now. Things that had to be done. And no matter what I wanted, it was time to focus and attempt to solve this riddle.

Thankfully, Luke and I had had a whole lot of practice with making things happen.

Stopping outside the complex where Laura and Mike lived, we both sighed with relief. Lights were still on in both places.

"Here." Luke handed over a business card with a police symbol and

Mike's name and contact info.

"Let's do this thing."

Luke squeezed my hand and hurried to take his position. I went upstairs and strategically placed the card into the crack near the bottom of Laura's door so that when she opened it, it would flutter to the ground and catch her attention.

With hardly a second to spare, I got out of the way as Laura rushed out. The card went right over her toes and she bent to grab it, reading the name of her neighbor.

She paused for a second, like she was trying to work out how the card could have possibly gotten up here. Then she dropped it into her pocket and locked her door.

Downstairs, Luke knocked at Mark's place and was instantly met by the muffled sound of children racing to answer it.

Laura went down the stairs, and was met by two kid's faces behind their screen door, peering out into the breezeway.

"Did you knock?" the boy asked, giving Laura a giant grin that would have melted anyone's heart.

Laura smiled and shook her head. "Nope, must have been the wind."

The kids giggled and the boy shouted after Laura's retreating form, "Have a good day!"

Laura walked backward for a pace to wave back at them. My heart tugged at the smile she wore—how could someone who obviously thought the little kids were adorable want to murder them? She couldn't be that big of a monster.

Round one was over. Now to guilt her into going to go talk to Mike before she actually finished her plans. Maybe there was something he could do to stop her. Some way to convince her.

It was a stretch, and a lousy one at that, but it was all we had to go on at the moment. After my flub the other day, we had to hope this angle would pan out. Or we'd have to take more drastic measures.

I definitely did not want to think about that.

"I'm going to go track down Mike. See what I can do. See you later, okay?" Luke swept up behind me, close, but not touching. Something about the wary look in his eyes told me he was worried about crossing some line between us, especially when everything was so blurry right now.

I couldn't begrudge him his doubts. Not with what had happened last time.

Grabbing him around the waist, I buried my face in his chest. I'd known he'd smelled good before, but somehow it now slid into my veins and made me incredibly grateful no one could see us.

"You. Are. Going. To. Miss. Her. Bus," Luke said, breathing heavily as we kissed out on the sidewalk. Despite his words, his tight hold around me made it very clear he didn't much care.

The rumble of the bus down the road confirmed Luke's assessment and we managed to break apart. Luke took my car keys and headed toward the mini "death trap."

I raced down the sidewalk, attempting to clear my mind a little before I reached Laura where she waited in a huddle with the other bus patrons.

Ducking behind a fence, I uncloaked and did my best to stand near Laura as we boarded. While we drove, I had to wait a few stops and one transfer to get a seat next to her. Which was fine, because I needed the time to get the appropriate images up on my tablet's screen.

Dropping onto the blue plastic chair, I gave Laura the customary little "sorry to invade your personal space" public transportation smile and pretended to read, angling the tablet so Laura would easily see it if she glanced over.

Which she did. Of course. Not obviously or anything, but she wasn't reading or texting, so taking a quick peek was just human nature. A fact I enjoyed capitalizing on.

As soon as she caught sight of the screen, she shifted in her seat, turning so it would be much harder to accidentally see what I looked at.

"This isn't bothering you is it?" I asked, giving myself a thick British accent. That wasn't hard—Luke and I had spent enough time in England to pick one up.

I tilted the screen again, allowing Laura to get another eyeful of the image as she responded to my question. It was pretty gruesome. Blood and crippled forms on the ground, images from the Boston Marathon terrorist attack.

She shook her head and looked out the window at the passing streets.

"I'll read something else. Did you hear about the scandal last night? The one about campaign contributions in Maryland's Senate race?" I asked, knowing full well she'd commented on several forums online regarding the findings.

She murmured some kind of response I couldn't catch.

Hmm. How far could I push this?

"Seems like someone needs to do something. Step in. The whole country's going to hell in a hand basket." It was nearly a direct quote from what she'd written in a comment on a Times article yesterday.

Keeping myself busy with my tablet, I felt her shift next to me, her eyes crawling over my skin.

Tension settled between us, almost tangible.

"Yeah, I thought the same thing." She hesitated over her words as if choosing them carefully. "There are some real scary things going on."

I nodded. "It's unbelievable sometimes."

We turned the corner and Laura pulled the cord to get off at the next stop. Somehow, we'd arrived close to where she worked. Too fast.

As Laura smiled and snuck past me, I wanted to grab her, throw her onto the seat, and demand she not do anything stupid. I was going to have to push her harder to hang up her vigilante hat and realize she had to stop her plans.

And yet....well, and yet, even thinking of that still set off the alarm bells in the head. They clanged out *wrong!* But, really, what else could we do? I couldn't let all those body bags happen.

Laura left the bus, walking toward her building. I called for the next stop and once on the sidewalk, found some convenient bushes near a parking lot to cloak myself.

As I walked, I went over every possible angle of attack. Anything and everything was fair game to get her thinking about what she was really doing, and how it was just downright wrong. Laura hadn't given any indication she was religious, but her father had been, according to what I'd found online. Might be some strings to pull there.

She loved kids. Not that she was about to have any herself— according to her bio on a dating site she'd last accessed two years ago— but she found in them the innocence she longed for in the world. Too bad they'd grow up to be shitty people like everyone else—according to comments on a blog post.

The thing was, she didn't seem like a lunatic. I skirted around an oncoming car, catching sight of it at the last second before it barreled into my invisible self. I couldn't finish this job injured, even if I did heal quickly.

Why did I think she wasn't capable of releasing the plague? She had means and motive. What more proof did I need?

I'd seen some wackos in my time, worked with a few on jobs, and basically the criteria didn't fit with Laura. Maybe that was what scared me most. She wasn't like the rest and that meant anything could happen.

Somehow, we had to stop her.

"Hey, how are things going?" I cast my thoughts out to Luke, a warm spot growing in my chest at the thought of him.

"Okay. I've been dropping hints about the FBI case, and trying to coax him to look into it," Luke thought. "I don't know if it's going to work yet."

"Sounds like fun."

Luke laughed. "I can think of plenty of things I'd classify as fun. This doesn't exactly count." It wasn't too hard to imagine what he meant from the low tone he used.

"Well, you'll have to show me later," I teased, jogging a few steps so I could slip past the door behind a bald man carrying a bucket of soda from 7-Eleven.

"You are seriously the worst distraction," Luke groaned.

Snickering, I took the elevator up to Laura's floor and scanned the room.

Laura exited the employee lounge and donned her white coat. She knotted her hair up into a messy bun and snagged some gloves as she made her way through the lab.

The other employees were gathered around in clusters, chatting, some trying to hide coffee cups behind monitors despite giant safety signs telling them they couldn't eat or drink in there.

Laura said her hellos, nodded, and waved as she made her way to her station in the back, but didn't stop to chat. Following behind her, it wasn't hard to miss the casual eye rolls between her coworkers about her behavior.

Maybe I'd misread her? Maybe she was more socially awkward than I thought. But that was a far cry from mass-murderer.

At her workstation, I stood off to the side while she gathered her paperwork and read through a list of things to do. She brought her computer to life and checked on some results, satisfied in her findings from the nod she gave her screen.

She then went off to scan a machine making random beeping sounds, while I took the opportunity to look over her files.

Not that I expected anything to read "Biohazard to be unleashed on the world" but there had to be something. I jumped when Laura started shouting at one of her coworkers to help her out.

After a quick inventory of how she'd left her computer, I started to click through her files.

Just a bunch of charts, strangely colored graphs, and data I'd need a doctorate to understand.

But, then, hidden amidst her Personal file, which she used her normal password to guard, I came across a group of documents simply labeled with numbers. I opened number '1' and realized they were notes. Anyone looking at them probably wouldn't have thought much of them, but after reading up on toxicity and delivery methods for different kinds of pathogens, the numbers and notes clicked into place.

Laura had been using company time and resources to help her plans.

At the bottom of the page of notes, one line chilled me to the core. "Simulated Death Toll: 1,000,000."

That was the first trial, dated months ago.

I took a quick photo of the file before I shut it down. But I left the file browser open with the list of trials showing. Another push. If Laura thought someone was on to her, surely she'd change her mind.

Maybe.

Or it could speed things up.

It was a risk, but one I had to take.

Laura returned a few minutes later, muttering to herself about stupid lab techs. She grabbed her mouse and went to click on something when she froze.

Her whole head bobbed up and down as she scanned over the files. She glanced around, her eyes narrowed, as she tried to guess who could have gotten into her private work.

But no one was around. And no one had been by her computer while they fixed the machine. I could see doubt filter into her gaze as she tried to figure out what had happened.

"I didn't open that, did I?" A shiver shook her narrow shoulders and she looked around the room as if she half expected there to be someone lurking in the corner.

Some people can sense when I'm looking at them while invisible. Not everyone, and not every time, but Laura looked over at me, her eyes meeting mine like she could see me standing there.

It was enough to send a chill through me. I moved away and Laura's eyes didn't track me.

Weird.

Later, after wandering the lab, I wound back to Laura and knocked the photo her neighbor had of her kids onto the counter. No way could it have fallen if I hadn't done it. And I took a small amount of satisfaction at Laura's wide-eyed response. It unnerved her for sure.

"Any chance you could hack into Mike's email and send something to Laura?" I asked later, sitting on the bench next to my mark.

She kept dropping things, peering over her shoulder, and anytime anyone walked close, she jumped about a foot off her chair. Basically, she was a wreck. And hopefully getting a lot of time to think about how horrible her plans were.

"Good thought, but Mike might get suspicious."

Okay, so he had a point. "I think it may be time to impersonate an agent."

"Be careful," Luke warned before going silent.

I brought my hands together, almost clapping before I caught myself. She'd hear that for sure and I didn't want to make her think she'd lost it completely.

Digging my phone out, I brought up a website that allowed me to email from what appeared to be official, dot-gov, email addresses. It wasn't legal, but considering we were trying to stop millions of deaths, that didn't bother me.

*'Laura, this is agent Ramirez from the lab visit two days ago. We have some additional questions for you regarding some of the operations ongoing in your lab. Could we set up a time for a phone call?'*

I read it over a few times, changing the wording to sound more official, and sent it. It only took a second for Laura's phone to sound.

Sighing so her hair pushed off her forehead, she peered at her phone sitting out on the counter. Then she peeled off her gloves and headed to the employee lounge. I trailed behind, phone out, breathless at the thought of her reply.

The lounge was empty. She grabbed a yogurt from the fridge and settled on the couch to stare at her phone again.

After a glance at the glass door where her coworkers were visible at their respective stations, I perched on the other armrest of the couch and did my best to be as silent as possible.

Finally, she wrote out a response and hit send. I fumbled with my phone to make sure I'd turned the sound off. Thankfully, I had. Because that would have been an awesome screw up.

Her email came through and I read it while she ate.

*'I'm afraid I have no additional information I can provide. I suggest you speak with my boss if you need anything more.'*

"Hey, Luke?" I called out.

"Yes?"

"I don't think Laura's going to budge. How much can we nudge Mike to investigate her?"

# CHAPTER
# 22

I waited around until most everyone left before it was safe to start pilfering things. In the interim, I entertained myself with sending Laura links from random email addresses that detailed the fate of people who threatened State security, as well as other reminders of the good things going on around in the Bay; the people she may not want to kill.

Most of them probably filtered into her spam, but a few made it through, as evidenced by the blanched expression she got when she checked her inbox.

If it did anything, I didn't know, but it was worth a try. And it was kind of fun, in a twisted sort of way.

Laura finally packed up her things and left. I debated tailing her, but instead worked my way through the darkened lab, gathering cards, letterhead, and several other small things to tip off someone about

Laura's work.

Once done, I called an Uber and rode back to my place.

Luke wasn't back yet, so I took the opportunity to compose a letter on Laura's company letterhead, plotting ahead on how I'd get Mike to see it. With everything in my bag, Luke and I had a pretty good chance of pushing him to investigate.

The back door opened and my stomach did a happy little flip. "Luke?" I called out.

"Sorry, sweetie, it's just me." Melody bounded down the hallway in clattering wooden clogs.

It took a moment to hide the bite of disappointment. I'd been hoping Luke might be up for something more interesting than saving the world for an hour or two. And, well, I didn't quite know how I felt toward Melody at the moment—grateful? Ready to tie her up in the garage and let her rot for a few days?

I watched her approach with one raised eyebrow, cemented in my position on the couch.

"Look, I know you're not really mad. You can cut the crap." She flopped down next to me, shoulder to shoulder, and gave me a saucy grin. She wore bright red lipstick that had gotten onto her teeth.

"Yeah? And why shouldn't I be mad? After all you two did." I shook my head. "So not cool."

Melody laughed and tugged on her braids. "Oh, that's just part of the beauty of it all."

I huffed and set my computer aside. I couldn't work on fake correspondence with Melody watching. "You could have done something to clue me in, instead of letting me freak out for all that time."

Melody's brows drew together and she stared at her hands in her lap. "Look, I really didn't want to make you mad. I just thought that you two needed to get on with things. I'm so—"

I cut her off and wrapped an arm around her shoulders. "Sheesh, you don't think I'd really give you that hard a time, did you?"

Melody met my eyes for a moment, then huffed out a deep sigh. "So, you're going to tell me everything, aren't you? Because I think you owe me that much at least." Melody arranged herself and kicked her noisy shoes to the ground so she could pull her knees under her funky forty's style dress, forgetting my attitude in a second.

"I don't really have much of a choice, do I?" I asked.

She shook her head, a grin as mischievous as it was proud pulling her lips wide. She was way too satisfied with herself over her little prank. Granted, she had been pretty amazing at it, and for that I could give her props. I'd spent centuries attempting to push people into doing stuff and she's managed it without even any kind of plan.

I stood and started tea before launching into my tale. I left out a few little things—like how long ago it really had been that Luke and I had our drunken night of revelry/shame, but mostly I was honest. She deserved it.

When I finished talking, she sipped her tea and dropped her head back against the pillows. "That, while being the most screwed up story ever, is also utterly adorable. I think I may have to become a professional matchmaker."

"Yeah. To help out the multitudes of gutless women who can't grab what's right in front of them? Because I'm sure there's just loads of us."

"Oh, you might be surprised. I'm just not sure how many hot men there are, pining away for these clueless damsels."

She had a point. "Yeah, Luke's kind of one in a million that way."

"Try one in a billion."

We fell quiet as I attempted to think of anyone I knew, anywhere, that might be a good match for Melody. She deserved someone awesome in her life, and despite all I had said, I still felt a little guilty/annoyed about how things had gone down.

The back door opened again and Melody jumped to her feet, giving me a wink. "I'll just get out of your hair." She dropped her mug in the sink and waved to Luke as she bustled past.

"She didn't have to run out like there was some kind of fire." Luke set his bag down on the armchair.

"Yes, she did."

Luke wrinkled his brow, his eyes meeting mine.

"She'd probably feel a little awkward if she saw us doing this." I stood and walked up to him, pausing only inches away, head tilted up to keep his gaze.

"Yeah?" Luke managed, his voice more a breath than a word.

I reached for his hand first. A little niggle of nerves settled in my stomach. What if he'd changed his mind? What if he realized it was better we just stay friends? That was the more logical thing to do and he was always so rational.

"You really think I'd change my mind?" Luke's thoughts skated through mine, laced with hurt.

I gulped. Damn it, why did I broadcast so much lately?

"I hope not. I certainly haven't." Far from it. I'd spent a chunk of my afternoon imagining just what I wanted to do to him. It wasn't like I was some kind of chaste woman, but I'd surprised even myself with the images I came up with.

Luke slid his free hand around my back, pulling me flush against him. Oh. Well, lust was certainly not something he'd changed his mind about.

"I've hoped for far too long that you might finally realize that we go together. That this," he tapped my sternum, then his own, "works."

I buried my face in his chest and pulled him as close to me as I could. He pressed his lips to the top of my head. The way he held me reminded me of someone cradling a vastly expensive or important artifact, and somehow that didn't seem strange, or cheesy, or anything. It was just right.

Loosening my grip, I stretched up on my toes. His mouth, so tender and warm, moved against mine. I parted my lips, tasting him, the kiss deepening into something more, something that brought fire to every last one of my cells, pulsing deep within me.

I didn't remember moving until my knees knocked against the couch, and then we were falling, Luke catching me above him, gravity tangling us even further.

I found the buttons on his shirt, some automatic part of my brain undoing them one by one when all I wanted was to rip them all off.

Exploring his chest and his abs that I'd ogled earlier, I trailed kisses over his collarbone, giggling at the way his breath hitched. I wanted, needed, to feel him against me, to explore the rest of him.

Reaching the bottom of my shirt, I slid it over my head, earning a lascivious grin from Luke, whose warm hands slid over my skin to cup my breasts.

"I think you need to pinch me," Luke whispered, finding the clasp on my bra and fiddling with it for a moment before I reached around to give him a hand.

My bra slid off, joining my shirt in the corner. A shiver went through me and goose bumps rose at the sudden exposure of skin.

Without thinking, I pinched his shoulder, twisting a little until he winced.

"Why?" I asked as he grabbed my hand away, kissing my fingertips.

He laughed. "I was pretty sure I was dreaming. Lucky for us both, I guess I'm not."

I balanced above him, crossing my arms. "Nope, not sleeping. Thankfully. If you were, I might be a little ticked."

"I sincerely doubt I could sleep through this." His hands ran over my stomach, caught mine, and he drew me back down to his chest.

Divesting Luke of his jeans gave me a moment to catch my breath. To let the truth of what we were doing slide through me. I wanted this. Needed it. Needed him.

Luke's dark gaze met mine and his hands fell to my shoulders as he blinked. "Are you sure?"

"Never more. And I'm sober this time." I forced a grin, shame coloring my cheeks.

Luke shook his head. "I always imagined this differently. I wanted to take you out. To court you like I should. Especially after what happened in Germany."

"Forget about before. Can we? This is what it should be. Us. Now. And there's plenty of time for being together. I'm not likely to forget you promising to take me out." I traced a finger across his shoulder, longing to do the same with my lips.

"I'm not certain I can forget about it. But we can go forward."

He captured my lips, drawing me against him. His warmth slid through me and it was like getting lost in a fog—I lost track of me, of him, of where he ended and I began, everything. There would be time later for specifics. For capturing details. Right now, all that was real was me and him, and finding what brought us together, what would make us a stronger whole than we'd ever been apart.

# CHAPTER
## 23

The clock read almost midnight when I woke. I pushed back the covers, trying to remember at what point we'd made it to my bed.

Luke was sound asleep next to me, his dark hair a wild halo against the pillow I grinned and resisted the urge to run my fingers through it. After the last few hours he had to be utterly worn out.

I had underestimated him when he'd asked for a rematch in the car that morning. He had stamina to spare, and if his kiss had been mind-altering with the tiny-car handicap, well giving him space paid off and then some.

Sliding out of the covers, I grabbed my robe, and padded out to the kitchen. My body felt heavy and light, tight and loose in all the right spots. I'd never experienced anything quite like that and even thinking about it made me want to go wake Luke just to continue the fun.

The living room was a disaster zone and I laughed as I surveyed the scene. It felt like someone had poured molten happiness into me, filling every nook and cranny of my soul. Not even Laura, the attack, Theo and Lexi—all of the horrible mess I'd gotten us into, none of it could break through right now. Right now, I just wanted to ride this high for as long as it lasted. I'd had precious few moment of bliss in my long life and knew enough to enjoy them while they lasted.

All I regretted was that I waited so long. We should have done this centuries ago. But we couldn't change it now, and only could enjoy what we had.

Snagging some crackers out of the kitchen, I settled back on the couch and grabbed my laptop. As amazing as things were with Luke, I hadn't forgotten we had a job to do. Too many lives were on the line to be a total slacker.

Plus, he needed to sleep. He'd need his strength for when I did give in and wake him back up.

Bringing up the letter I'd been writing before, I finished the thing and read through it a bunch of times to ensure it worked. Mike had to be convinced, and I didn't know just how much of a push that would take.

"Hey."

I jumped at the disruption from my work. Somehow I caught my computer before it crashed to the floor.

Luke chuckled and sat next to me. "Sorry, didn't mean to startle you."

"I should have heard you. Just got sucked into writing the letter to nudge Mike into investigating Laura."

Luke nodded and leaned around so he could read the letter over my shoulder. "That sounds perfect. Are we dropping it off tomorrow morning?"

I nodded, planting a kiss on his cheek. "And a few other things."

Luke snaked a hand around me and tugged me close, so my back rested against his chest.

"I hesitate to mention this, but we might need some kind of contingency plan. If we can't find a way to stop her." Luke's tone held untold amounts of wariness.

Which was a good thing because his words made my stomach clench and me scoot away so I could look him in the eye. "A contingency plan? I'm not doing that, Luke. Never again." Ice shot down my backbone and I grabbed a blanket to try and stifle my shivers. Gods, no, not a contingency plan. Not after last time.

Luke pressed his lips together. He had to of known this would be a touchy subject. Why bring it up now?

"I don't like it," he brushed a lock of hair behind my ear, "but we can't let her do this. We may have to have to find another way to stop her."

A contingency plan. That meant taking out a mark to ensure we fulfilled the coincidence. It was the failsafe when attempting to stop something, like what Laura had in mind. And I hated the thought of just killing Laura, and not just because I tried to never eliminate a mark if I could help it. To me, it meant we'd failed. That we hadn't been able to accomplish the job without anyone knowing what we'd done. And while the logical part of me knew it would save a whole lot of lives, I also knew it meant that I really fucked up when I'd let Laura evade the FBI. Not that I didn't know it already, but still, it stung.

"We'll figure something out. But I can't do that. You know I can't." I closed my computer, wiping my palms on my robe.

Luke fell silent, knowing there was more I had to say.

"I won't kill her. I can't. I know what she's trying to do is so wrong, but Luke, she's not completely horrible. There's something off about all of this mess. I just don't know what. We'll find another way."

"And if there isn't another way?" Luke asked in a soft voice.

My mind went to the last time we'd had to put this kind of plan into action. It had been a while ago, but definitely not long enough for me to forget. We'd just made it to the Colonies, though we wouldn't stay here long. It had been around the American Revolution and an ambush had been planned against one of the vital rebel colonists. We'd been charged with stopping it.

My mark had been the rebel. Jeremiah. I'd done everything I could to try and dissuade him from going in the direction of the ambush. Luke's mark had been the one leading the ambush. His mark was dead set on killing the other man.

As the hour drew closer, we were supposed to allow Jeremiah the chance to slip through the enemy's defenses, but we ran out of options.

Except one.

I still thought about what else we could have tried. There had to have been something. But at the time, all we'd known was there was an event we needed to make happen and every option led to a dead end.

Luke, hating what he was doing, brought a 'message' to the group his mark led. Because Luke had access to inside information, he convinced them his mark had turned and was a spy.

This didn't end well. The group killed Luke's mark. Shot him. And Jeremiah got his lucky coincidence that the adversary was occupied so he could sneak past enemy lines.

I never forgot what that coincidence cost. A man's life. Because we'd been too incompetent to find another way.

"This is worse than that," Luke said, no additional clues required to know what I thought about. "It's millions of lives."

Gulping, I nodded. "I know. But I can't. I can't do it. I don't know why, but something just seems wrong. And I can't bring myself to hurt her."

Luke set a warm hand on my arm and I wanted to shake it off. I couldn't handle this all right now. Instead, he drew me against him while I covered my face with my hands.

Somehow his proximity eased the tension in my chest, let me breathe.

"It will be okay. It'll only be something we do if tomorrow doesn't pan out," Luke whispered in my ear.

Fighting back tears that threatened to spill over, I nodded. "Tomorrow will work."

Tomorrow. July 3rd. It had to work. Had to.

Luke gathered me against him and stood, carrying me back to bed. He tucked me in tight and pressed his lips to mine.

"You're joining me, right?" I asked, my voice strangely tiny.

"You don't mind?" He peered down at me, his eyes too dark to read.

"I would only mind if you didn't."

Luke went around the bed and disentangled the rest of the covers. I laughed, watching him attempt to get them organized.

"How did we even do that?" he asked as he settled down next to me.

"I think it might have involved some kind of blanket fort."

His laughter warmed some part of me that had gone cold at the thought of harming Laura. He wrapped the covers around us both and my body felt drenched in heat.

"Do you feel like you've finally found home?" I whispered, nuzzling into the crook between his neck and shoulder.

"Definitely."

# CHAPTER
## 24

**M**y alarm buzzed in time to The Doors far too early the next morning. I slapped my hand along my side table, then the bed, until I finally found the thing and turned it off. I flopped back down onto my pillow and groaned.

Laura. I'd been dreaming about her, sitting next to her in the lab while she held up little vials, explaining to me how many people she could kill with each one. I'd been nodding along with her like for some reason I was part of her plot, at least until the music filtered in to wake me.

What on earth did that mean?

The soft chuckle next to me shot my eyes open and my heart rate through the roof.

Luke watched me, pure amusement setting his dark eyes dancing. His lip caught in his teeth as he fought to keep from laughing.

"Did I scare you?"

"I had no idea why someone was in my bed for a second there," I said and laughed at my own ridiculousness.

Luke reached from under the covers to draw me closer. Every place his hands touched flamed and a delicious shiver raced down my spine. "I hope it doesn't take too long to get used to waking up to someone."

There really wasn't any hope of responding, verbally, mentally, or any other way, other than to arch into his body pressed against mine.

I soon discovered another random fact about Luke—he hogged the bathroom. I only had one full bath in my part of the house and I finally had to kick him into the half-bath in the guest room.

He thought it was hilarious. I still had wet hair. It would take a little getting used to.

Of course, when I did make it into the kitchen, he'd managed to make tea and toast so it was difficult to be upset. Even with cold wet hair hanging down my back.

Grabbing my keys, we took our breakfast down to my car and Luke drove us to the apartment complex.

"Okay, you seriously know every street in this city, don't you?" I asked, amazed as Luke took us down a narrow alley that opened into an otherwise hidden parking lot where we could leave my car.

"I used to get bored and driving was a way to keep occupied. I found a lot of interesting places." He shrugged and turned off my car.

We got out and made a quick sweep to see if we were alone before we cloaked ourselves.

"Driving around?" I shook my head, "Really? Doesn't that get annoying? With traffic and all?"

Luke held his palms to the sky in front of him. "At times. But, it kept me from pestering you, or going out of my mind. Don't you ever get bored?"

Thinking about it as we rounded the corner and headed toward the complex up ahead, I had to shrug. "Sometimes. But I find a book, or watch a movie, or something. After so many years, it's hard to not find something to do with my down time."

"I sometimes find myself needing to do something different. Outside. To see the real world. Every once in a while, it feels like things are slipping, not real any more. I worry I'm losing touch."

My brows felt like they hit my hairline. I'd long figured I was the only one who felt that way. "Yeah?"

"Sometimes."

I fell silent, his words rattling around in my head as we walked. It was true that so much had changed in the last couple of decades, and I felt like I was playing a constant game of catch-up. It wasn't hard to understand what he meant. Still, I'd found myself treating the world around me like a game—a hundred and one ways to make sure I kept up with the times. Luke, well, that just wasn't his style.

"Maybe it'll be easier, together."

He took my hand, lacing his fingers with mine. "I hope so."

At the apartment complex, I dug out the supplies I'd confiscated from Laura's lab. The first was the letter I'd printed off this morning, which I sealed into an official envelope, then ripped open to give an authentic look. Handing it to Luke, he set off to strategically place it.

I grabbed several small clear plastic sample tubes, filled with water, along with some official looking buccal cell swabs, and went to work by Laura's door.

"He's going to come out in a second," Luke thought from downstairs.

The screen door slammed from the downstairs apartment. It was early—too early for his kids to be up—and Mike swore under his breath at his lack of stealth.

With careful aim, I kicked one of the small tubes from the landing over his head so that it fell next to him.

Mike leapt like I'd dropped a grenade. Perfect shot.

He examined the small tube, reading the neat handwriting on the top, and frowned at the upstairs landing.

"Weird," he breathed, pocketing the tube and making for the parking spaces.

Luke rustled the paper, half stuffed into the envelope, across the ground, like a non-existent breeze carried it. It was rather authentic looking, but Mike paused and looked around like he expected someone to jump out with a camera and say, 'gotcha!'

Luke tugged on the paper again so it scratched a few inches across the ground. The fact that I could see him, glowy edges and all, toying with the piece of paper made it really hard not to laugh.

Mike picked up the letter and turned it over to see Laura's typed name and the name of her company.

He paused. He had to recognize the business. It was the one he'd sat outside of a few days ago while tailing the agents. According to Luke, he'd been researching them on the web. Putting two and two together, his eyes widened as he peered upstairs to Laura's apartment once again.

"Come on, be nosy!" I silently urged him. The letter was half open already, the words visible on the page.

Mike gave in to his curiosity, just as I'd known he would. I rubbed my hands together, enjoying watching his frown grow deeper while he read the letter detailing the FBI's interest in the company, and the company's concerns over employees utilizing company resources to carry out their private research.

Mike pulled the tube from his pocket, inspected it, and folded the letter back into the envelope.

"Come to mama," I thought, earning an eye roll from Luke. Mike went to the stairs and climbed like his feet had weights on them. His eyes never left Laura's door.

I'd 'dropped' a couple more tubes up there, varying the sizes. Someone who didn't know much about lab stuff would have been thrown by them. And the best part was the small amount of rubbing alcohol I'd poured around Laura's door. It carried a pretty strong scent, and while not exactly lab-ish, it was enough to draw attention.

Mike inspected the random assortment of things staged to look like they'd spilled from Laura's purse.

"If he knocks and you have to figure out how to deal with the letter, you're buying us donuts," Luke said from below.

"He's not going to knock." I narrowed my eyes at Mike and willed him not to. Not that I'd have any influence, but I wished I did.

Mike pulled the letter from his pocket again and rubbed his jaw. I held my breath. Do not knock on that door, dude! Then, he turned and walked down the stairs, taking the letter with him.

"Donuts?" I asked, gathering the litter of supplies and bounding down the stairs.

"Lucky." It was all Luke would think on the matter.

I glanced back at Laura's door, debating my next move. Pulling out my phone, I brought up the email I'd hijacked yesterday to impersonate the agents, typing out another message.

*'Laura, we would like to urge you to reconsider speaking with us. Could we meet you this morning briefly before work?'*

If she said yes, we'd get Mike to intercept her, talk with her, get her to stop. Somehow. But when my phone beeped five long minutes later, I wasn't surprised by her curt response.

*'Again, I suggest you meet with my bosses. I don't have any additional information to offer.'*

"She has to know we're on to her," Luke thought.

A tingle of electricity zipped across my back as I looked up at Laura's door. "She does. But does that mean she's going to reconsider her plans?"

Luke took my hands and our eyes met. Neither of us had any ideas. And that was the least frightening part.

# CHAPTER
# 25

"Y**ou owe me a donut," I called after Luke.

He laughed, waved, and jogged back to my car to find Mike.

I couldn't quite seem to get the stupid grin off my face and was grateful no one else could see me perched on the stairs to Laura's place.

I'd left a lone sample tube sitting in front of her door, one more little reminder that things were not as they seemed. When she bustled out, late for work, she noticed it and stopped dead in her tracks. Her keys clattered from her hand onto the cement.

"What the hell?" she swooped it up and held the tube to the light, licking her lips like they'd dried to Sahara levels.

She disappeared back inside and I took advantage of her open door to look around.

If we'd thought the place was a mess before, now it looked like a bomb had gone off. Files and papers were on every available surface and racks and racks of tubes spilled out from the kitchen.

Was that her stash of what she was going to release? But it couldn't be—that had to be kept cold, or warm, didn't it?

Laura had gloves on and was investigating the tube with her back to me. I'd clearly freaked her out, much more than I'd intended. But what did that mean? What did she suspect?

She took a couple of minutes, while I poked through her room, looking for anything specific that might be of interest. Nothing stood out with the 'See, This is Proof' label that I wanted to find.

Shit.

It still felt off to be there. As if something about Laura's part in this was not right. But the evidence was overwhelmingly against her. How could I deny everything in her room? Yet, the persistent tug in my gut hadn't picked up and left, no matter how much I told it that it was wrong.

Stupid intuition. What good was it if it couldn't even realize that Laura was in deep?

Laura let out a long sigh and her shoulders slumped at the kitchen sink where she drained the tube's contents. I guess she'd figured out it was water.

Taking my cue, I went back outside, not wanting to get trapped in her place when she grabbed her purse and raced out the door.

She hurried down the block to the bus stop and pulled out her phone to call work.

"Yeah, I have an appointment this morning. Totally forgot about it. I'll be a little late," she assured the person on the other end. I couldn't make out what they said, but the tone that came through wasn't the slightest bit happy.

"Moron," Laura grumbled as she dropped her phone back in her bag.

She flagged down a bus that was just about to pass us by and I stepped on after her, grateful this one was a lot less crowded than yesterday's. Invisibility, crowded places, and my toes did not mix well.

Laura slumped into an empty seat and massaged her forehead. The bus went in a different direction than her work and I wished for the ten-thousandth time that I could read my mark's mind.

"We're headed in your direction," I thought to Luke.

"Mike is having a fit over the letter. He's tried to get in touch with the agents for the last half hour, but the bureau won't give him anything. His boss is off today because of the holiday tomorrow, and the guy above his boss is a tool and refuses to even meet with him."

"Did you just use the term 'tool'?"

Luke sighed. "You're rubbing off on me."

As much as I wanted to enjoy that little moment, there was too much else going on. I sighed, causing the woman I stood beside to give the seemingly-empty aisle a concerned look. "Okay. Well, this might get interesting."

Laura pulled out her phone and scrolled through it. I couldn't see without alerting her to my presence. She changed busses once then set off walking, her brisk pace leaving me to run behind her.

It became clear where she headed about a block later, and despite a deep sense of relief, I frowned.

"She's headed to the police station. What's she going to do?" I asked, mostly to myself, but also to clue Luke in.

"She wouldn't turn herself in. She hasn't done anything. Yet."

"Exactly," I thought, edging around her to get a better look at her expression. A fierce determined frown brought her brows low over her eyes. It was not a good look on her.

Something niggled at the back of my mind. There was more to this situation. But, I was going to have to wait to figure out what.

It was then I noticed her dress. The same one from the image Luke and I got back when this mess started. So, I guess it hadn't been a ticket she'd gotten, right? She'd been telling Mike something. But what?

Maybe, finally, this whole thing would make sense?

"I think we're about to see what happens in that one scene we got," I thought at Luke.

At the doors of the police station, she paused and stared inside the glass like she didn't know what to do. She touched the door handle, then her hand fell away.

She'd come all this way and was going to chicken out!

Not if I had anything to do with it.

"Can you get Mike to get out here?"

"Maybe." Luke sounded occupied and I took that to be more of a 'no.'

Looking around, I tried to think of some way to push her inside. A little jolt that would make her do the right thing even if she didn't want to.

Down the street and headed our way was a mom with her little girl. They walked fast, eager to get away from the odd crowd that mingled in the area. Pulling a quarter out of my pocket, I waited until the little girl was a step away from us, then made it look like it dropped out of Laura's bag and rolled right in front of her little patent leather shoes.

Her ponytails swung around as she picked up the money while her mother managed a weak grin.

"Is this yours?" The girl tugged on Laura's bag strap.

Laura, who had been utterly lost in thought, blinked and looked down at the pigtails and pink cheeks on the little girl who held up the quarter, "I don't think so."

"It fell out of your bag," the girl said, trying to hand off the coin.

"Well, then you keep it. Thanks though." Laura smiled at the girl and nodded to her mother.

The girl shrugged and pocketed the money before setting off.

That was one hell of a nudge.

Laura took a deep breath, watching the little girl skip a couple of steps to keep up with her mom's clip. Then she pushed open the door to the station and entered the craziness inside.

"We're headed your way," I called to Luke.

Luke made some kind of non-committal noise in response.

Laura waded through the crowd of people in different lines to the desk.

"Could I speak with Mike Nowak, please? I have some information for him."

The woman behind the desk pressed her lips together, scouring Laura's cute sundress and otherwise wholesome appearance. In comparison to a lot of the people in the station, Laura looked like an ad out of a magazine.

"Let me call him up here." She grabbed the phone and spoke swiftly. "Take a seat and he'll be here shortly."

Laura nodded and went back to the cramped waiting room and looked around for an empty seat. Finding none, she leaned up against the wall and pulled out her phone, staring at the screen with glassy eyes.

"You have a competitor for the title of most stubborn person," Luke noted a moment later.

"Excuse me?" I replied. "What's that supposed to mean?"

"He is nearly impossible to push. But we're coming out now."

I wanted to be annoyed but couldn't. Luke had a point. I probably did have some kind of market on being obstinate. It was going to take a good long time to live down what we'd both kept hidden from one another.

The door to the back buzzed open and Mike strolled out, Luke squeaking through behind him. The woman at the counter pointed to Laura and Mike made his way over.

Laura watched him approach like he was going to lead her to the gallows.

"Laura?" Mike extended a hand, which Laura shook with a limp grip. "You live above me, right?"

She nodded and glanced around. "Can we go somewhere else and talk?"

Luke and I exchanged a look. This was going to be interesting.

Mike frowned, and after turning to inspect the back office, took Laura's elbow and steered her out the main doors. They walked down the sidewalk for a minute or so in silence, Mike's face an unreadable mask, while Laura looked close to tears.

They finally stopped, each of them appraising one another with hooded glances.

"What's going on?" Mike asked.

Laura fumbled with her bag. "Something's going to happen. Tomorrow. Down by where the fireworks are going to be set off. I don't trust the FBI agents."

# CHAPTER
## 26

**M**ike's eyes went big and Luke's jaw dropped. I came within a millimeter of dropping my phone to the ground and screwing everything up.

"What in the hell is she playing at?" I asked.

"Do you have any kind of details? Information that I can check up on? And why don't you trust the FBI agents?" Mike fired questions, taking out a notebook, apparently not caring how Laura knew about the FBI. His hands shook with either excitement or nerves; it was impossible to tell which.

"The agents, I don't know—something was off about them. I, I don't think they're here to help. I don't trust them. But, I know you. At least, I see you around all the time. I know you're not up to something."

Mike frowned at Laura's confession. "I haven't been able to get in touch with the agents all morning. I don't know what's going on, but they were supposed to stay in contact with the department, at least my partner and me."

"There's something else going on. Tomorrow. You know where all the crowds gather for the fireworks by Crissy Field?"

Mike took notes in handwriting I was sure couldn't be read later. He nodded at Laura's question.

"It's going to be there. You need to scan the crowds more. It's going to be bad. Really, really bad." She suddenly covered her mouth like she'd said too much.

"What's going to happen? Laura, you have to tell me." Mike pressed a hand to his forehead, frustration evident in every line of his face.

"I can't. It's not safe if I do."

Luke's eyes snapped to mine. "What?"

"I'll protect you. The whole force will. But, you've got to get me some more information." He reached out to touch her arm, but thought better of it and dropped his hand to his side.

Laura looked like she might keel over right on the sidewalk. Her head hung from her shoulders and she bit her thumb. "Tomorrow. I'll meet you there. Show you what I can. I don't know all the details, but I'll show you. Just make sure that you do everything you can to get people searched. Maybe you'll get lucky."

"Who's doing this to you?" Mike asked in a low voice.

She met his eyes. Wrong thing to ask. Her lips pressed together in a fine line.

"I can't help you unless I know what to do. Please, Laura," Mike pressed.

Laura's eyes dropped to the ground and her shoulders slumped. "It's too big to share right now. We'll only get one shot at stopping this. This is my card. Call me. And tomorrow night? Be there at eight. I'll meet you out in front of the St. Francis Yacht Club."

Laura spun away and almost ran in the opposite direction of the police station.

Mike stood there on the sidewalk until long after she turned the corner. "Okay, translation, please?" I threw my hands up.

Luke shook his head, eyes wide. "She's either being manipulated by someone into her plan tomorrow and is scared for her safety, or she's trying to lure as many cops down there as possible to make sure they're infected."

My stomach dropped. I hadn't thought of Luke's last suggestion.

"I'm going back to her place to see if there's anything I can learn." I pressed my hands against my eyes until lights sparked. "Maybe she'd got it all written down somewhere in plain English and I'll be able to figure out just what I'm supposed to do."

Luke wrapped an arm around my waist, pulling me close. "Good luck. I'm going to keep watching Mike. See what he does with this information."

With a kiss, Luke followed Mike into the station while I snagged my car and drove over to Laura's place. I should have taken the bus after I ran two red lights and totally cut off some poor guy, but my brain had to work out all the possible implications of this new information.

There had to be something in her apartment.

Getting inside took some work. I was nowhere near as proficient at B&E as Luke, and even with his detailed instructions, it took me close to an hour to get all her locks undone. I politely told Luke that next time he could take my job, or at least give me a lesson in lock picking.

Inside, only dim light filtered past the blackout curtains. Without Laura there to worry about, I didn't concern myself with being silent, or with not bumping into things. I doubted she'd be able to tell if I disturbed any of the boxes, stacks of paper, or newspaper clippings spread everywhere.

"Okay, Laura, let's see what you've been up to."

Her notebook sat on the counter, closed with a sharpie resting on top. Finding a spot to open it forced me to sit on the floor in her tiny kitchen, cracking the big book like it might explode.

The top sheet was decorated with black inky lines surrounding a single word: 'Success!!'

Below she'd noted it was none too soon—only two days to spare. A host of other notes accompanied it, detailing what she'd accomplished in undecipherable lab-speak.

Other than notes on how to ramp up production, her only other comment on her plans were 'Two days' from yesterday. That didn't bode well.

Peeking into her fridge, several boxes of vials sat open and waiting on the top shelf. A big warning labeled the side: 'Biohazard. Open only in designated clean room.'

Yeah, that was not comforting. Whatever she was doing with all that junk had finally worked and now she was about to use it.

I considered destroying it all, right then and there. Or taking it with me. But there were too many problems with that—I didn't know how to dispose of the stuff, and no way would I risk infecting people. That was what we were trying to stop in the first place. And, if I took it now, then there wouldn't be any damning evidence against Laura if we did get some cops to check this place out.

Closing her fridge, I leaned my forehead against the cool metal exterior.

I should have let the agents find her the other day. My stupidity got in the way. Laura was responsible for what was about to happen, and I'd cut it so damn close. All those body bags. I'd almost let it happen.

The thought made me retch and I leaned over the sink full of dirty coffee mugs. So many deaths. All of them my fault.

No way I'd let that happen. Gripping the edge of the counter, I took a deep breath and tried to settle my stomach. We could still stop this. Whatever I'd done to get Lexi and Theo in trouble was out of our control, but at least we could finish this job. Stop Laura. Stop the attack.

Fix some of my stupid actions.

My stomach twisted even more painfully at the knowledge of what we had to do. My palms slicked with sweat; I closed my eyes.

"Luke? I think we may have to find a contingency plan after all."

〤

"If she can't make it to the marina, then there's no way she can carry out her plan," I said, grabbing the last wonton and dropping it in my mouth. I'd brought home Chinese take-out—my favorite comfort food—and Luke and I dug in at the breakfast bar.

"And if she finds another way?" Luke raised his eyebrows.

"We don't let her. Look, I'm not going to hurt her, okay?"

"I don't want to hurt her either." Luke leaned back in his seat, arms crossed.

"I know that. Really, I do." I placed a hand on his chest. "But, we can't. I don't know why, but we can't. Just trust me on this. We have to keep her from the marina tomorrow."

"Shouldn't we have Mike arrest her beforehand?" Luke suggested for the third time.

"Are you going to be able to push him to do so before then? And we're going to need his help if we can't contain her for some reason."

We bounced ideas off one another for way too long and the food disappeared in the process. Not that we'd gotten very far in our plans—neither of us had any good ideas of what we could do. Just what had to happen—we had to stop Laura.

And I was not going to hurt her. No way, no how.

Luke wasn't advocating that—he was just a little more open to the idea if we had to. Which might have bothered me if I hadn't kept flashing on all those dead bodies—that had to be our first priority when it came to what we did. As much as I didn't want to harm Laura, I'd do what had to be done.

It was my fault we were in this situation. We had to fix it. Even with drastic measures. But, I couldn't admit that aloud—the feeling of wrongness overwhelmed me even at the thought.

Damn, did I wish my random sense of protectiveness for Laura had an off switch.

"Fine. We do what you suggested. But if something goes wrong, I will take more drastic action. Okay?" Luke eyed me like he expected me to protest.

Our discussion tonight had been a bit different. First of all, it was rare that we had marks that were close together and allowed us to discuss things about them. It happened, but not often. Nor did we usually talk about this kind of thing. Sure, we told each other what we were up to, but planning together? Totally not our normal style. Throw into the mix that a part of me couldn't help imagining him naked, and we might as well of been on Mars.

"Fine." I sighed, realizing it was the best compromise we could to come to. "But it's going to work."

Luke grinned. "Double down on the donut bet?"

"I think we've moved from donuts to Danishes. Don't you?"

Luke laughed, leaning in to kiss me. He tasted like salt and rice and I gripped his shirt, desperate for the distraction he offered. I couldn't handle being in my head with all my mistakes for one moment more.

"Last night wasn't enough?" Luke teased, tracing his lips down my throat. I was so, so glad I'd worn a low-cut blouse today.

"Funny." Lifting the bottom of his t-shirt, I teased my hands underneath, all too caught up in the smoothness of his skin, the way his muscles tightened under my fingertips. "If it was enough for you, I'll just leave you alone." I dropped my hands to my thighs and went limp in his grasp.

He bit my earlobe, a little hard, and chuckled. "Who's the funny one now?"

Picking me up and pressing me up against the wall, his knee slid between my legs.

I gasped.

His shirt was off in a second.

We never made it anywhere near the bed.

# CHAPTER
## 27

The Fourth of July. The morning dawned clear and warm. Every summer we had a few of these scorcher days, far too hot in a city where air conditioning was normally never needed. Luke had one leg tangled in the blankets and not much else to cover him.

Even with everything hanging over me with Laura and tonight's events, I couldn't help the small smile at the sight of him. If one good thing had come from this shit-show of a job, it was that we'd come to our senses. Not that that would balance out millions of people dying, but it made a whole lot of the rest of my life make sense.

Laura. Gods. Today was D-Day. I left Luke to get some more sleep and padded out to the kitchen. The sooner we got started, the better, despite the fact that I wanted nothing more than to just skip today and pretend we never had to do what was coming.

I started the kettle and grabbed my tablet to delve into Laura's recent activity. She'd been awfully quiet last night, which made sense if she'd been working.

"Anything interesting?" Luke asked, planting a kiss on my shoulder. He still hadn't come up with a sleep shirt, which didn't bother me in the slightest.

"Nope. She hasn't been up too much. I imagine she's super busy working, putting all those final touches on ending the world." I clicked over to the San Francisco Chronicle and read through the events planned for today. So many people. So much potential insanity.

Luke had his laptop out and clicked around. "Mike searched for Laura's company last night. That's about it."

"You ever wonder about how many laws we're breaking by looking all this stuff up? If anyone ever found out, we'd be screwed." I went to grab the kettle before it screamed, pinching Luke's butt as I went by.

Luke's grin was infectious and he took my seat at the counter. "I have wondered about that. If the FBI ever does come looking for us, we won't stand much of a chance."

I wrinkled my nose. After tonight, the FBI would take top priority and entail a change of venue for Luke and me, once we'd located Theo and Lexi. We couldn't face issues with the government. There were too many things we'd been involved in. And the whole invisibility thing only went so far, as had been demonstrated all too well the other day. If the FBI had keyed into the other partnership, it would only take a little digging to realize Luke and I were known associates.

"Ready to leave in five?" Luke asked, taking my mug from me.

"Yeah." My stomach tilted at the thought. Luke must have noticed the bitter look on my face and pulled me to his warm chest.

"We are going to stop her. We're not going to let those people die."

I wanted to agree, but I couldn't form the words. I couldn't lie. I just leaned my forehead against his chest and breathed in his scent of spices and sweat. It didn't alleviate my frustration at what I'd done, but it did help. "I don't deserve you."

Luke set my mug down with extra force, taking both my shoulders in his broad hands. He stepped back and leaned down to meet my eyes. "Don't say that. Ever."

I tried to swallow back the tears that gathered in my eyes and closed off my throat, but there was no stopping them. One by one they slipped under my lids and down my cheeks. Luke's thumbs brushed them away and I couldn't help but flash back on the time he'd done that before, right after we'd finished a job.

We'd been heading home and my horse threw a shoe and I'd ended up in a heap on the ground. I probably broke my leg, but it wasn't like we had x-rays then. It hurt, a lot, and as hard as I'd tried to keep from crying, I couldn't help it. Luke had pulled me close and let me cry into his rough wool coat. Then he'd lifted me onto his horse, done his best to make me comfortable, and walked us back to where I'd been living. He took care of me the whole time I'd healed—a week at least.

How much had it hurt him to tend to me like that, thinking I didn't reciprocate his feelings? How had he not let his emotions sour into hate? Especially after our 'Night of Shame'? I at least had the benefit of memory loss, otherwise no way could I have been that strong.

But, that was just him. He had that ability. I may not have deserved it one little bit, but I loved him for it.

"Ami, listen to me, unless you've figured out how to time travel, what's in the past is the past. We can't change it. We can only move forward. And all I want to do is move forward with you."

I opened my eyes, the kitchen a blurry grey swirl of sunlight and shadows. "Me too. I just wish," I sighed, "I wish I hadn't been so stupid. I wish I hadn't give up, hadn't gotten scared and tried to find some way to work things out after Egypt." My heart squeezed in my chest with my words, a witness to the truth.

"I wish I'd figured it out all those years ago. I was scared to death when you kissed me that one time. Freaked and pretty horrible. This is just as much on me as it is you." Luke tucked my head under his chin, his fingers trailing up and down the bumps of my spine.

I tilted my head up to try and catch his expression, though I couldn't see much. "Scared?"

Luke's laugh was felt more than heard. "I thought then that giving in to how I felt would make everything we did impossible. That we'd be too distracted. And then I was sure I'd fucked it all up when you barely spoke to me for just about forever."

"You looked like I'd tried to bite your head off, not kiss you!" I protested. The flash of horror in his eyes was definitely not something I'd imagined.

"Oh, I'm not trying to excuse my behavior. I was a damn idiot. But if we let ourselves get lost in the past, how the hell can we enjoy the present?" He peered down at me and lifted a brow.

He was right, even if it wasn't easy. The only way either of us could keep going, when everything around us shifted in a kaleidoscope of color and people and faces, was to try not to dwell on the past. It haunted us from time to time—there were always reminders of things we'd seen over so many years—but we had to let details fade. Names and faces slid into obscurity. Or we'd go crazy. We'd both been around for far too long to carry the weight of all that history.

In order for us to be together, I was going to have to learn how to do the same with my own inability to tell Luke how I felt. For the hurt I'd carried for too long from his rejection. Because there was no other way we could be together—not with my guilt strapped onto our relationship. It was not going to be easy, but I had to lose that baggage.

Luke lifted me onto the counter and I wrapped my legs around him, kissing him until my tea was cold and I couldn't see straight.

"Don't we have to save the world or something?" I cradled his face in my hands and dropped a peck on the tip of his nose.

"Damn world. I'm so sick of saving it."

We both laughed, but Luke regrettably settled me on the floor and urged me toward the shower.

"Just don't use all the hot water," he whispered in my ear, patting my butt.

The sizzle and pop of someone setting off an illegal firework outside reminded me we had serious work to do. The world wasn't going to save itself.

# CHAPTER
## 28

pproaching Mike and Laura's apartments, I could hear kids screaming and playing out back in the yard. My heart flopped. Before Luke could stop me, I walked back there to see the sprinkler Mike's wife had set up. She sat off to the side while the two kids ran and jumped in the water. Little bits of my heart crumbled as I stood there.

"Some days I really hate whatever the hell I am," I thought at Luke.

He pressed his hand against the small of my back. "I know what you mean."

With a shaky breath, I spun on my heel and went back to the stairs. With the kids making so much noise there was little chance of anyone hearing Laura while we secured her.

Luke set to work on her locks while I listened at the door, then the window, to see if I could catch anything inside. I didn't hear even a footstep.

"She better be in there." I joined Luke at the door.

He just shrugged, sweating a little as he worked the locks. His pick and rake were twisted and contorted in the last one and his tongue poked out of the side of his mouth as he concentrated, turning the lock slowly so it didn't draw attention.

There definitely had never been a hotter lock pick in the history of the world.

A soft click and Luke pocketed his tools. "Ready?" he thought.

I shook my head. "No. But do we have a choice?"

"I don't think we do." Luke met my eyes, his brow pinched with his silent words. "But, if we keep her from the marina, hopefully all those people…"

I held up a hand to stop him. The body bags hadn't left my mind all morning. "I hope this works. Because it sure as shit feels wrong."

I did the honors with the door, Luke right behind me. It took us a second once inside to let our eyes adjust to the dark. A single lamp in the kitchen lit the lab.

Laura lay sound asleep, her cheek pressed to her notebook page.

"I imagine we didn't have to be quite so stealthy," Luke thought.

We closed the door and made our way across the room. Once next to her, she shifted in her sleep, groaned, and settled again.

"This is just so wrong," I thought, more to myself than to Luke.

It had to be done though. All those bodies….

Luke removed the piece of duct tape he'd cut from the main roll and placed on his sleeve for easy and quiet access. He readied himself while I lifted Laura's head to allow Luke to affix the tape before she could wake up.

As soon as the tape was in place, Laura blinked twice and her hands twitched to remove the tape. But she couldn't. I had a firm hold on her wrists, held behind her back, and Luke took the rest of the tape from his bag and started to wind it around and bind her.

Laura couldn't quite seem to figure out what to do. I had to admit, two invisible sets of hands tying me up would have confused me, too. Her bewilderment lasted just a moment before she started to buck against us, screaming into the tape.

Luke switched me, using his much larger frame to hold her down so I could secure her feet.

"Bathroom," I thought as soon as I finished.

Luke hefted her up and cradled her against him. We made our way down the hall, careful about not bumping her against the walls or doors.

Tears streamed down Laura's face and her hair was a wild mess that stuck in the damp. Luke set her down on the tile floor.

"I hate this." I held the tape as he grabbed a few towels from her cupboards and set them under her head.

"I do too." Luke's thoughts were tight, anxious. "But I'm not letting all those people die. I will do anything to make sure that future doesn't happen."

I gulped. The edge to his tone was final. I didn't blame him, but it settled wrong in my gut. This wasn't right. But what choice did we have?

Using the handcuffs we'd picked up, the kind with the extra-long chain between the cuffs, Luke secured Laura to the shower fixture, giving her just enough room so she could move around a little on the floor and not hurt herself, but not enough so she could get loose.

As soon as we let her go, Laura started thrashing, kicking against the wall with both feet tied together, shaking her head and crying into the tape across her lips. I wanted to comfort her, let her know that this was only temporary until after the threat had passed and we worked out how to get her to the correct authorities.

"We've got to go." My stomach ached like I'd eaten something foul.

Luke escorted me from the bathroom and we locked her in there, securing the door from the outside.

Laura wasn't going anywhere. There was no doubt of that. And tonight, all those people watching the fireworks would be safe from the terror she'd wanted to release.

I felt like the worst person on the planet for doing that to her.

In Laura's living room, I slumped to my knees. My forehead hit the floor and I held my stomach as my chest squeezed and sobs wracked my body.

This wasn't right. But what choice did we have? The thoughts were on an endless loop.

Luke settled next to me, a strong arm circling my waist. He pulled me into his lap and stroked my hair until the tears subsided. My stomach ached from crying so hard.

"This is all my fault."

Luke frowned down at me and shook his head. "No, this is Laura's fault. She's doing this. We're stopping her."

I wanted to argue. To point out that no, really, if I just had done what everyone thought I should back at the lab that day, we wouldn't be here tying Laura to her shower. But I swallowed back the thoughts. I didn't have the energy to argue. I knew I was right.

"We'll figure something out. About what to do with her. She's going to be fine," Luke added.

I managed a miserable nod. "It just doesn't seem right."

# CHAPTER
# 29

U sing Luke's keys, I pushed open his back door and looked around before stepping into his mudroom. Something smelled kind of funny, like new plastic, but everything else appeared in order as best as I could tell.

"Anything strange?" Luke came up behind me and placed his hands on my shoulders.

Together we walked inside, studying every detail. I wasn't sure what I should have been looking for: I doubted there'd be some giant sign that said 'hey, the FBI's been here.'

"It has only been a few days and this place feels strange," he noted, going to his fridge and grabbing out an apple.

Together we swept the rest of the downstairs, including his library/reading room that I longed to chill in for a few hours. Then Luke led the way up. In his bedroom he went through his drawers to gather a few things, sleep shirts included, despite my protests. I perched on the side of his bed, watching him, jumping at every unaccounted for sound and feeling like I was one of those old toy cars that had been wound past the point of no return.

Flopping back against the comforter I remembered the random photo I'd found the last time I was here. It somehow felt like just the perfect thing to drag my mind off everything it didn't want to think about.

"Hey, wait, I was going to ask you something." I reached over snagged the photo, holding it up so he could see it in all its 80's glory.

Luke's face turned a brilliant shade of crimson—seriously, red enough to mimic a stop sign. I couldn't help laughing, the tension of the day adding to the hilarity.

"You know I've dated other women occasionally." He kept his hands busy, not even able to look in my direction as he spoke. He ducked low in front of his dresser while I propped myself up to look over at him.

"And this woman gets a place of honor by your bed, because?" I couldn't help the giggling challenge in my words. Had that photo really sat there for the past, what, nearly forty years? What in the hell had made her so special? Not that I was really jealous, but my curiosity was certainly peaked.

Luke kept his eyes elsewhere and his response was somewhat muffled. "She was the only other woman I've ever really loved. When she died, it took me ages to get over her."

Any amusement I might have felt zapped out of the room like fog under the afternoon sun. "Oh. I'm so sorry. I didn't know."

"I imagine there's a few things that we haven't had a chance to really learn about what we've been up to lately." He stood and met my eyes. "I seem to remember some guy hanging around back in, what was it, the sixties? Pretty sure he had hair down to his waist."

"Ah, yeah," I rubbed a hand over my face, cringing a little. "That would have been Bobby. Good guy. Great guitar player. Definitely not someone I loved. I don't have any photos of him by my bed." I turned and replaced the little memento in its spot, touching the woman's face. While a little part of me burned with jealousy, I also couldn't help being grateful that she'd been a good thing for Luke. One of these days I'd ask about her and learn what happened to her.

"So, any other boyfriends I might need to worry about?" Luke asked, shoving things into a duffle bag.

I rolled my eyes. "Nope, kinda been avoiding anything serious for the last decade or so. It just gets too messy and I hate hurting people."

"Ah, yes, hurting other people but never being the hurt one?" Luke arched a brow, tossing a pair of socks at me.

"Well, maybe that, too." I giggled, flopping over on his big poofy comforter. It felt good to talk, to open up, to be able to share so openly about everything with someone who understood all the little weird issues with dating a mortal.

It took Luke a moment to join in, but soon his rich, deep, humor joined mine until he grabbed and wrestled me into the blankets and pillows.

Luke was in the process of removing various pieces of my clothing when something cracked downstairs.

We both froze. "What was that?" My grip on his arms left indents in his muscles.

"Get dressed." Luke stood up and tugged his clothes back on.

I did the same, my heart beating so loud I wondered if I'd be able to hear anything else.

"I guess they were watching the house."

Luke swore profusely and after hunting out his shoes, grabbed his bag, and helped me disentangle myself from my shirt I'd been too hasty to pull on properly.

"Is there another way out?" I asked, turning in a slow circle. We could go out the window if need be, but it would be a long drop.

Luke nodded and went to a far door that blended in with the wall—I hadn't even noticed it before. He must not have used it often as paint crackled when he opened it. Beyond was a small balcony on the roof. I would have been delighted if I hadn't heard muffled footsteps on the stairs.

Luke waved me over and we stepped out into the heat of the afternoon, sunlight baking the dark roof.

"The heat might hide us if they're using the goggles." Luke peered around the edge of the balcony. He swore again and I had to look. At least five men in bulky gear and the awkward looking headset things were planted around the yard. Only the small alcove around the balcony door, and the afternoon heat, shielded us now.

"Looks like we're officially fugitives." Inside, the bedroom door slammed open and two sets of footsteps charged inside.

Luke looked pained, patted the side of his house like he said goodbye, and dropped low to swing his long legs off one side of the balcony and onto the street-side of the roof.

From our vantage we couldn't see anyone waiting in that direction, but as Luke slid down the slate and landed in one of his flowerbeds, a shout went up from somewhere.

"I'll catch you." Luke waved for me to follow.

With a shaky breath, I swung over the ledge, my shoes catching on the rooftop. Behind me, the door to the balcony opened and one of the agents came out. He took too long to spot me. I skidded down the incline, the edge of the roof slipping by me as I headed for the ground.

Luke's arms circled around me, taking the brunt of the force. The fall still jolted up my legs and my teeth bit into my lip so that I tasted blood.

"Thanks." I took Luke's hand as a contingent of agents made their way through his carefully cultivated garden toward us.

"Move." Luke pushed me in front of him toward the street.

A part of me wanted to look back, to collapse in the fetal position, but Luke kept us going. We vaulted the low wall that separated his property from the sidewalk and Luke stayed behind me as we took off down the street.

Heavy booted footsteps kept up after us, shouts to stop and give ourselves up lost in the erratic beat of my heart.

"Where?" I managed to think as reached the corner. I didn't know this neighborhood, didn't know where there was the possibility of cover.

"Left!" Luke grabbed me and propelled me in that direction.

The street was lined with shops, coffee houses, and galleries. Crowds were far too thick to make our getaway easy, and I found myself dodging strollers, couples, elderly women with shopping bags. I hit a few, undoubtedly freaking them out that something unseen had been so close.

The chase the agents gave had to scare them more.

I risked a quick glance back at the ten men and women after us, thundering down the sidewalk, gear rattling and goggles bouncing on their faces.

"We've got to get another route. They'll head us off," I thought at Luke.

His response wasn't verbal—just confirmation—but he had no idea where to go.

My foot caught on the uneven sidewalk and I struggled to catch myself before face planting. Luke's arms went around me and hefted me to my feet, the footsteps drawing ever nearer behind us.

"Get in the street, dodge the traffic," Luke shouted at me.

Great. Invisible frogger. But it would slow down the agents. And lessen the chances of an ambush.

Sliding over the hood of a shiny Porsche, I skidded into traffic. It wasn't terribly busy, just enough to slow down the agents. Freaked out drivers started honking as the agents entered the street. Cars clogged the lanes.

"Keep moving," Luke called from my heels.

I could stick to the lines between the cars and dodge as they slowed. I watched as drivers looked around to see what was going on and some moron changed lanes right into another car. I jumped up onto the mangled hood and dented it. The driver looked out, clearly confused, then even more so when Luke followed me.

"Over here!" Luke shouted, turning so we went down another street. My lungs were about to explode and I was going to eat cement any second, but I managed to do what he asked.

What Luke aimed for became clear. The BART station up ahead. Blessed public transportation and all the crazy people who would be there.

We could blend in and lose our tail. If we were really, really lucky.

Behind us a couple of the agents broke free of the traffic snarl and gained on us. We reached the subway entrance and flung ourselves down the stairs to the dank, piss-smelling interior.

"Go visible," Luke thought at me.

"People!" I thought back in horror. All around us individuals milled in the tiled underbelly of the station.

"We will be harder to pick out if we're visible to everyone."

I didn't buy the idea but trusted his reasoning. I dropped my cloak and earned more than a few gasps from those around me. Apparently invisible people stood out even in the weird world of San Francisco, which included a man dressed as a giant pink penis who danced at one end of the platform.

After walking for a bit, people's stares stopped and Luke grabbed my hand. We both feigned calm, though we were heaving for breath and sweat dampened my whole shirt.

Catching the next train without bothering to look back, even at the frustrated yelling of a couple of agents, we stepped into the car and ducked into a corner. The white walls had been decked out with scratched in names and dates.

"So, looks like we're going to be relocating. Maybe Argentina?" I dropped my sweaty brow against Luke's chest.

He wrapped an arm around me. "Mi Español sucks."

I laughed, the sound strangled by the adrenalin high still pumping through my veins. "We could do Brazil, but I'm going to need to remember Portuguese."

The automated voice called the next stop and Luke maneuvered to the door.

"We're not riding around for a while?" I thought, not wanting to get out and run any more. The rush was abating and it felt like my shoes were made of lead.

"Any more time and they will start an organized search."

I wrinkled my nose. "Yeah, okay."

The stop was still a good long way from the car, but there wasn't much we could do. Sticking to busy pedestrian streets, we hoofed it the couple of miles, and one giant pain of a hill, to where we'd left it.

"Any chance we were followed? I really don't want those guys as dinner guests," I peered over my shoulder for the hundredth time.

"If they were following us, they would have already stopped us."

I rested my head against the steering wheel for a long moment.

"That was exciting." He'd run his hands through his hair so many times it stood out in a wild array.

I just nodded. There were no words to describe today. Which, really, was probably a good thing. "What do you think the chances are that they can track us back to my place?"

Luke shrugged. "I have no idea. We're going to have to get out of this city aren't we?" He let out of a long breath. "Damn."

I felt the same way. This city was home. We'd never spent so much time in a single place. And I loved my house and everything else. But keeping our cover meant our safety and we couldn't risk that.

"Tomorrow. We plan that all tomorrow. After we let Laura go, and get her to confess to Mike. Then we worry about moving."

I pulled into traffic, driving as slow as a tourist all the way back to my place.

"Tomorrow," Luke echoed. "They shouldn't be able to find us before then. You don't have any documents linking your face to your house, or your car. That's got to make it harder."

Tomorrow. Tomorrow we'd leave everything we knew, all that I'd grown to love about this place. Unless Luke was wrong, and then we'd be on the run. Or worse.

# CHAPTER

# 30

We decided to walk to the fireworks show because neither of us felt like dealing with parking. It wasn't too far and we grabbed some street tacos along the way, the crowd of people accumulating as we drew closer.

"Their meeting spot is there." Luke pointed with his taco to a ritzy building where a police car sat parked in a handicap spot up front. "Mike's waiting."

We kept off to the side as we approached and did our best to look inconspicuous, though I suspected we looked like we'd just robbed a bank or something. Mike leaned against his patrol car, alone, his eyes never leaving the gathering shadows.

"How long do you think he'll wait?" I watched the skinny man from where we positioned ourselves on the grass that led down to the water. I'd brought along a blanket that we spread out and settled onto.

"All night? He knows something is going on. He researched Laura and I think he has some idea of what would have happened, if we hadn't done something."

I bit into my fourth taco, unable to look at him. We hadn't eaten all day and a headache had begun to pound behind my eyes, but I might as well of been eating sawdust. It was going to take freeing Laura and being damn sure the threat of the attack was gone before I could even hope to feel okay with what we'd done.

"Wouldn't have happened if we'd pushed him the way we should have," I said.

Luke poked me with his toe. "We did everything we could."

I nodded, head still down. "Maybe whoever gives us these jobs will see that we can't handle the big stuff and downsize us to missing objects. Personally, I don't want to deal with this whole saving humanity from extinction thing ever again."

"Yeah, you say that now, but give it a couple of decades," Luke said.

"Yeah, yeah, a few decades and all the humans won't even need us to save them."

A cop, one of the half dozen we'd seen since arriving, gave me a funny look.

"You don't think the FBI agents spread our picture around, do you?" I asked.

Luke shook his head. "Not today. It's too busy with the holiday. But by Monday we'll be celebrities."

I wrinkled my nose and returned my attention to Mike. At least he wasn't going to get sick and die a grisly death. Even if the means to get that outcome made my tacos want to make a repeat appearance.

"This was supposed to be our date night," Luke drew my focus back to him.

I made an effort to smile and force Laura's freaked-out face from my thoughts. I reached over and wrapped my arms around his neck. "So, you owe me a date. Can I vote for a day where we don't have people chasing us through traffic, or I have to learn the best way to use duct tape to secure someone?"

"You're not upset?" Luke's hands rubbed circles onto my lower back. He was trying to distract me and I let him. Wanted him too. One more minute of thinking about how bad I'd screwed the pooch might lead me to run screaming into the bay.

"About this being our date? Why would I be?"

"Because, people do this differently, don't they? Date, get to know one another, then start sleeping together? We skipped several important steps."

I raised an eyebrow. "You do realize that we've known each other for longer than this city has stood, than anyone and anything around us has been here, and I'm relatively certain I know more about you than anyone on this planet. Right?" I thought the words, not too keen on allowing anyone to hear how old I was.

Luke's laughter built in his chest, rumbling through him. "That may be true, but I always imagined this differently."

"Yeah? Do tell." I settled back on my elbows and propped my feet across his lap.

Luke shook his head. "There were plenty of permutations over the years. It's not like you ever had a father or someone I could ask permission from."

"Thank heavens," I cut in.

"But most versions did involve me taking you out somewhere elegant. A formal date. Wine and flowers. Perfect gentleman sorts of things."

I chewed my lip. "Well, I really did screw that up, didn't I? Damn. I'm sorry."

Luke shook his head, his eyes full of laughter. "Saves me the trouble, doesn't it?"

"Nope. Not really. Because I think I'm going to have to hold you to that sort of thing as soon as humanly possible."

"Might be a bit difficult seeing as how I'm not completely sure you're human." He grabbed my foot and tickled the soft spot behind my knee.

Our laughter brought way too much attention, and after the reproachful gaze from several parents, we settled down, my cheeks flaming. From the way one little girl stared at us with her mouth hanging open, her stuffy parents obviously never displayed any kind of affection, ever.

The show started a minute later. Even as old as I was, there was something about the boom and thunder-like clap followed by the brilliant sparkle of fireworks that got to me. They made me oooh and ahhh, and clap as the flashes of light lit up the grass and the Golden Gate in the distance.

Memories of the first time I'd seen fireworks brought a small smile. We'd been on one of our rare trips to China, having taken a boat there. Our journey took ages and I remember being so confused why we were the ones chosen for it—surely there had to be another partnership in the region who could handle it. Now, I knew that may not have been the case, as we were often spread too thin to do all that we had to. Still, the evening had been warm and Luke and I had been walking along a harbor. I couldn't even remember the city's name, though surely it had changed in the intervening centuries.

Luke had headed off to look for his mark and the sound of the display starting had made me duck and search for cover, certain we were under attack. But the cries from the people around me, in a language I had only just begun to understand, made me look up at the sky. Out over the water, brilliant plumes of color exploded like flowers of light and sound. As the next few fireworks were set off, Luke appeared at my side, the two of us watching with mouths hanging open at the sight. I'd wanted to take his hand that night and somehow make the evening more real by sharing it. I hadn't then, but now I reached for him, the memory fading away in the glow of the present.

We were about halfway through the display when Luke looked up and around in search of Mike. I felt tension rip through his body from where I leaned against him.

"What's going on?" I got to my knees so I could look too. There was no sign of Mike anywhere near the Marina Club.

"Mike went over to the parking lot, but his car's still here. Something feels, off."

If it had been under any other circumstances, I would have taken great pleasure in rubbing it in that Luke admitted to 'feeling' something about his mark. But the wrinkle in his brow and flat line of his lips kept me silent.

Our eyes met in the flash of red light from the next explosion. We got to our feet, threw the blanket in my bag, and raced to the parking lot before the next one went off.

# CHAPTER
# 31

The parking lot lights had been turned down low for the show, which was not the safest thing to do and made things more dire for whatever Mike had gotten himself into.

We cloaked ourselves and came up on him, crouched behind a car while he spied on several men working out of the back of a white delivery van.

"Why do those guys look familiar?" I asked, walking around so I could see the others better.

"They're Laura's bosses," Luke said.

He grabbed my shoulder and we paused to watch them assemble multiple syringes from small vials they took out of a Styrofoam ice chest.

"What are they doing?" he asked.

"Getting ready to release the plague," I said.

Of course. Laura wasn't working alone. She couldn't have been.

There were more people to finish the job, even if she'd been taken care of. Of course, of course, of course. How had I missed that?

"We have to stop them," I stated the obvious.

Mike decided the same thing and chose that moment to make his entrance, gun trained on the two would-be terrorists.

"Stop. Drop what you're doing and put your hands above your head." Mike held his gun level at the two men.

"Shit." A flare of panic rose in my chest and my breathing became shallow and quick. We had to intervene, but how? How did we avoid everyone getting hurt?

"I'm going to uncloak and help him," Luke said.

I nodded, mute and frozen in the middle of the aisle of cars. Behind us, more crashes and booms from the show drowned out any possibility of screaming for help.

"I'll," I gulped, "I'll get the syringes."

Laura's bosses paused in their movements and seemed to size up whether Mike posed a real threat.

The back of the van they worked out of yawned open under the small light by the door, and neither of them looked inclined to stop their methodical work. The peel of the paper wrapper, snap of plastic covering the tip, and puncture into an upside-down vial to suck up a small amount all seemed rote. Then they capped the syringe and plopped it into a steadily increasing pile. Just how many people did they plan on infecting tonight?

None, if we had any say in the matter.

Luke edged off around a blue sedan and nodded to me before his cloak fell away and he stepped out at Mike's side.

"What's going on?" His voice dropped an octave and carried enough weight that said he was more than willing to create some trouble.

Taking courage (or insanity; I wasn't sure which) from Luke's actions, I went around the other side of the van. The side door was open a crack and I could get in that way.

"You should clear the area," Mike replied, his gun never wavering from the guy holding the cooler full of vials.

Two against two. And only one gun. I could see this information pass in a glance between Laura's bosses. They still held the vials and syringes, neither bothered to set them down.

The van creaked as I worked my way through the door, bent at the waist to walk across the empty cargo area. The space was cramped but it was one of those big delivery vans made for lots of stuff, and right now only several ice chests occupied the area.

"I said, put the vials down. Do it!" A hint of panic filled Mike's voice.

Not good.

The two men seemed to sense this and went back to filling the syringe in hand as if there weren't a gun trained at them.

"You should listen to the officer." Luke glanced between me and Mike and drew closer.

Mike followed suit. Hadn't he called for backup? Weren't a billion cops wandering around? Why were we doing this alone?

I was just behind cooler guy and waited for Luke and Mike to creep closer before I made a move. I wasn't inclined to get shot, though the chances of it killing me were almost nil and I'd rather get the box of deadly stuff out of harm's way.

Syringe guy looked up at his partner. The two of them looked alike. Brothers, I'd read online. Wealthy. Smart. With a sadistic edge.

A quick nod and they swung into action. Syringe guy ducked and made to run around the other side of the van. I ripped the cooler from the other guy's hands and dragged it back inside where I hoped it'd be safe.

Outside, Luke went after cooler brother and I could hear him slam the man up against the van next to me, his face plastered against the side window.

I screamed.

Mike faced down the tall and lean brother—the one I'd seen flipping off the FBI agents back at his lab—past the open back doors. The man held tight to the syringe he'd just filled while Mike tried to figure out how to disarm him and keep the gun aimed.

My head pounded like too much blood flooded through it. I couldn't even make out what they said. The whole world seemed to flash shades of white and blue and red, the finale full of brilliant colors in the sky.

Behind the syringe brother, I hesitate for a second. There had to be a good way to stop him, make sure Mike could get him secured. Preferably without anyone getting shot.

Someone hit the side of the van again. Hopefully not Luke.

The syringe caught the light, a drip of liquid trailing from the pointy end.

Taking a shaky breath, I lunged and grabbed the guy's hand to pull the syringe out of the way. Mike took the split second to rip the man's other hand down and spin him so it was behind his back.

But as the man turned, I lost my grip. Mike managed to secure his hands, but I lost track of the syringe in the process.

The rapid snap of Mike's handcuffs secured the brother.

Only, the man started laughing.

I uncloaked, earning a freaked out look from Mike. But that wasn't what I cared about. His leg. The syringe poked through the fabric there.

"He got you." The words felt thick on my tongue.

"Too late, asshole. You'll be dead in three days. And everyone you come in contact with will be dead too."

Mike stared down at the plastic tube, his eyes wide with horror.

Luke came around the van, blood dripping from his eyebrow, dragging the other brother.

He stared at Mike's leg, then met my eyes.

"We can't let this happen," I breathed.

"Too late. It's been foretold. We have to bring the apocalypse or the

Gods will be displeased. Don't you know that? It's the end times you stupid bitch. You two especially should know that," the man jutted his chin at Luke and me.

Guess he'd figured out Luke and I weren't totally normal people.

Mike, seeming to regain his motor capabilities, grabbed the back of the man's loose blue jacket and flung him into the van. He handed Luke a zip tie to secure the other brother. Luke loaded him into the van while he spit insanities about the coming of the End Times and other stuff that sounded like a mash-up of every dystopian movie from the last decade.

"Who are you two?" Mike sat down on the bumper and proceeded to remove the syringe from his leg. He glared at it with narrowed eyes and picked up one of the little packet things they came in to store it.

Luke glanced at me and I shrugged. "We're here to help. We were supposed to make sure that didn't get released," I motioned toward the syringe with a grimace.

Damn had we fucked up.

"The government?" Mike asked, peering at us like we might sprout horns any second.

"Not exactly," Luke said.

"Then who?"

I smiled. "That's a very good question."

Mike's eyes went wide for a moment, then he shook his head, clearly coming to the conclusion he wasn't going to get an answer.

"Well, I think you've officially been exposed to whatever this is. Which means, well, who knows what."

"That you're going to die," the still conscious brother snapped from his huddle on the floor.

"There's a woman involved with their plot. We left her…indisposed. This morning. We might be able to get her help," Luke suggested.

Behind us, people started to filter away from the shore, and load into cars far too close to us.

"Get in." I forced Mike into the van and hurried around to close all the doors. "We don't want anyone else in contact."

Mike's face blanched. "Oh."

"Do you think we could get Laura to help?" Luke settled into the driver's seat. Mike propped himself up in the back of the van and stared at the wall with a comatose look about him.

I searched through the brother's pockets, earning nasty comments and nearly getting bit, until I came up with the car keys. I tossed them to Luke and sat into the passenger's seat. "Just drive. We need to get away from here. And hope no one else gets close to that stuff."

"We should call the CDC. They are better set up for this," Luke said.

"Like the fucking CDC's ever seen this strain. You're going to die. Might as well get used to it." The brother laughed. "Welcome to the end of the world."

"Do you mind?" Luke asked, navigating around people and cars that would have had me white-knuckling the OS handle if anyone other than Luke had been driving.

I grabbed out the tape I still had in my bag and ripped off a piece. The brother landed a good spitball on my cheek before I managed to slap the piece over his mouth.

"Help me hold his legs," I said. Mike managed to shake off his blank stare enough to restrain the thrashing man with several rounds of tape. My skills in binding up a person were getting a little too good.

The other brother wasn't waking up any time soon.

"I'm going to Laura's," Luke said when I crawled into the seat next to him. We'd managed to make our way out of the parking area and onto a main street. The crowd was behind us but traffic would be a nightmare in a matter of minutes.

"Laura?" Mike asked, perching next to brother who hissed from behind his tape.

"Your neighbor. I don't know if she can do anything," I said. Either she'd make things worse, or we'd get another person exposed. "She was supposed to be helping them. We thought we'd stopped this all from happening when we secured her earlier." My stomach churned over what we'd done all over again. And for what? So these wackaloons could just release the pathogen on their own? Damn it! Why hadn't I seen this coming?

The conscious brother kicked against the side of the van and when I looked over at him, he shook his head vehemently.

"What? You don't want to go to Laura?" My tone slid into snide.

The brother just shrugged.

"She's working with you, isn't she?"

The man shook his head and rolled his eyes with disgust.

For a moment, I thought about removing his tape enough to get a complete explanation, but I wasn't up for more of insanity. Let him be cryptic and annoying in relative silence.

Something about the way he'd responded didn't sit well though. They weren't working with Laura? How was that possible? She knew about their plans. She'd had to have been doing all that weird stuff in her apartment with them as accomplices.

"Something's strange about all this," I thought at Luke. "I don't know what, but something."

Luke glanced away from the road and caught my hand for a moment, squeezing. "I know. Something's off. But we're going to get Laura to help Mike. There has to be a way."

"I hope so." Peering over my shoulder, I watched Mike rock with the van, huddled against the side. His eyes had glazed over again and he twirled the syringe between his long fingers.

# CHAPTER
# 32

Luke parked with two wheels up on the curb outside of Laura and Mike's apartment complex.

"Stay in here," I said over the back of the seat, reaching for the handle.

"Don't go out there! You could meet someone, one of my kids!" Mike's voice rose and he grabbed my shoulder to pin me to the seat.

Luke, lines of strain crisscrossing his forehead, touched Mike's arm. "We can't get sick. We can't pass it along because we can't get it."

Mike shook his head. "You heard what he said. You've been exposed! We could be contagious."

"Mike, look, we can't get it. It's impossible. I've lived through a bunch of plagues before and never passed anything along." Keeping my tone calm and almost undid me. I was so beyond my breaking point I wanted to scream at him to take his hand off my shoulder before I broke it. I was trying to help—couldn't he see that?

Mike rocked back on his heels and shook his head, his hair falling into his eyes. At least he'd stopped touching me. "Wait, what?"

I took a deep breath and forced words from between my teeth. "I am not sick. I won't get sick. And I can't pass it along. I can't say the same for you, so stay here. Please. We're going to try and see if we can get help."

Before he could say anything else, Luke and I got out of the van, taking care to not open the doors any more than necessary in case the thing was airborne. But if whatever was in those vials could be spread through the air, why would they need a syringe? The brothers weren't going anywhere, and Mike could handle them for a little while—he wasn't sick yet—and Luke would need my help with Laura.

My brain felt like an egg frying—like from one of those old don't-do-drugs commercials. Every synapse fired and everything felt too bright, too real.

We took the stairs to Laura's apartment two at a time.

Luke didn't bother with the locks, just put his shoulder to the door and busted right through with a giant crash and flying splinters of wood.

Why, why did that seem so damn hot, now of all times?

Luke must have caught on to my line of thinking and winked at me before his serious mask went back on.

Laura.

I was never, ever going to not feel terrible about what we'd done to her. Even if she had worked with her bosses on the attack. It felt like one of the splinters from the door had lodged in my chest, twisting with every pang of guilt.

We barged into the bathroom and flipped on the lights, flooding the room with images I didn't want to see. She huddled on the floor, asleep. Blood from where she'd tried to free herself caked onto the side of the tub and around her wrists. Her hair matted around her face, salt flaked to white from her tears.

"I think I'm going to be sick," I whispered.

Luke checked her pulse and set gentle hands on her shoulders. "Laura? Can you hear me?"

Her eyes fluttered open and she started to cry, whimpering against her gag. Bloodshot sclera showed all the way around her irises.

"This will hurt, but it will be fast," Luke explained, taking an edge of the tape on her face.

She nodded and closed her eyes as the silver tape peeled away with a quick ripping sound. I heaved at the bloody chap of her lips and had to rest my forehead against the cool of the mirror to keep from losing my tacos. A pool of fog grew and shrank with my deep breaths.

"I thought no one was ever going to find me," she said, voice all wobbly.

"Don't tell her it was us," I thought at Luke. "She'll never help."

"Well we're going to get you out of here. But we need your help," I said aloud.

I'd thought Laura looked pale in the dim lights of her bathroom, but she went white. "They released it, didn't they? Oh shit. Maybe we should just lock ourselves in here. Maybe we could wait it out."

"They injected it into a cop at the park. We have him in the van downstairs, with all the vials. And the two guys." I handed Luke some scissors I found in one of the neurotically organized drawers.

"Are you sure he was the only one?" Laura asked. She cried out a moment later as Luke released her hands and her arms swung free.

Her wrists were raw and I went in search of something to spread on them. Anything that would keep me from staring at her and the raw guilt that ate at me.

"He's the only one. We are sure," Luke said.

"We have six hours then. Until he's contagious. So long as they didn't get anyone else, and we can get him treated, we might be able to stop this. I have a few doses ready in my fridge." She held out her hands as I found antibiotic salve and coated the mess that had been her wrists. I wrapped several layers of gauze over it, grateful to hide the evidence of what I'd done.

Luke had to help her get up. She stumbled and grabbed the wall before she managed to get her feet under her.

"I can't believe they did that to me." She clutched her head as she made her way to the kitchen. Luke kept hold of her arm to steady her drunk-like walk.

Luke and I remained silent aloud. "We really screwed this up," I thought to Luke.

He gave me a wide-eyed look, somewhere between horror and self-loathing.

Neither of us wanted to admit how bad this was. How close we'd come to creating the scenario we wanted to stop. Another twist of guilt that was almost physical pain.

"What are you doing in here?" I stepped into Laura's lab/kitchen where she dug around in her refrigerator, her rear sticking out into the room.

Laura paused and looked at me in the brighter lights of her kitchen. "I know you from somewhere, don't I?"

How many times had she seen me recently? Enough that she recognized my face. But I just shrugged and shook my head. After the day she'd had, the chances of her second-guessing herself were high. Not that I wanted to screw with her any more, but I would not put our secrecy at risk. "I don't know. We've been working undercover here and we were tipped off something had happened to you."

"You two are with the cops? Or the government?" Laura's eyes darkened and her hands stilled, still holding several small tubes she'd extricated from the fridge.

"No. Not like that," Luke fumbled and looked at me with a blank expression.

"More like, well, just, not the government, okay? It's hard to explain." Not that I did any better than my partner.

"Great." Laura gave us both a strange look and gathered up several more vials from her fridge. "Just, honestly, don't even bother with an explanation."

I sighed. "Later. We'll explain later, okay?"

Laura pursed her lips, grabbed a large cardboard box from the counter, and went around to throw things into it.

"Her mind will blow if she ever figures us out," Luke said.

"No doubt." Laura's scientific world didn't have room for whatever Luke and I were.

"Where's this cop?" Laura held the box in front of her, swaying a little. Her wild hair and wide-eyed expression left her looking a whole lot like a mad scientist.

Luke took the box and I directed her toward the door. "Downstairs. In your boss's van."

"You're lucky it's only one guy. I didn't have a chance to make more treatment drugs today, because someone…something…tied me up." She shook her head, confusion clouding her gaze.

"That's what you've been doing in your lab?" I asked, trying to keep her focused on anything other than what we'd done to her.

"I've known for a while what my boss was up to. He knew my feelings about the government and brought me in on his project when he started his new company. I played along, hoping to get enough information to stop them. And I snuck as much denatured sample home as I could, using it to create that." She tapped the box Luke carried down the stairs. "A way to treat it."

"Thank the gods you've got it," I said. "Mike doesn't deserve this happening to him."

"Why would they do this?" Luke asked as we reached the back doors.

Laura paused, negotiating the curb like a frail old lady. "Wait, Mike?

As in, my neighbor, Mike?" Laura looked between us.

I nodded, not sure of the best response right now. Her eyes filled with tears and her chin quibbled.

"Shit. That guy's got kids and everything." She grabbed the box from Luke and reached for the door.

We all jumped when Mike's face appeared in the small back window of the van, his lips curled back as he shook his head. He raised a fist and banged on the glass. Laura released the handle with a little shriek.

"They've started vomiting. Blood. And they don't look so good," Mike yelled, his voice muffled but his panic more than clear. If he didn't calm down quick he was going to hyperventilate.

"They must have injected themselves a few hours ago," Laura muttered. "They'll be contagious. If we keep them sealed in the van, maybe we can contain it, but..." she trailed off, looking around the neighborhood.

Despite the late hour, there were plenty of kids around, and a bunch of other people. Someone had broken out sparklers and they fizzed up and down the sidewalks. The crackle and pop of other families out enjoying the festivities sounded from nearby. The warm night and lack of fog had everyone enjoying the holiday.

"You've got to call someone. The CDC!" Mike screamed through the glass before he disappeared into the murky gloom of the van.

"Laura, we have to do it. They'll be able to do something, use your treatment." I kept my voice even and touched her arm, wishing I could make her see that it was our only option.

"But," she shook her head. I could imagine what went through her mind from all the posts I'd read online. She didn't trust them. But right now we didn't have a choice.

"I'm calling." Luke pulled out his phone.

Laura slumped onto the curb and dangled her head between her knees. "At least we'll be able to save Mike. I hope." Her voice was small, but I wasn't imagining the faint relief that resided there. "They'll probably arrest me for not calling them before, or for my lab, or something."

She had a point. I doubted she'd get out of this. Even if Luke and I had been morons about everything, what she'd done still fell into illegal territory. I patted her shoulder and listened as Luke started to speak with someone, blurting out information and begging for help to hurry to our location.

"It's one hell of a coincidence that it's Mike, isn't it? That the one cop in the whole city that got into this was my neighbor?" Laura glanced up at me, a glum expression pulling her lips to one side. Someone's sparkler reflected off the wetness gathered in her eyes.

"Yeah. One crazy coincidence."

# CHAPTER
# 33

"Explain to me why." Luke settled onto the curb after he filled us in that the CDC had been on high alert, thanks to the FBI, and a team would be here soon. Mike watched from the window, fear lining his face despite our assurances that we'd get Laura's treatment to him in time.

"They have this thing, this belief, that the end of the world is here. That they're supposed to help usher it in. That humanity's beyond saving and that the only way to make the world work again is to kill everyone off." Laura shook her head. "It's nuts."

I bobbed my head in agreement. "Where did they get that deranged idea?"

Laura shrugged, her fingers playing with the bandages at her wrists. "Other than some novel? No idea. I know there's gotta be something, but they never filled me in on those details. And I never asked. I mean,

I'm no fan of the government or some of the shit that goes on in this country. But to kill so many people with that strain they created? It's horrible. That's why I had to stop them—no one else would do it, could do it. The CDC would just lock me up and never get out ahead of this. We'd all be dead first."

Luke and I didn't have an argument for that—there was no way to know if Laura going out on her own had saved lives or was about to cost Mike his. Her boss' attempt had been scary enough to drag us into the fray, along with Theo and Lexi. Considering we'd only ever worked with other pairs a few other crucial times throughout history, that was monumental in and of itself. Of course, we'd also almost managed to botch up everything.

Behind us, a door opened and I twisted around to see a woman step outside into the yellow light of the apartment breezeway. "Is everything okay?" she asked.

Mike's wife. My heart collapsed as Mike pressed up against the glass to see her. Tears dripped down the inside of the window.

Laura got to her feet and stumbled to the woman's side. Their hushed conversation was inaudible until Mike's wife let out an anguished cry and raced to the van.

"Ma'am, don't open that." Luke had to pry her away from the handle, and pick her up to set her back a foot.

She wriggled free, but instead of opening the door, pressed her nose and hands to the glass. Mike placed his fingers on the other side, his breath fogging the window as he pressed his forehead against it, his eyes wide in the dim light.

"It's going to be okay. The authorities will be here soon. I have a way to treat it. He's going to be okay," Laura repeated from off to one side. She kept her chin tucked to avoid looking at any of us.

A black van/bus hybrid thing roared down the street, sending kids scuttling to their parents, and screeched to a halt behind the van. A door opened and men and women in full body suits emerged, their breath hissing through some kind of ventilators strapped to their backs. A chill curled up from my toes at how much they reminded me of the first image that sent us on this crazy chase.

Luke clasped my hand as I wavered on the spot. How close had we come? How many lives had we nearly been responsible for losing?

Mike's wife almost collapsed onto the street and Luke left me to collect her and set her on the sidewalk, while he went to converse in low tones with the suited-up people. My brain felt like I'd tuned it to static that pressed against my ears from the inside of my skull.

Laura limped over to the man ordering the others around and ticking things off of a clipboard, and launched into some kind of explanation. Within minutes the place lit up like midday with massive spotlights from the van sending every shadow into retreat.

Luke left Mike's wife in the hands of several of the alien-suit people and grabbed my arm to tug me away from the madness. How long had I been standing there, mouth hanging open, watching them all?

The next hour was a blur of the CDC setting up a perimeter, moving the van, running tests, and a hundred other things. Luke and I tried to answer as many questions as possible, careful to keep our stories straight and avoid any potential exposure from having information we shouldn't have been privy to. A telepathic link and lots of practice made that a whole heck of a lot easier.

Later, once I could break away, I found Laura in her kitchen, slumped onto her stool, gathering paperwork into a huge box. Her lips pressed together more with each thing she dumped in.

"Everything okay?" I leaned up against her doorway and managed a small grin, despite the guilt that seemed to gnaw at my heart.

She started and looked up, eyes blurry with fatigue. "They're making me take everything to their lab to run some extra tests, but I guess it's okay. It's better than the alternative."

"It's going to be alright. You know? You've saved the day, really. You should be proud." I meant it, too. She may not have done it the way I would have, but she'd still made sure Mike would live. That the kids downstairs would have a dad.

Maybe, just maybe, it was a good thing I hadn't gotten her caught in the lab. Not that it excused my inability to work out the real situation, but it was some small consolation. Still the gauze on her wrists and the way her lips looked more like something from a zombie movie drove home how much I'd screwed up.

Laura quirked a grin. "I'm not sure everyone sees it that way, but thanks. I couldn't let so many people die. Not without doing anything."

I glanced around her kitchen, grateful for the mess of machines and other unidentifiable goings-on to distract myself. "Well, I do. So thanks. For what you've done. And I know Mike and his family feel the same way."

Someone dressed in uniform knocked on the door. "Can I help you carry that? They want you downstairs," he said.

Laura nodded and dropped another notebook into the box before she handed it to the officer. I slipped out of her apartment while she went in search of shoes. Cloaking myself on the landing, my feet felt like they were tied to cement bricks with each step down.

"Luke? I think this calls for ice cream. And we've gotta start brainstorming how the hell we're gonna find Theo and Lexi." I shot the thoughts at him, sidestepping the crowds of onlookers and workers surrounding the clear plastic tent erected around the van. More lights had been set up in the tenant parking lot and the whole place bustled like the stock exchange. Neighbors and news people milled around barricades the cops set up and contributed to the dull roar of conversation, punctuated by the occasional yelp or laugh.

As best as I could tell, the coincidence had worked out in the end. Well, worked in the sense that it looked like we'd avoided an outbreak of some horrible plague, and Laura would save Mike. Not that I felt any

213

better. Things should have resolved long before tonight's near-miss.

Frowning, I turned in a slow circle, searching for Luke's dark head. He was tall enough to stand out amidst most everyone. He'd been there five minutes ago, talking with someone I couldn't see, before I went in search of Laura.

"Luke?" I called again.

No answer.

Strange.

I tried again while I wandered around the building. My fatigue melted away as my heart rate picked back up. Flashes on the days I'd been unable to reach him echoed in my mind until I found myself pleading with whatever unknown deity governed our lives that Luke hadn't been hurt.

"If you're playing some kind of trick on me, I'm so making you sleep on the couch." It may have been an empty threat, but my gut knotted tighter the longer he stayed quiet.

"LUKE?" I mentally shouted, officially crossing into pissed.

No answer.

My heartbeat hit hummingbird speed. Where the hell could he be? I tore around the yard, searching every face. No Luke. I went through the apartments in Laura's complex, then those in every direction.

Nothing.

No Luke. No response. Nothing.

Gulping air to keep from screaming, panic crept through my system, a ravenous beast.

I searched everywhere three time before I collapsed against the side of Laura's building while hot tears spilled down my cheeks. I buried my face in my hands, unable to stand seeing so many people when the one person I needed to be there, wasn't.

Where the hell could he be? He'd just been there!

The silence in my head felt like my brain had swollen to twice its normal size and pressed against my eyes. I thudded my head back against the rough wall behind me, wishing it would settle the whine in my ears.

Something wasn't right. Not at all.

First Theo and Lexi disappeared.

Now Luke.

# CHAPTER
# 34

The first streaks of dawn stretched through the fog when I called a cab to take me home. I had the guy drop me off a block away and kept my sweater wrapped tight and head down as I trudged through the sleeping neighborhood to my place.

Inside, I tiptoed through the rooms, praying Luke somehow ended up here. That for some reason he fell asleep and hadn't heard my calls.

But the rooms were empty, cold, and far too quiet. My footsteps echoed against the walls and I shivered even with my hood pulled up and the heater blasting.

Exhaustion rolled over me and I slumped onto the couch. Luke's socks were tucked under one of the pillows and I threw them across the room.

"Luke?" I called one last time before curling around my knees and dropping my head against my jeans.

My brain felt like it had been stuffed full of the fog that swirled outside. Thoughts were impossible. So was any chance of coming up with a plan, figuring out my next step. Some logical part of my brain screamed that I had to do something, but I didn't have a clue what. Calling the cops was out. Luke didn't 'exist', and the agents had undoubtedly made sure someone hunted us.

Plans would have to be made. But right then, I had to close my eyes and soak up my tears on my sleeves.

ℳ

"Ami?"

Someone's voice filtered through my dreams and consciousness settled over me, unfriendly and cold. It took a second for reality to settle into place, and during that time I allowed myself to wish Luke called to me.

"Ami? What's going on?" Melody stepped into the living room, worry creasing her brow.

She looked ready for work, wearing a prim vintage brown dress with a full skirt and short boots. Settling next to me, she pushed my hair away from my face and repeated her question.

My tongue felt too clunky to respond. "Luke's missing."

Her eyes went wide. "What? How? When?"

"We were working last night. Once the job was done, I went searching for him, but he was nowhere. I can't, well, I can't get ahold of him."

Did I explain all the intricacies of what Luke and I were? We'd never had a rule against it, but it was not something we shared often. It never seemed to end well. Even if I thought Melody would handle it, it was a lot to dump on someone.

"Have you called the police? Or anything like that?"

Worrying my lip, I shook my head. "I can't. For a whole lot of

217

reasons, but mainly because I just can't."

Melody sat back and her hands fell to her sides. "What aren't you telling me?"

So much for keeping secrets. I couldn't process why it might be a bad idea to tell her, and I needed someone to talk with. "Just, just, Luke and I aren't exactly here legally. I mean, the police or government don't have real records of us. And I'm more than a little sure the FBI's looking for us."

Could the FBI have gotten him? After the chase yesterday, it was obvious they were trying to apprehend us. But then why would Luke not give me any warning? Any mental communication? This silent business was just too strange. It hinted at something sinister—explanations I didn't dare let myself consider.

Melody took a long minute to process that. "So, wait, you're here illegally? Like from another country?" She shook her head. "That doesn't make any sense."

"Not here from another country. Well, not any time recently." I ran my hands through my tangled mess of hair, tugging at the loose strands, "Honestly, I couldn't even begin to say what we are. It's not natural, and I'm not totally sure what to call it."

"If you're some kind of vampire, I'm so leaving, Ami. I hope you know that." Melody narrowed her eyes and huffed out a breath that blew back her bangs.

"Good grief, what is everyone's fascination with vampires lately?" I grumbled. "No, not a vampire. Look, Luke and I have jobs we do around the city. We make coincidences happen. The important ones. The ones the world kind of needs."

She laughed, her head tipped back in mirth until I could see her molars. Then she caught sight of my expression, stood, spun in a circle, paced to the door and back, and sat down next to me. "That makes no damn sense."

I shrugged. "Yeah, I know that. But that's what we are."

"And Luke? He's what, your partner in crime or whatever?"

Instead of answering, I closed my eyes and cloaked myself. Sometimes going invisible was the only way to convince someone of what I was.

Melody fell off the couch, her rear hitting the ground with a giant thump. "Holy shit, Ami! Ami, where are you?" She reached out and patted my invisible but very solid form. She got to her feet, tapping her hands along my arms, legs, missing my boobs by a millimeter. Her expression was an impressive mix of disbelief and total amazement.

I dropped my cloak and Melody looked at me like I just sprouted antlers. "Damn. And I thought I'd only ever get to read about something this cool!" She clapped her hands together and settled next to me, bouncing on the cushions. "Tell me more! Everything!"

"Luke is my partner. He works one side of the coincidence and I work the other. Basically, we make things that would statistically happen very rarely happen more frequently."

"And now, Luke's missing?"

I nodded, my stomach twisting so tight it was only a matter of time before I had to make a run for the bathroom.

"So, how are we going to find him?" She tucked her feet up under her, her big brown eyes meeting mine.

Shit. I should have seen that one coming. "Not 'we', just me. It's too dangerous. I can't ask you to do that. I won't let you."

Melody held up a hand. "I get that. But Luke's my friend, too. I'm helping."

There was a part of me that wanted to take advantage of her offer. I had no idea where to start and any help would be amazing. I could use the moral support. But I was not dragging Melody into anything that made the FBI tail her.

"It's better to just give in now, before I just stalk you and make more trouble than you want," she noted.

A dull facsimile of laugh escaped me. "You couldn't follow me if you tried. I can go invisible, remember?"

"Wait, have you ever, you know, gone in a guy's locker room? Because I totally would do that if I could." She waggled her eyebrows, tugging on the end of her braid.

I might have laughed but my heart felt like it had been wrung out like a wet rag and I wasn't into it. "Sauna's are better."

Melody chuckled but sensed my mood and sobered. "Look, I'm calling in sick. And then we're going to find him. I swear."

"Seriously, no. Give me today. You go to work and I'll see what I can do. If I need someone to give me a hand, I'll call you, okay?"

She looked like she wanted to argue until her expression softened. "Anything, anything at all, call me, okay? I've just got storybook time later and otherwise I can get someone to cover for me. And I want to help." Her expression begged me to reconsider. I walked her to the back door and watched as she headed off down the street, turning to wave three times before she stepped onto her bus.

As much as I wanted her help, there was no way I could allow it.

Even if I had no clue what to do to find him.

"Luke?" I put as much power into his name as possible, making it ring in my own internal ear.

Nothing.

While I'd hunted around Mike and Laura's apartment complex last night, I'd tried his phone about a hundred times. This morning, I did the same—calling, texting, and then resorting to the web to try and track down its location. I didn't know Luke's passwords to get into the tracker systems, but I stared at the cursor for a long while. Then I started to guess.

No one knew Luke like I did. How hard could it be to predict what he'd set when I could hear his thoughts?

Ten guesses later, I was feeling a little less confident. I glared at the screen for a moment when inspiration dawned over me. I typed in the keys, half hoping I'd be wrong, if only because it proved how long the two of us had been ignorant of our feelings.

'LukeAndAmi'

The website refreshed and I was in. I sat back and closed my eyes, my chest tight and my throat closed off. Damn it.

A few clicks later and there was a ping on Luke's phone.

At Luke's house across town.

My whole body tensed. That couldn't be a good sign. It smelled like a trap and a half. Who, other than whoever/whatever had Luke, would have taken his phone there?

Not after the agents flushed us out of the house yesterday. He hadn't left his phone behind while we were there—I'd seen it on him after.

I swallowed bile. There weren't any other choices. I didn't know where else he could be. I had to try and track him down.

Closing my computer, I stared out the window for a long moment to collect my scattered fragments of thought. Luke was out there. Somewhere. I couldn't imagine the alternative.

If the universe was a big enough bitch to have stolen away Luke after giving me a few measly days with him, I was so not going to play along with any attempts to make it run according to whatever guidelines we were given.

I had no idea if I could even quit my job but if something happened to Luke, I'd find out. After everything I'd done to fuck up this last job, maybe that would even be for the better. No one needed someone like me screwing up millions of lives.

Getting ready took extra effort. What did I take with me? What would just weigh me down if I had to run? What other contingency plans did I need to make?

I settled on plain jeans, grey sweater, and beanie, along with shoes I could run in. Several other needed supplies went into my bag, along with mine and Luke's passports and other vital documents. This trip could take me anywhere and a quick getaway was almost assuredly necessary.

At some point I made myself some tea. I needed food, even after finishing off the last of the stale crackers that stuck to my throat and made me cough.

My kitchen felt too small and yet too comfortable. There was no choice but to leave, but I couldn't help the sliver of fear I'd never come back. Sure, I could start over again somewhere else, though nothing could replace this little space. My haven. It had been for so long I couldn't imagine anything different.

At the same time, I couldn't have a future without Luke. I may have had trouble with grasping that before, but now it felt branded onto my soul. And if that meant losing my home, all that I knew? So be it. I'd be happy to trade.

Grabbing my bag, I went down to the garage and settled into my car. Time to find Luke. And kick the ass of whoever took him.

# CHAPTER
# 35

Luke's house looked altogether strange. The flowerbeds wilted in the warm temperatures and paths of giant footprints wound through them, including a flattened patch where Luke and I landed after jumping from the roof. Had that only been yesterday? It felt like a decade.

There was no chance I'd see who or what watched the house. As much as I hated going in blind, no other option presented itself.

The back door was nudged closed, the lock not secured properly and the chain dangling. The hair on the back of my neck stood on end.

"Please let the agents have just not closed it all the way," I murmured. I didn't believe it for a second. With trembling fingers, I pressed against the door to open it.

What greeted me inside was almost awe-inspiring. The place had been opened and spilled from top to bottom. Like someone gutting a fish, cupboards and contents had been tossed across the floor.

My heart went out to Luke, even if he never saw the mess. The sight would make him scream—all his careful organization flipped and shattered. It also made the fact he was missing all that more real, all the more underhanded. That truth lodged below my ribs, sharp, pointy, and stabbing with every breath.

What had happened to him?

Avoiding broken glass and sugar spread like snow across the floor, I snuck into the rest of the house. Books were scattered across the floor, loose paper tucked here and there like a tornado had gone all Wizard of Oz on them. The mess was the same in the guest room, library, and bathroom. It was almost as if someone looked for something, but I couldn't begin to guess what it might be.

So, where was Luke's phone? At least a hundred missed calls and texts were on there, my ever-increasing stream of panicked attempts to reach him.

Wandering from room to room, I couldn't locate it downstairs. So I climbed up, each step as deliberate and silent as possible. The seventh one creaked and I cursed it in an inaudible torrent of swear words.

At the top landing, I pushed open the door to Luke's bedroom, the mid-morning light spilling around my feet, muted as it filtered through the sheer cream curtains.

What I saw inside made me rear back and nearly topple down the stairs.

"Careful there, Ami. We don't want you to harm yourself." Theo's rich deep voice rose from within.

Gathering myself together, I went back to the door. It creaked as I leaned a shoulder against it. My knees needed the support.

Theo and Lexi lounged against the end of the bed, watching me with interest that rippled against my skin like someone ran an ice cube against my flesh.

"What's going on?" I stepped over the threshold despite my desire to turn tail and race in the opposite direction. Everything inside me screamed wrong.

"Take a seat, why don't you? We'll explain what we can," Lexi said, her tone just as snooty and annoying as I remembered it. She extended a hand toward a kitchen chair they'd placed in the middle of Luke's room. All four legs were intact, unlike those downstairs.

"I'm fine standing." I hovered by the door with my arms crossed. "Just answer my question."

"Oh, sweet Ami, you think you have any choice in the matter?" Lexi chided, sarcasm drenching her words in filth.

"Actually, I know I have a choice in the matter. Just tell me what's going on." I tightened my grip on the strap to my cloth bag slung across my chest and shifted my weight from foot to foot. The door looked pretty damn good.

"Really? Well, I imagine you would think like that. You were always a bit thick. Delusional, really. The way you denied what was right in front of you and made Luke hurt like that for so long proves my point."

Now there was no possible way I'd get in that chair. Bitch.

Lexi must have guessed my thoughts because a small grin split her lips. "And if I told you Luke's safety depended upon it?"

My breath left me in a whoosh. "What have you done with Luke?"

Theo chuckled. "We haven't hurt him, if that's what you're worried about. Well, permanently."

"What have you done with him?" I was a millimeter away from launching at both of them. I would take a great deal of pleasure in breaking Lexi's nose.

Lexi smiled and pulled out Luke's phone. She typed in his passcode and turned the screen around to me. "See for yourself."

A video played and I had to lean in closer to watch. When I did, I really wished I'd stayed by the door where I left my stomach.

Luke's face had been worked over by someone with a blunt

instrument and an eye for detail. He moaned for water, then for me, his voice a broken facsimile of its normal richness.

Fire slid through my veins. "What. Have. You. Done. With. Him?" I lunged close to Lexi, my nose nearly pressed to hers. Her dark eyes flashed with mirth.

"Oh, calm down, Ami. It's going to be fine. We just need a little favor is all." Lexi's grin was predatory, all teeth and vinegar.

"A favor?" If they thought I'd do something for them they were mistaken.

"Yes. A favor. Luke's our leverage to ensure you carry it out. Obviously." Lexi shook her head like I was a few ingredients short of a cake.

But why? Why couldn't Lexi and Theo just do whatever this was on their own? It made no sense and turned room turn red around the edges.

"What do you need?" I already sensed I'd wish I never asked.

"We need a little help in procuring that biohazard you so heroically kept from being spread."

# CHAPTER
## 36

"Excuse me?" I reared back. "What the hell do you want that for?"

Theo motioned to the chair. "Take a seat. It looks as if you might need it."

They could have taken a bat to my knees and I would have left that chair vacant. "Just talk."

Theo and Lexi exchanged a glance that spoke volumes about what they wanted to do to me. Fine. Bring it. I'd take them both down with the amount of adrenaline singing in my veins. The whole room was in sharp relief and I longed to do something, anything, to get them to talk. Anything to get me closer to Luke.

"Luke and I stopped that stuff from getting released. On our own. So what do you want it for?" What had I missed about them? Something felt poised to hit me between the eyes.

Lexi cocked her head to the side and narrowed her eyes. "That's what you think? That we were here to stop the spread of the disease?"

I threw my hands up. "Of course. No one wants all those people dead."

"Are you sure?" Theo's deep voice was full of enough conviction it almost felt like a blow. "How do you know that for certain?"

What the hell was he playing at? "Because that's how these things always work. The first clue. The one of all those," I gulped as the image surface in my mind's eye, just as horrible as ever, "dead bodies. The first one is always of what we're supposed to avoid when we get big jobs." I wadded my bag's straps between my sweaty palms, desperate for something, anything to make sense.

Lexi shook her head. "How do you know that?"

Her question made me take a step back. I hated that I had allowed myself to react. "That's how it's always worked, Lexi. Forever and always. It just is." A fist of uncertainty tightened around my throat. Right? That was how things always worked—not that anyone had ever written that out for us.

"But you don't know that. It's not like anyone ever gave you those instructions personally. Told you how this whole thing works." Theo cut in and stepped in front of his partner, realizing there was a good chance I would knock out Lexi.

"Well, no. But there hasn't had to be. We make the coincidence happen. It works out. It's worked for all this time." It took a whole lot of effort to clamp down on the panic that seemed to seep into my mind like something sticky, bewildering my thoughts.

Luke's comments about me following directions from some unknown source for millennia filtered through my mind. We'd talked about it, but we didn't understand it. Didn't know what had given us our abilities, our tasks. But we loved our work. It made our lives worth it. And when we did our jobs right, good things happened. Mostly. Lives were spared, people found, happiness happened.

And when we screwed up, people could die. Like today. Mike, and so many more, almost lost their lives because I'd screwed up.

Lexi shook her head. "I'm not terribly surprised by you. But Luke had to have figured it out at some point. I thought he'd share it with you. He's always been the brains of your operation."

My hand stung with a million little pricks and burned with heat. Lexi clutched her cheek, her eyes wide for a moment before a calculating smile settled over her features. "Theo."

A huge hand settled on my shoulder and before I had a chance to respond, Theo's muscled form crumpled me into the chair like I was a tin can. I struggled against him and tried to slide off the edge, but he held me in place and wrapped several of Luke's belts around the chair and me.

"Let me go!" My breath hitched as I fought to free myself, wildly tipping the chair legs as I threw my weight against the bonds.

"We will. But you'd better calm down to hear what you have to do. No more hitting my wife."

Lexi gave me a little smirk, marred by my handprint against her pale skin.

Why couldn't I shoot fire out my eyes or something? Invisibility was so useless.

"Where were we?" Lexi asked once Theo had ensured there was no way I was getting out of the damn chair. "Oh, yes. The lack of supervision. Instructions. Don't you think that's a little convenient? It leaves some things so open ended."

"Open ended? Stopping a whole lot of deaths doesn't seem open ended," I cut in.

"Sure about that?" Theo asked.

"Think about this city. The others you've been to recently. All those homeless. The lack of jobs. Infrastructure falling apart. Corruption at every level of government. All of it. What's so bad about a plague? They helped clear out the riffraff in the past," Lexi spoke like I was a two year-old.

"You've got to be shitting me." I shook my head, unable to comprehend what Lexi said. "It won't change anything! We don't manipulate things to work how we want them."

Lexi shrugged. "There's no one to stop us. We realized a long time ago that pushing people to do what we thought was right was impossibly easy. Like the FBI agents. This way we can really change things."

"By killing millions? Billions? That makes no sense!"

"Doesn't it? We're trying to give the world a fresh start. Hit the reset button. The fit will survive." Theo's deep voice almost lent an air of authority to what he said.

"So, what, you want me to get the plague vials? I'm sorry people, those were already taken by the CDC. No way I can get them now."

Lexi grinned and took her time to lock eyes with me while she leaned in close. "Then you can say goodbye to Luke."

"You do know what happens when one member of a partnership takes a bullet to the head, don't you?" Theo asked.

Something hot and squirmy settled into my gut. We were hard to kill, but a bullet could do the job if aimed well. My expression must have given away my panic.

"Killing one of you means you are both dead." Lexi took a whole lot of satisfaction in telling me this, her perfect little white teeth catching the sunlight.

I hated them so much right then it caused me physical pain being in the same room, same city, same universe, as them.

"Now, if you had just let Laura be caught the other day at the lab, this would be so much easier. But seeing as how you were so 'in-tune' with your mark and kept her safe, you'll help us acquire at least one vial of the plague. Call me from Luke's phone." She dropped the device onto my lap. Somehow it made me even angrier to realize I had it when Luke didn't.

And Laura—damn it, I had been right in keeping her away from the agents.

"You have twenty-four hours. That should be plenty of time," Theo added.

Lexi held up a finger, like she'd just remembered something. "Oh, and I've always wondered—just what did happen that night we went to the bar, the four of us? Did you ever notice that last glass you drank tasted a little, off?"

It took me a second to process that, my mouth opening and closing like some stupid fish. "You put something in my drink?"

"What do they call it these days?" she looked at Theo, eyes sparking in the light. "A roofie, I think. It worked something like that—the antique version, you could say. It worked well to put a nice wedge between you two, keep you two on the small assignments and out of our hair. Well, until this one."

Oh holy hell. At least that explained why I didn't remember a damn thing for so long. Which was so sick and twisted. Luke and I had both been far too out of it for anyone's good that night. And what happened had almost ruined any chance we had together. Would things have worked out between us sooner if Lexi hadn't messed with us? No way to tell for sure, but right about then I blamed her entirely.

"I hate you both!" The words came out strangled through the cloud of frustration that suffocated me.

Lexi just giggled and went around behind me. I squirmed, not at all okay with the fact I couldn't see her.

Something slammed into the back of my head and pain bloomed behind my eyes until a shower of white sparks erupted and I slumped forward, slipping into darkness.

# CHAPTER 37

My head felt like someone had poured acid in my skull. If my brain melted out of my ear I wouldn't have been surprised.

Blinking my eyes open, the grey light in Luke's bedroom felt like a million suns. I reached up and touched the back of my head. A knot the size of an egg swelled at the bottom of my hairline. My hair crunched around it, bits of blood flaking between my fingertips when I looked.

"Bitch," I said through clenched teeth.

At least they'd loosened the belts.

Feeling like an arthritic old woman, I rose to my feet. The room spun a few times and I had to grab onto the chair to keep from going over. Something clattered to the hardwood floor and once I could open my eyes, I searched for Luke's phone. Picking it up made my head pound with every heartbeat and my feet dance like I'd tried to stand up on a Tilt-o-whirl.

I clicked the screen on and noticed a timer ticking down the seconds. Twenty-one hours left. How convenient of Lexi to think of something like that.

Moving on sheer hatred, I managed to get myself downstairs. The freezer, while ransacked, was closed and Luke's icemaker still functional. I found a towel and wrapped up some cubes and gingerly pressed it to the back of my head. My breath hissed through my teeth at the contact.

"It's going to be a great pleasure taking her down." Saying the words aloud made them feel more real and sent a zip of electricity through my body.

As my brain came back online, I thought about what Lexi and Theo said about our jobs and our role here. They had a point that we didn't have anyone to answer to, just the knowledge that if we failed unpleasant things could happen. Like all those body bags. For Luke and me, that was enough. More than enough. How could it not be? No one wanted to let people get hurt, killed, or even with the smaller jobs, miss out on something good in their lives. And sure, I'd totally fucked up a few times. Hell, I'd been doing this for so long I couldn't even remember when we started. I couldn't always manage the impossible. But never, not even once, had I considered going against the images I was given, the jobs we were assigned.

And I never wanted to, because what we did was important. It wasn't my place to go against that—even if sometimes I questioned if I was the right person for the job. Lexi and Theo missed the bigger picture of how our work brought together so many pieces of the lives we intersected with. They thought they had some control over what we did here.

I'd be damned if I let them get away with it.

With Laura, I'd trusted my gut. While it hadn't been a smooth path to save all those people, I'd been right to do it. Doubting myself had made this job so much harder and almost led to failure. But now it was time to fix it.

Starting with finding Luke.

How I planned to do that ran around in the muddle of my mind as I cloaked myself and walked back to my car. I bumped into several people along the way, barely able to keep my feet, let alone control my trajectory.

Driving would not be easy, or all that safe, but once I settled in the seat, I was able to focus a little better. I took it easy as I made my way across town while cursing the traffic. As I drove, I planned. First: save Luke. Second: take Lexi and Theo down.

For the first time since the images for this job poured into my mind, a steely resolve circulated in my blood. I could do this. I had to do this. I'd been right about Laura, and my instincts about Lexi and Theo had been spot-on. Time to put that to good use.

I made it into my house after pausing on every step on the way in. My heart beat like I'd run a marathon by the time I collapsed on the couch.

How did Lexi and Theo think I'd be able to do anything after they brained me? It would serve them right if I'd been unconscious the whole twenty-four hours. I had to blink a million times and swallow back bile to even move into a more comfortable position.

Pulling my laptop over, I plugged in Luke's phone. First things first. I had no idea how tech savvy the other pair were, so there was a chance they'd given me more information with Luke's phone than they thought.

The crappy thing was that I had to see Luke's face, frozen in the first frame of the video, as I attempted to pull the geotagging information from the file. He looked horrible—almost to the point of not being human. How could anyone do something like that to another person? How could anyone do that to Luke? Beating him was like shooting Bambi. It just made no sense.

"Hah!" I exclaimed and pumped my fist into the air as I located the data. I regretted my move as a fresh wave of pain shattered my skull.

The other partnership hadn't spent the time Luke and I had keeping up to date on recent technology. The GPS location where the video had been taken was listed and a quick search with Google maps gave me the exact address.

The back door opened and I looked around for any kind of weapon I could grab while not moving from the couch until Melody poked her head into my living room. I dropped my cloak, earning a little yelp from my friend.

"You look worse! What the hell happened?" Melody rushed to my side, eyes wide with concern.

I pointed to the throbbing lump on my head and she gasped. "I know who took Luke. And where he is. Or was, at least. But there are a few problems." I explained the rest of what happened, along with who Lexi and Theo were, while Melody's grip on my throw pillow grew tighter and tighter, until I had to remind her not to shred the thing.

"Holy crap." Melody shook her head. "What are we going to do?"

I wanted to protest, tell her there was no way I wanted her involved in this, but my current plan required her help. That, and I was about to pass out or puke from how bad my head hurt.

"Have you taken anything for that?" She motioned to where I cradled a fresh batch of ice. I shook my head and she got to her feet. "Stay here."

Like I was going anywhere.

She clipped out of the room in her heels and I heard her climb the stairs. I went back to mining the information on the phone while wishing I could march over and get Luke and be done with this. But the chances they'd kill Luke, and therefore me, were too high. I was going to have to be smarter about this.

Melody returned a few minutes later, dressed in jeans, a black sweater, and running shoes, carrying a plate with a sandwich on it. She handed me half, along with several small brown pills. "Motrin. It'll help with the swelling. Have a few bites before you take them."

Breathing out a small sigh of relief, I let Melody take care of me. "You know, I've only ever told a few people about Luke and me. None of them took it that well," I noted between bites. "One guy seriously tried to get me burned at the stake."

Melody grinned and bit into the other half of the sandwich. "Yeah, well, I read a lot. I guess I'd always hoped something interesting would happen like in the books."

"You may reconsider. Being afraid for your life is a little different in the real world."

She rolled her eyes. "Yeah, I'm not delusional. So, are you going to tell me your plan? Or am I going to have to guess?"

I swallowed the pills and rested my head back against the couch, organizing all the pieces of what I had to do. Melody listened, commented on several bits, but by the time I finished looked ready to take on the world.

The Motrin started to kick in and I stopped feeling quite so miserable. Or maybe it was the food. When had I last eaten?

"Let's do this thing." I pushed myself to my feet. Thankfully the room spun only a little.

"They're going to be sorry they messed with us." Melody grinned and rubbed her hands together like some old-school villain.

Together, we made our way down to my car.

Time to save Luke, stop a plague, and bring down Lexi and Theo.

# CHAPTER
# 38

I filled Melody in on everything I could think of on our way to Laura's place. All the information I'd gleaned online and snooped out about Laura and her boss's throughout the past week.

She crossed her arms and slumped in her seat, grumbling about how stupid she thought Laura had been by not going to the authorities earlier.

"She's going to get jail time for that, for sure." She pressed her mouth into a thin line.

I didn't doubt her.

We pulled up to Laura's complex where a low bustle of activity still hummed. Nothing like last night, but crime tape draped around the building like sad birthday streamers and several police officers kept guard over men in space-suit-like-things, working in the contained van. I'd thought they'd have hauled the thing away ages ago but guess not. The activity out there at least meant I'd have a clear shot of Laura's apartment.

"You're getaway, okay?" I pulled into the hidden parking lot Luke and I found the other day.

Melody nodded her head once, all business. She scooted over behind the wheel as I got out. I could hear her gasp as I went invisible. As cool as she may have been able to play things, that had to freak her out a little.

I made my way toward the complex and took care to keep out of the way of anyone from the neighborhood wandering around, curious about the strange activity and masked men.

Getting up to Laura's door required a little creativity. A cop stood guard and I ended up throwing one of the kid's toys against the fence in the backyard, forcing him to investigate while I took the stairs two at a time. I gripped Laura's door handle and said a silent plea that it be unlocked. The knob turned under my sweaty hand. Success! I threw myself inside and closed the door before the cop got a chance to return.

"Who's there?"

Oh shit. I pressed myself against the wall, even though whoever heard me couldn't see me. I'd expected the place to be empty. All I needed were the keys to Laura's lab and to get the hell out of there.

The last person I expected to see was Laura herself.

Holding my breath, I watched her walk into the living room, now cleared of a lot of the creepy pictures and other clutter. She looked around and wrung her hands. Dark circles ringed her eyes and her hair stood out in a frizzled mess. A ping of guilt at Luke's and my involvement in her state didn't help matters.

"I heard you." Laura turned in a circle to search the shadows like she half expected an axe murderer to jump out at her.

After we tied her up in her bathroom, I didn't doubt she was more than a little paranoid. I'd be. I edged my way toward her kitchen, hoping her keys were somewhere accessible.

Laura, still peering over her shoulder every couple of steps, went back to her bedroom and I breathed a small sigh of relief. This was meant to be a quick trip. In, grab the keys, and get out. I didn't need Laura to screw that up. Too much hung in the balance.

I'd seen the keys in her kitchen drawer yesterday, but after the upheaval of her gathering things for the CDC I doubted they were still there. It was a place to start though. Inching into the kitchen, I glanced around at the haphazard way items sat jumbled on the counters and the papers strewn across the floor. Most of the larger machines were gone, leaving gaps like missing teeth.

The drawer in question opened with a whisper. I only dared pull it a few inches, recalling that the keys were nestled toward the front edge in a muddled pile of paperclips and hair ties.

A warm hand wrapped around my wrist and I screamed. Laura peered, unfocused, at where I stood.

"I knew it." Her voice was low and her other hand searched the open air until she brushed against my other arm and grabbed hold.

I couldn't unscramble my brain enough to do anything other than stand there, my eyes aching from how far they'd bugged open. My heart thundered against my chest and I half wondered if that's what allowed her to find me.

"Who are you? Show yourself," Laura said.

The front door of the apartment opened and the cop from downstairs poked his head inside. "Everything okay in here?"

"Yeah, yeah, I just found a huge spider in here. Freaked me out!" Laura forced a laugh. The cop snickered and shut the door behind him.

"I know you're there. Tell me who you are. How you're doing this. Or I'm hauling you to the guys downstairs and telling them you work for my bosses. They're going to be really interested in how you do this invisibility thing."

I wriggled against Laura's vice-like grip, trying to formulate a plan. No way would Laura help me once she found out what I did to her. But now that she knew I was in here, no way would I get away without a lot of trouble. One word from her and the hunt for Luke and I would be amped up, and every cop given goggles to spot us.

Think! Damn it!

Laura narrowed her eyes and searched the empty air as if she looked hard enough she could spot me.

"I'm not going to harm you." I kept my voice low, gravelly, hoping she didn't recognize it.

Taking advantage of the second of surprise at my words, her grip weakened and I twisted around and wrapped an arm around Laura's torso. "I just need your help. Otherwise your bosses will win."

To Laura's credit, she didn't panic, though her breathing accelerated under my grip. "You work for them. Why wouldn't you want them to win?"

"I don't work for them. I'm trying to stop them and the others who are trying to do what they failed to accomplish. But I need you to keep quiet."

Laura huffed. "After you tied me up? Hell no."

I tightened my grasp, a sour taste filling my mouth. I didn't want to harm her. "It's not what you think, Laura."

Running on instinct, I dropped my cloak and let Laura loose. I placed myself at the entry of the kitchen—she couldn't escape. I just needed to convince her to give me the keys. Just that little tiny thing.

As much as I didn't deserve her help, or even want to have anything else to do with her, I needed those keys.

Laura spun to face me and her jaw dropped open with a little snip. "Shit."

"Yell, and I'll go invisible and you sure as hell won't catch me again."

Laura nodded and I could see her calculating this turn of events in the way her eyes flashed from me, to the door, to the drawer I'd opened.

"There are more people trying to finish your boss's job. And they have my partner. The guy with me last night. I need to stop them." I hated giving her this much information but something inside told me it was the only way. I'd learned the hard way that if I didn't trust myself, this would be a whole lot harder.

"Why haven't you gone to the authorities? They'll help."

I rolled my eyes. "Seriously? You saw what I just did. Do you think I can just ask for their help? They'd do whatever they could to get their hands on us."

"Oka-ay."

"Look, I need some kind of fake plague. Something that will throw them off. At least until I can get my partner and get them taken care of." I shoved my hands in my pockets to wipe the sweat off. No way was I letting her see how nervous this all made me.

Laura let out a puff of a sigh and slumped against the counter. "So, you're breaking in here for what?"

"Keys. To your lab. I know the security system there won't give me enough time to pick the locks." At least not without Luke's help. The thought tightened my throat and I had to shake away my frustration. "I need to get something good enough to fool them."

"The CDC has been there for hours. There's nothing left," Laura said.

I'd worried about that and planned on breaking into the CDC's lab if necessary. But I'd been praying something might pass for what I required.

"I need something." A note of pleading entered my voice and I wanted to scream at how weak I seemed. There had to be a miscellaneous vial of stuff. Anything.

"I might be able to help," Laura breathed. "But it's not going to be easy."

"I'll do anything."

Laura pressed her lips together and nodded. "I got that impression."

She moved to leave the kitchen and I let her pass, following her into the back bedroom. There she sat down on the edge of the bed. "They can't hear me as well from back here. If anyone's outside the door," she explained.

I hesitated but leaned up against the closet door and crossed my arms. I didn't have much of a choice.

"Can you get me out? Make me invisible, too?" Laura asked. A hint of hope shimmered in her eyes.

"Why would I want to do that?"

"Because there's another lab. I told the CDC guys about it, but they're waiting to take me there personally. If we got there first, we'd be able to get what we need. And then I can get out of the country."

Holy shit, she wanted me to help her escape. "Just tell me where the other lab is. I'll get the stuff. They're obviously not going too hard on you."

"Only because I said I wouldn't help them if they didn't give me some kind of deal. I'm only here to get some of my belongings. They're going to keep me under watch until they can bring charges against me. I am not going to stick around for that." Her eyes flashed and something twisted in my gut.

To be honest, I was surprised they allowed her to do anything that didn't involve bars and a shared toilet. They must have assumed Laura wasn't much of a flight risk. Her online record must not have been well known. No way would she subject herself to a government and judicial system she saw as corrupt.

"I really don't think I can make anyone else invisible. And I don't know how else to get out of here." The cop downstairs was only the start of the problem: there were still a couple more guarding the hoard of CDC workers, all of whom would recognize Laura's wavy blonde hair in an instant.

"You don't think you can? Have you ever tried?" Laura fixed me with a calculating look.

"No. I know I can do little stuff. When it's in close enough proximity to my body. But anyone person sized? No idea." Luke's comment about wanting to make a car invisible flashed through my thoughts, making my heart ache.

"How does it work, the whole invisibility thing? Do you have a device? Some kind of program or little machine? Or is it in your clothes, bending the light or something?"

"No. Nothing like that." Hysterical laughter bubbled up in my chest.

Laura pursed her lips. "Then, how?"

"I don't really know how it works. It just does. I've been able to do it for as long as I can remember, and that's one hell of a long time."

"How long?" Laura breathed the question.

"I don't know. Time erases the details." Some part of me relished the shocked wide-eyed, jaw-hanging look Laura wore. Her world didn't allow for whatever Luke and I were.

"You know, I believe you." Laura shook her head, rose from the bed, and reached over to pinch me.

I yelped and rubbed my arm, jumping out of her reach.

"I think you can make me invisible, too. But you're probably not going to like it."

Was she ever right about that. In the next twenty minutes, Laura experimented with my ability, figuring out how far the bubble of invisibility extended (basically several inches all around when I focused and wanted it to, a few more in one direction when I really focused).

"I'm going to need a lift." Laura took the piece of paper my invisible fingers held out to her.

Which is how I ended up with Laura plastered against my back. She may have been petite but that didn't make it any easier to negotiate walking across the living room. And if I wasn't careful, her butt—the farthest part away from me—became visible. A bodiless ass bouncing across the street was going to draw attention no matter what.

Laura dug out a small bag from the back of her closet, "Passport, money, and essentials," she said in response to my unvoiced question.

She'd prepared for the possibility she'd have to run. Didn't surprise me much.

Back in the kitchen, she pulled down two large glass tumblers and fixed me with a long look. "Ready?"

No. Not at all. "Let's do this."

She raised the glasses over her head and brought them down in two massive shattering crashes. She screamed and dragged her shoes through the glass. "Help! Someone's in here! Help!" Her scream was real enough to bring goose bumps up along my arms. Damn if Laura didn't have a potential future in acting.

Outside, the cops thundered up the steps. Laura grabbed my shoulders and I helped her wrap herself around my torso before I cloaked us both. Navigating to the door, we stood off to one side, my breath caught in my lungs as the it swung open.

The cop had his gun drawn and scanned the room, but looked right through us. Laura tightened her grip as he did so, echoing my own nerves. He stepped into the apartment and headed toward the kitchen where Laura left a window open. We took advantage of the lack of guard and navigated our way down one slow step at a time.

Sweat pooled on my lower back and trickled between my boobs. Somehow, we made it down the stairs. The other cops raced over, orders shouted into radios, feet pounding up the space we'd just vacated.

It took until we were across the street for chaos to erupt and Laura tilted her weight as she twisted around to watch. If anyone saw a floating body part it must have gone unnoticed.

As soon as we were out of her apartment's line of sight, I let her down and dropped my cloak. Without saying anything, our feet slapped the pavement away from her apartment. The world felt like a blur—the goal of my car the only thing in focus.

Melody started the car as soon as she saw the two of us round the corner to the little parking lot. Laura slid into the back seat and I heaved a huge sigh as soon as my door closed behind me.

It was to Melody's credit that she managed to get us out of the neighborhood while driving very much in the tradition of a San Franciscan. Laura flattened herself against the back seats and sniffled.

"Okay, what's going on?" Melody demanded as soon as we'd put good distance between Laura's building and us.

"She's going to get us what we need. But I had to break her out." I took a deep breath, all kinds of doubts over my decision coming to mind. What if Laura did all this to play me? Get back at me for the bathroom incident? Too late to worry about it now, but somehow my insides twisted tighter.

"Who are you?" Laura's voice was muffled against the back seats.

I made quick introductions and ensured it was clear to Laura that Melody was not to be screwed with.

"So, where am I going?" Melody did yet another quick scan through the mirrors to ensure we weren't being followed.

"It's by my regular office," Laura said.

"Get on One," I translated.

Melody gave me a frightened look, but did as I'd said. I leaned back against my seat and closed my eyes for a moment. How had all of this spun so far out of control? Luke was missing. Lexi and Theo were working for the dark side. I'd managed to drag Melody into this mess. And to top it all off, I'd just broken out a criminal.

# CHAPTER
## 39

We managed to arrive at the other lab without incident. Melody's death grip on the steering wheel hadn't abated any and she kept looking over her shoulder the whole way. I thought she might scream when someone cut us off on the freeway. Laura didn't say anything beyond basic directions, but her stifled sobs made me wish I'd brought Kleenex.

I couldn't quite decide if I wanted to kick her out of the car or if I was grateful she planned to help me. If she planned to help me.

We ended up in the same business district as Laura's other lab, only tucked around behind the other buildings in an area in need of new paint. Laura told us where we could park and from the car, we surveyed the two-story building, dull grey with too few windows. It looked like the last place on earth I'd ever want to work.

"You up for getting us in there?" Laura asked, leaning through the front seats, her chin resting on her fists.

"Why don't you wait here? Give me directions by phone or something?"

Laura shook her head. "You'll need my help with the security system."

I cursed under my breath. Of course. Picking up Luke's phone from the center console, I dropped it back into the cup holder upon seeing we had fifteen hours left.

This had to work. How much time would it take to get into the CDC labs? I didn't even know where they were. That kind of break-in would require planning. And skills I didn't have, invisibility or not.

"Wait here. Any sign of something suspicious, drive away and we'll meet you wherever you text from," I told Melody.

She nodded and shifted her gaze to Laura and back to me. I wanted to tell her I trusted Laura probably less than she did, but it wasn't like I could say that with Laura watching me with red-rimmed eyes.

We exited the car and Laura resumed her stranglehold on my neck, her feet crossed in front of my stomach. Once this was over, I was so getting a very long massage. From Luke. Naked.

I had to shake those thoughts away, along with the possibility that it might never happen.

Navigating my way around oil slicks, random curbs, and potholes that filled the lot, I managed to make it to the back door. Laura produced keys and used her thumbprint to let herself in.

"See why you needed me?" she asked, her breath hot in my ear.

I didn't answer. Okay, yeah, that made things easier, but it also placed Laura at the building, which meant if anything went wrong there would be evidence of her being there. The confidence she had in making it out of the country was kind of amazing and kind of insane.

The long, blank, white hallway stretched before us, doors shut, only the faint emergency lighting casting small pockets of illumination. My breath sounded like a gale-force wind in the silence.

"Second floor," Laura said.

"Please tell me there's an elevator."

There was. And the upper floor of the building looked like a space station. A long glass wall separated a large lab space with shadowed forms of machines sitting idle in the dark. There were lockers past the elevators, outside the doubled set of doors into the lab, along with a shower and a whole lot of other equipment that had to be donned to get inside the lab itself.

"I'm going in. Alone. Just wait out here. Okay?" Laura pulled on a Tyvek suit and tied her hair back before she put on a hairnet, cap, and zipped on a pressurized helmet.

She couldn't see me nod—I was still cloaked—but it didn't matter. She wasn't about to take directions from me. As much as I hated having to trust her, there wasn't much of a choice.

The doors unsealed with a hiss and click and she waited for them to close completely before she stepped into the next room. I watched through the windows as she navigated around the stainless-steel tables and other machinery to the row of refrigerators and freezers against the far wall. She rummaged around in two of them before pulling out several vials that looked identical to the ones I'd seen her bosses with.

She held them up for me before she tucked them into a little freezer box and slid them through a contraption that allowed items to cross out of the sealed space within.

I picked up the box like it might explode at any second. Laura had to be smart enough not to get the real thing, right? Whatever was in there was freakish enough. But if it saved Luke and fooled Theo and Lexi, it had to be worth it.

The sound of glass shattering slammed me back from my daydream of forcing the vials down Lexi's throat.

Laura stood in the center of the lab, a metal stool lifted like a battering ram as she crashed into the counter before her. Bottles and vials flew through the air and spilled across the floor.

Not content with that, she took the stool to the glass-fronted cupboards against the wall and smashed each while knocking the contents in every direction. The jar and containers ricocheted around the room, the crash of glass making me press my hands up against the windows to watch.

Screaming like a banshee, she made good work of the stool before she dropped it in favor of a long iron rod she wielded like a sword. She looked like someone out of a movie, dressed in her space-suit outfit, and I was kind of glad not to be in the same room as her.

The old expression "bull in a china shop" flashed through my mind. It suited things a little too well.

It didn't take long for a strange yellowish smoke to billow up from the floor where Laura spilled some kind of nasty chemical. I banged on the glass to catch her attention. Even though I didn't dare drop my cloak, she saw the sickly cloud.

And just stood there. Staring.

"I'm not going in there," I screamed into the glass. She didn't move.

Damn it! No way was I walking into that insanity. I didn't care if it wouldn't kill me. I had way too much other stuff to do than to save this crazy woman.

I kept repeating that as I yanked on one of the suits hanging in an unlocked cubby. It hung to my knees and I couldn't seem to find an opening for my hands, but I managed to get my skin covered. That had to be better than nothing. I hoped. The last thing I wanted was to end up covered in sores and blisters from whatever was in that gas. It may not kill me, but it sure as shit could hurt me.

Beyond the glass, the cloud grew. Laura didn't budge an inch, the iron rod dangling in her fingers as she stared.

"Laura! Move your ass!" I yelled.

Not that it helped.

Setting the box of vials by the elevator, I followed Laura's example of how to get through the series of lab doors. I imagined a trip to some other planet felt like this.

Drawing in a deep breath of clear air, I danced from foot to foot as the doors did their seal and hiss, a blast of air hit me, and I was inside.

My eyes started watering within a second. I hadn't had time to find any of the rest of the protective equipment that covered my face, but Laura was only five yards away. I could get to her and back out in under a minute. Theoretically.

Racing around the piles of mess she'd made, I knocked into Laura in an effort to get her attention.

She just stumbled a few wobbly steps and folded to the ground.

The skin around my nose burned and I longed to take a deep breath, but that couldn't be a good idea. Already the noxious cloud obscured the door. I wasn't letting the stuff into my lungs. I grabbed Laura under both armpits and heaved.

She didn't come without a struggle, wiggling and straining against me. But I was determined and managed to half drag her through the glass and other debris to the doors. I dumped her inside and crammed myself in there, continuing to hold my breath until the blast of air cleared out the trailing tendrils of fumes.

Gasping, I dropped my hands, still in their sleeves, onto my knees and hung my head.

"You should have left me." Laura managed to get to her feet and stumbled out the second door into the locker room.

"Was that your plan? To get in there and kill yourself?" I had to gulp air to speak and my words lacked the true degree of pissed-off-ness I felt.

Laura shrugged. She peeled off her equipment and left it in a pile like a shed snakeskin. She slumped in front of the sink to dip her face under the stream.

Man, did I want to kill her myself.

"What the hell was that?" I kicked off my suit and stalked to her side. Dropping my hands onto the counter, I glared at her.

She just shook her head and looked away. Tears gathered in her eyes, clotting her already mussed mascara.

Damn it, she was a mess. And for good reason. I hadn't helped with that. Sucking in a deep breath, I forced my anger back. I couldn't make this worse. She'd helped me, and Luke, and had saved Mark's life. Even if she went about it all wrong, she wasn't evil. My shoulders slumped and I leaned up against the counter.

"Look, I'm not going to let anything happen to you. Got that? You'll get out of the country. Find somewhere else to make a life."

Laura's eyes snapped to mine. "Right. While all my research will be discredited. While I never get to work in a lab again. And I'll be really lucky if I don't face extradition if I ever visit a country with a decent science program. They ruined my life. Ruined me." Her shoulders shook as she attempted to wrestle her emotions into check.

I wrapped my arms around her, petting her head as hot tears seeped through my sweater. "It's going to be okay." The words rang false, even to me.

She sniffled and shook her head but remained silent. I wanted to remind her she'd had a choice to go to the authorities ages ago. That it had been her decision not to, to keep quiet about what was going on. Even if she'd managed to find an effective treatment against the infection, she made the choice to keep herself from those who would want to take her to trial.

If Lexi and Theo had their way, she'd be sitting in some FBI interrogation room, and her bosses would have released the pathogen before she figured out a cure. Still, I wished I'd come up with a better plan for this job, had pieced everything together sooner, better, so that she hadn't ended up in the crosshairs. I think that just made me even more frustrated. At myself, not her.

"Look, let's get out of here, okay?"

Laura nodded and helped me wash my face and eyes with saline solution, which helped with the burning.

"You're lucky you didn't get more hurt. That stuff is really dangerous." She dabbed my face where the salt water trickled down my cheek.

"What is it?"

"Mustard gas, I think. Probably a few other things mixed in. Bleach doesn't go well with many of the chemicals in there."

We looked at the window to what used to be the lab. There wasn't much that could be seen past the glass, just swirling noxious yellow clouds. Gross. I'd escaped seeing much of that in World War I and was very grateful Luke requested we stay in San Francisco at that time.

Laura ended up piggyback again. We took the elevator down and left the building through a side door that led to a small grassy area with a picnic table under a few bedraggled eucalyptus trees.

I kept a firm grip under her knees and made it around the back of the building toward where we'd left Melody and my car.

Except that wasn't who met us. At least three police cars and a town car with the FBI agents pulled up next to the building.

I think my heart flipped backwards in my chest, trying to get the jump on where I needed to run. Fast.

"Shit." Laura echoed my thoughts.

"They just got here. Let's move before they cover the building," I said in a low voice.

Not that running with a full-grown woman on my back was easy, but now we had to track down Melody. I hadn't heard my phone and said a silent plea she hadn't been tailed.

# CHAPTER
## 40

**W**e made it all of two blocks of squat office buildings and ugly parking complexes before I had to stop. My breathing sounded like someone trying to start a lawnmower.

"What are we going to do?" Laura's voice whined like a mosquito.

We rested in an alcove reserved for a recycling dumpster, which smelled like cardboard. It didn't allow us to see out, but we were at least well hidden.

I pulled out my phone and was dismayed that Melody hadn't texted. Did I call her? Or would that draw too much attention?

We both screamed a little when my phone started to buzz in my hands.

"Oh, thank heavens." I hit the accept button and pressed it to my ear.

"Ami? Are you guys okay?" Melody's voice squeaked as she spoke.

"Yeah. We made it out. Where are you?"

"I'm so sorry I didn't call before. I saw the cops enter the lot and I had to go. I didn't want to make it obvious I was calling you on my way out. But I think they may have gotten the plate numbers on your car."

Of course they had. Shit. I rubbed a hand over my forehead and tried to plan out the next step. Laura had the vials. We had a few hours to get down to where they held Luke. What next? What next?

"Melody, we're going to come to you, but you should probably not stay in any one spot for long. And you're going to need to ditch the car."

We made plans to meet Melody a couple of blocks away, and after a quick sweep of the parking lot to ensure we were alone, set off at a brisk run toward her. I cloaked myself, but no way could I carry Laura any longer. She handed over the box of vials and accepted my light touch on her shoulder so she'd know where I was.

Sometime in the last couple of hours she'd come to trust me a little. That was both comforting and daunting. I had no idea if I'd be able to get myself out of this situation, let alone Luke, Melody, or her. After all that had happened, I felt a sense of obligation to ensure her safety, but Luke came first. He'd always come first.

Melody waited for us around the side of a gas station, tucked in next to the trash and air pump. She hadn't released her death grip on the steering wheel.

I crouched next to the driver's window and dropped my cloak.

"You're not coming with us, are you?" Melody's voice didn't rise above a whisper. Her eyes were huge and I reached through the open window to give her a hug. I tried not to think about the chance I'd never see her again. The very real possibility this would be it. Because, just, no. It couldn't be. I'd get to say a proper goodbye later.

"I can't. You two have to get to safety. Ditch the car after you clear out anything with a name on it. Make sure there aren't any cameras. One of those crappy lots where you pay without an attendant will probably work. Then take the bus back to my place. Okay?"

Melody managed a weak grin. "We can do that."

"Where are you going?" Laura clambered into the passenger's seat, her brows drawn together in concern.

"I have to get my partner back. You two should be safe at my place for a bit. When I get Luke, we'll figure something out."

The two women looked at one another then back at me and nodded in unison. I grinned. They were smart, resourceful. If anyone could lay low for a few hours, it would be them.

The real question was whether or not I'd manage to get Luke out of this. If the tables were turned and Luke had to save me, I wouldn't doubt him for an instant. But I had to believe I could do this. Trust myself and my ability to get in and out of difficult places. If this job taught me anything it was that if I could just do that, the rest would work out. Hopefully.

Waving as Melody pulled out of the lot, I dropped my cloak back around myself and took a deep breath. Now for the fun part.

)X(

I caught a bus for several stops in the opposite direction of where we'd been, just in case someone tracked us. Getting off in a neighborhood that made me super grateful I was invisible, I walked around until I found a little alley where I could safely use Luke's phone. After making sure no one was around, I ducked into the relative privacy of a backyard.

Lexi and Theo had left their number as the only contact in Luke's list. I held my breath as it rang three times.

"Well, seems like you made good time," Lexi's voice came through loud and obnoxious.

"I have what you want. Where did you want me to meet you?" I already knew, but I needed them to say it.

Lexi's joy seemed to leak through the connection, as noxious as the gas back at the lab. She listed the address I'd found before. The hotel where Luke and I found their trashed room. Guess they were still staying there.

"I'll be there in a half hour. Be ready to hand over Luke." I ended the call before Lexi could drive me any more insane.

I closed my eyes and leaned against the yard's rickety gate. My headache had returned and I rummaged for more meds in my purse; they stuck to my throat as I forced them down. I needed sleep and a shower.

More than anything, I needed my partner.

"You can do this," I whispered to myself. I had to.

Taking mass transit downtown took longer than I wanted it to. I walked from near the diner where we'd met those few nights, what felt like years ago. Evening had just about given in to night and the fog thickened to drown everything in a damp grey.

There was no time to appreciate the growing quiet of the city, the shush of traffic on the wet pavement. I all but ran toward the hotel, the small Styrofoam box of vials wedged into my giant bag where it rattled with each footfall. Laura had better of gotten the right kind just in case this all went to hell. I really didn't want to be responsible for unleashing something horrible, even second-hand.

Even if it meant I lost Luke, or myself.

I'd never be able to live with myself if we killed so many people. Without even having to consider it, I knew Luke would feel the same.

The marquee cut through the gloom and I slowed to force deep breaths into my lungs and wipe the sweat from my brow. The closer I got, the slower my feet went. If this all fell apart, would this be the last time I was outside? The last time I saw the city I'd come to call home?

Shaking my head, I refused to let myself think like that. I had to do this. Luke was inside there and I'd be damned if anything else happened to him.

Cloaked, I slipped past the doorman, asleep, and into the lobby. I took the stairs and cursed every last one of them. Why the hell couldn't they be staying on the second floor instead of the seventh?

The hallway was just as I remembered it—all mirrors and garish patterns. There must have been a factory somewhere that designed hotel hallway carpet and they must have provided some good drugs to their workers. That was the only explanation for the globs of colors that looked a lot like a lava lamp on overdrive.

Room 709's door opened before I had a chance to knock. Goose bumps rippled up my back as it swung to reveal a slightly improved version of what we'd seen before. Most of the furniture had been repaired or replaced, though now it all sat against the wall.

Theo blocked the doorway and grinned down at me like I was some kind of favored child bearing gifts. I wanted to kick him in the balls.

Instead I extracted the box from my bag. Standing in the hallway, I opened it and held up a single vial of the nasty stuff and shoved it in front of his face.

He reached out to take it, but I swooped back. "Look but don't touch. I'm not handing this over until you give me Luke."

As if on cue, Luke called my name from inside the room before someone or something stifled his voice.

It took my fingers cutting into the dense Styrofoam to keep me from launching past Theo's bulk. Rage dotted the hallway red before several deep breaths cleared it.

"Let me see," Lexi pushed her partner out of the way and I held the vial up to allow her to look it over. It was all I could do to keep my hands from shaking.

Finally, with a nod of satisfaction, Lexi motioned to Theo. He disappeared into the room and returned a minute later with Luke supported on his shoulder.

I sucked in a hard breath at the sight of him. The cuts I'd seen in the video had started to heal, replaced by nasty green and yellow bruising that ran under his skin down his neck. His eyes were alert though and he looked like he could mostly carry himself. Maybe not take the stairs, but I could at least get him home.

His grin at the sight of me looked like it hurt. My knees shuddered beneath me. How could anyone hurt such a man?

"Oh, gods, I thought I'd lost you." I whispered into his chest and pulled him in so close he winced. It was going to take a crowbar to get us apart any time soon.

"We have to get out of here," he thought.

My vision went blurry at the familiar sound of his thoughts. I'd never thought I'd miss them so much. "Are they really just going to let us go?" I asked.

"I very much doubt it."

Keeping an arm around Luke's waist, I handed Theo the box. "What are you going to do now?" I asked.

Lexi laughed. "You'll see."

With that, she tugged on Theo's hand and drew him back into the hotel room. The door slammed shut behind her and we found ourselves alone in the hallway.

Something didn't sit well with me. That had been freakishly easy. Something else was up.

# CHAPTER
# 41

Luke's eyes met mine, his gaze almost a caress. The sight of him made anxiety in my gut begin to unwind. I stood up on my toes and pressed my lips to his. "Thank the gods you're okay."

Luke closed his eyes and rocked back on his heels, his eyes closed as his fingers tangled in my hair. "Let's get the hell out of here. We have to figure out how to stop them," he thought, urging us toward the elevator.

I was never so grateful when the doors slid shut and we were alone in the little box. Luke half leaned on me and I had him in a bear hug, wrapped around his middle. I didn't dare shift his weight in case I touched some part of him that hurt.

"How come I couldn't hear you?" I asked as we watched the lit numbers flicker from floor to floor back to the ground.

"They did something. I don't even know what it was. A patch they put on the back of my neck. It kept me from responding." The strain in his tone drew my eyes to his.

"You could hear me?" I asked. Why that made things so much worse, I couldn't explain, but it did.

Luke brushed the loose strands of hair from my messy bun back from my face. "I knew you were okay."

Swallowing hard, I really wished we were alone at my place, because all I wanted to do was kiss away everything that happened in the past couple of days.

"Laura, she's okay?" Luke asked, worry creasing his forehead.

"She's okay. With Melody at my place." I thought to tell him more, to explain how we'd need to get her out of the country, but his next words stopped me.

"I should have listened to you. Gods, I should have. You always sense the way things should be." His hands cupped my face and he touched his forehead to mine. "I know better than to doubt when you sense something's off."

My throat tightened. All this time, centuries, I'd assumed Luke hated it when I got my little 'feelings'. That I didn't lead with my head, but with my heart. I'd always assumed Luke went along with things just to put up with me, but maybe I'd been wrong.

I opened my mouth to say something, but the elevator reached the ground floor and the doors rattled open, revealing the old-fashioned lobby.

It was now decorated with at least thirty men in SWAT riot gear.

Melody and Laura stood out as the only normal people in the middle of the crowd of flack gear, helmets, and bug-eyed goggles.

"I'm going to kill her." I stepped out onto the plush Oriental carpet with Luke next to me.

Lexi was toast. Screw getting her captured. I was going to take great pleasure in kicking her ass.

The two FBI agents stood next to Melody and Laura, smug with their goggles trained on us.

"You might as well become visible. We can all see you." Agent Ramirez stepped in front of the mass of cops. He was not much taller than Melody and the grin he wore reminded me a little of Napoleon. Short man syndrome, plain and simple.

"Why?" Luke asked. He stood up straight, though a flash of pain pinched his eyes closed. He took my hand and we walked forward to greet the assembly.

Ramirez chuckled. "Your little game is over. And unless you cooperate, your friends here will be in jail for a very long time."

Melody's expression blanched and Laura muttered something that sounded like a string of curses.

"We can't let them do that to Melody," I thought at Luke, careful not to look at him. I had no idea if they knew we could communicate telepathically, or if they could tap into it, but I wasn't about to make it obvious.

"Their involvement is unnecessary in this proceeding. Let them go." Luke didn't look like he was about to back down as he motioned to the confused Melody and Laura. When he moved toward the group, several of the officers fell back, exchanging glances and shifting their grip on their weapons.

"They must not know much about us," Luke said.

"Let's just avoid getting shot, yeah?"

"Give yourselves up and we'll see to it that they're taken care of," Ramirez said.

"No deal. Let them go first." Luke had stood with way too many armies. He tried to draw a low profile, but when he wanted to, he could be pretty damn powerful. His height, broad shoulders, and deep rumbling voice conveyed the truth; he wasn't pulling any punches. No way were the agents getting away with this.

Agent Connic whispered in her partner's ear, and with a huff of a sigh, they motioned toward Melody and Laura. It took less than a minute for the cuffs that held them to be loosened and for them to be led toward the doors.

I let out a little sigh of relief. Even if I had no idea how Luke and I would get out of this mess, at least we wouldn't have two more lives to worry about.

Through a part in the crowd, I saw Melody stumbled outside and push off the helping hand of a cop before flipping him off and stomping off down the street.

Laura looked like she was about to follow her before she turned and peered back inside. I was still cloaked, but somehow she seemed able to locate my face in the crowd. Even with the distance and dirty glass between us, I could see emotion flash across her features.

With that, she flung the door back open and stepped inside. "You know, they're not the ones you want. They've only been trying to help with this whole fucking mess." Her voice rose in a strangled shout.

There was a clanking, clattering wave of sound as everyone shifted to look at her. She ducked her head and ran a hand through her frazzled mess of hair. With a deep breath, she squared her shoulders and pushed through the group, coming back to the agents. Ramirez fingered the cuffs at his side, like he itched to latch them back on her.

"It's not them. They've only tried to stop things. The real ones you want are upstairs. Ami's been trying to stop them the whole time. Make sure they didn't have the real vials."

"What in the hell are you talking about?" Ramirez crossed his arms and looked between Luke, me, and back to Laura.

"We're not the ones you want. There's another partnership upstairs. They've been using you for ages. Go check room 709 if you don't believe us," I said.

The female agent pursed her lips and gestured for two of the uniformed guys with guns to check it out. They slipped up the stairs with cat-like silence.

Too bad I wouldn't be there to see them take down Lexi and Theo. That would have popcorn-worthy.

"And how do you know this?" Agent Connic asked while she looked Laura over like she might pull out a syringe filled with plague right then and there.

"Because she's with us." A tall, grey-haired man pushed inside the lobby and made his way toward Laura.

I recognized him from last night and the CDC crews outside Laura's building. He frowned at the agent's goggles and the hand he clapped on Laura's shoulder didn't seem 100% friendly.

Laura cringed but didn't make a run for it.

"What the hell are you all looking at?" the man asked, peering around the empty area in front of the elevators where Luke and I stood.

I rolled my eyes at Luke and he smirked.

Someone toward the back of the group handed forward some goggles, which the man donned and peered around the room, doing a double-take when he caught sight of us.

"Boo!" I thought and Luke snorted a laugh.

"Wait, you seem familiar," the man said. "You were there last night. You helped get the cop to safety, right?" How he pieced that together from the blurs of orange and red that our faces must have looked like was beyond me, though maybe these goggles were more high-tech than that. Still, I edged a few inches close to Luke.

Connic gave us a quizzical glance and Laura stumbled into an explanation of last night's events.

"You should really read my report of our progress with this case," the grey-haired man admonished, arms crossed.

"You really shouldn't interfere with our business," Ramirez pushed back into the conversation, hanging up a call and dropping his phone into his pocket. He glared at the CDC guy who just shrugged and guided

Laura toward the front door.

"Wait! You really don't have the right people," she called back.

Laura flashed a panicked look in Luke's and my direction, but had no choice than to be led out by the other scientist.

So much for her getting out of the country. A heavy weight settled across my shoulders at the thought of what she'd given up. Her whole situation was a maddening confusion of no good choices.

Two faint gun reports from above us settled a hush across the room.

"Oh no!" I covered my mouth, bile rising. I brokered no love for Lexi or Theo, but I didn't want them dead. Well, not really. Tortured, maybe. That lasted longer.

As if the shots were some kind of order shouted amongst the assembled men, everyone snapped to attention with aimed guns and shifting gear, focusing back on Luke and me.

"We're going to get out of the way of the elevator and stairs," Luke announced.

When no one responded, we made our way with careful, deliberate steps toward the far wall near the concierge desk. Several men kept their eyes on us, like they knew we planned on making a break for it.

Ramirez's radio crackled to life. "We're coming down. Two suspects. One's injured. Call an ambulance."

The words made me gasp and tighten my grip on Luke's already sweaty palm.

The elevator dinged and everyone watched as the little gold light marked off each of the floors down to us.

Several of the men had swarmed up the stairs earlier and now returned to flank the doors, guns up and faces unreadable behind their masks. I swear the whole room held its breath as the elevator opened.

Lexi and Theo, both cloaked, were supported by the men inside. Lexi had her hands cuffed behind her back and Theo slumped against the other agent, crimson blood soaking his t-shirt so that it stuck to his broad chest. A hole sputtered blood from his throat, a wound that even we couldn't survive. A low groan made it past my lips.

The rest of the men in the room broke into action. Several came to guard us while others went to help get Theo stretched out on the floor. Others kept Lexi between them.

The agents fought their way through the assembled mass, elbows flying, until they reached the other partnership.

Something in the way Connic held herself said she recognized Lexi. How long had they been pushing these agents? Getting them to do their bidding? And how much did the agents suspect? It was anyone's guess, but if I were to bet on it, I'd put good money on Connic knowing more than she let on from her pinched expression.

"I'd bet on Ramirez, too," Luke thought at me, frowning as we watched the room swarm with armed men and women. They reminded me of gnats.

Paramedics were wrestling with the front door and their gurney when Lexi gasped. Loud. Enough to draw everyone's attention to her petite form, bent double with her long blonde hair sweeping the carpet.

"No!" She screeched and broke free of the two guards holding her. She stumbled toward Theo's prostrate form, her hands still secured behind her.

The other agents stood back and watched with wide eyes.

From where I stood, I could see an unmistakable stillness in Theo. No breath lingered in his body.

Lexi looked around wildly. "Someone help him! You've got to do something!"

But it was too late. Her cloak began to unravel like a sweater with a loose thread and Lexi became visible to everyone in the room. Theo did too. Several of the armed guys removed their goggles to watch as Lexi's petite form emerged inch by inch. Starting from the crown of her head, face, body became visible. Her hair spilled forward as she rested her forehead against the man she loved and sobs shook her slim shoulders.

What was worse was her expression. Even in the dim faux-lamplight of the lobby it was possible to see how pale she was.

In slow-motion Lexi slumped to the side, her head coming to rest on Theo's arm with a little bounce.

No life resided in her eyes.

In the second of calm after Lexi's life leaked out of her, her body became swathed in darkness. It seemed to leak out of her, pooling in the air above her chest like a shadowy cloud. Theo had the same, though not quite as midnight black as Lexi's. The darkness wound together, twisting in a sinuous cloud, before popping into nothing.

I doubt anyone else in the room saw what Luke and I did. If they did, and managed not to react to it, I'd be impressed, because I held Luke's hand in a death grip.

Luke's dark eyes met mine, shock at what we'd seen evident there.

"I hope I never see anything like that again," Luke thought. I could only agree.

# CHAPTER
## 42

The paramedics fought their way through the doors and raced over, going to work on the bodies in a flurry of activity. Everyone in the room knew it was too late.

Swallowing hard to try and wash down the lump in my throat, I pressed into Luke, grateful for his strong arms around me. I wanted to sink to the ground and sob.

"We're not out of this mess," Luke thought at me. "Keep it together."

He was right, even if it sucked.

Pandemonium broke loose once more as the uniforms backed away or tried to help the paramedics take care of the bodies. The guards watching us were distracted by the events and two of them removed their goggles to better watch the show.

"Ready?" I asked. It was now or never if we wanted to make a break for it.

Luke nodded.

A door opened to the office portion of the ground floor just to the side of the concierge desk. I'd noticed it when we'd been here before. When no one was looking at us, we backed away. Luke reached the door first and edged it open so we could slip through.

Beyond was a series of dim little offices and a laundry room that made the whole place smell like detergent. Luke leaned against me as we raced down the hall. We nearly reached the back exit when the lobby door crashed open behind us.

"Stop!" One of the armed guys shouted. I spared him a glance but had no intention of listening.

The heavy back door swung open like molasses but we managed to get through it and into the blackness of the back alley. A cop car blocked the single exit to the left and Luke tugged us toward the right. A solid wall of dark stood there, taking on the shape of a concrete barrier, taller than my head.

"Luke! There's no way to get out!" I screeched while I tried to pull him in the other direction. The cop from the cruiser peered into the alley, with a glint of goggles catching the light.

Shit. Just shit, shit, shit.

"Stop! Hands where I can see them." The cop boomed down the passage, his voice echoing around us.

Neither of us paid attention. The cop yelled again, but Luke tugged me toward the black wall to trap us in. The sound of a gun going off made us both duck low. The bullet pinged off the wall ahead of us and I caught my whimper of fear before it escaped.

"They're going to corner us!" I shouted at Luke, panic bubbling up and over as the cop continued to screech and I waited for another bullet to find us.

"Here." Luke pressed on my shoulder and motioned toward a darker square of blackness ahead of us. I reached toward it. Nothing met my fingertips and I crouched down into the cubbyhole with Luke's breath warm on my neck.

The small opening went all the way through the wall, not more than a few feet. A latched wooden door took ages to open but emitted us into a patio area set up between the tall buildings.

"It belongs to the hotel." Luke pushed the gate closed behind us and wedged a lounge chair in for added measure.

"You couldn't have known that was there!" I pressed both palms against Luke's chest, half wanting to pull him closer, half wanting to push him back against the wall. No way had he known where we were going.

There were a few low lights scattered around and I could just make out Luke's sheepish expression. "Well, no, not really. It just seemed like the thing to do."

"So you're the one listening to your instincts now?" I rolled my eyes. No way would I let on how annoying that had been, or would be in the future. Payback was a bitch.

I threw my hands up and started looking for another exit. Adrenaline still sang in my veins and we had maybe thirty seconds before that cop got through the gate and started shooting at us at close range.

There was a more solid door on the other side of the patio, beyond the smattering of tables and folded umbrellas. We hurried over and pushed through to the bustling sidewalk on the other side.

The commotion at the hotel had drawn a crowd. No one paid any attention to the door opening as Luke and I merged with the group of people who tried to catch a peek at the city's police force amassed with their lights flashing, with several large trucks from the FBI and CDC added to the mix.

It took exactly ten seconds for someone to step on my toes.

So not one of the perks of being invisible.

Doing our best to stay out of people's way, I led us back down the sidewalk, away from the group and bright lights. Things thinned out quick the farther we got, and within a block we were alone on the sidewalk.

We had, what, three minutes tops, before the armed guys made it down this street? Luke stumbled next to me as his injuries caught up with him. My heart rate, still competing with a hummingbird's, went up a notch. We had to find a way out of here.

"There's got to be somewhere to hide." I scanned the dark storefronts and debated which to break into.

"Is that my car?" Luke asked as we came up behind a dark sedan pulled over to the sidewalk, idling with the driver's window down.

We crept forward and just as we got close, Melody poked her head out of the driver's window. "Gotcha!"

I screamed, loudly, until Luke clapped a hand over my mouth.

Melody wore a pair of goggles that had to have been lifted from the crowd back at the hotel.

"Get in you two, we're getting the hell outah here!"

She flung open the door and got out, her hands on her hips and a very self-satisfied grin on her face.

"You've got to be kidding me." Luke laughed and shook his head as he grabbed Melody into a hug.

"Seriously, let's go!" Melody pushed Luke toward the car and he slid behind the wheel with a grimace.

"You going to be able to drive?" I asked while I got into the passenger's seat.

"Yeah. I think." He managed a little smile.

Melody plopped into the back seat. "I knew you two were going to get out of there. And what's the fun of being a getaway driver if I flake out?"

I twisted around to peer into the back seat and shook my head at Melody, while Luke peeled away from the curb. "I swear you have some kind of death wish."

"What? They have nothing on me. You got them to let me go. And there's no way they can pin anything on me."

I laughed because I really hoped she was right.

"Where to?" Luke asked.

I leaned back against the cool of the leather and wished I didn't have to think about it. There was nothing I wanted to contemplate other than a bed and maybe a shower. With Luke.

"You're going to drop me back by the house. But where are you two going?" Melody asked, her exuberance dampened.

I met her eyes in the dimness of the car and hated that we had to say goodbye for good. No way would Luke and I be welcome in the City by the Bay from here on out. Maybe in a few centuries we could come back, when no one was looking for us.

"I think we're headed south. We'll let you know when we figure it out."

Luke reached over and took my hand. Neither of us were happy about leaving. This was home. But we would manage. We'd had plenty of practice. "At least this time we'll be doing this together," I thought.

Most of our other moves had been done alone, with only basic coordinating on timing and location.

"True. And will involve finding just one new house."

I raised a brow. "You think you're moving in?"

Luke sputtered for a moment. "Well, I mean, I don't know. I just thought maybe…"

"Come on you two, no silent convo's around me, okay?" Melody chided from the back seat.

"The only way we're getting a place together, wherever, is if it has two showers. And a giant hot water tank," I said aloud.

Luke laughed, shaking his head. "Fine. I think we can manage that."

Melody squealed in the back seat and clapped her hands. "Oh, you two are just so cute!"

I stuck my tongue out at her, both of us giggling.

"We'll remember who got Ami out of at least one of her stubborn ruts," Luke noted.

"Psha, and you out of yours, by the way," I glared at Luke. It was much easier to tease than what I wanted to do: sob at the thought of Melody not living in my upstairs.

Melody gave me an evil grin and pushed Luke's shoulder. "Sheesh. How long did you make him wait for you?"

I glanced at Luke, worrying my bottom lip. She was right. We'd waited far too long to be together. That would wear on me for a long time to come—a constant reminder that I needed to listen to myself.

"I'd have waited another century, if I had to. Wouldn't have liked it, but if there were no other way, I would have done it," Luke said.

That tipped me over some ledge inside and tears started to prick. A minute later I was wiping my eyes on my sleeves and wishing I could get myself under control.

All too soon we pulled up in front of my place. Luke figured we had about five minutes before the cops, FBI, or both showed up. I would have put money on both. We'd pissed off plenty of people today—a new record.

We raced inside and Luke grabbed his bags, already packed. I'd thrown most of my vital belongings and documents into a suitcase earlier, but walking from room to room reminded me of so much more I wanted to take.

"You can always call me and I'll mail you anything," Melody said, sneaking into my bedroom where I wrestled one last trinket into my bag.

I looked up at her and a fresh wave of tears overwhelmed me. My sleeves were still damp from the last batch. "I have something for you."

"No way. I just want you to not be a stranger, okay? I'm going to need to chat. Like, a lot." Her voice wobbled but she took a deep breath and managed a little smile.

272

I picked up the envelope I'd put together earlier, extricating it from the pile of paperwork shoved in my purse. "This is something you'll want. I promise."

I held it out to her and she took it with a begrudging look. "What is it?"

I lugged my suitcase off the bed and heard Luke making phone calls in the other room. "Just open it."

Melody pulled out the small stack of papers. Her brow furrowed as she read.

"Nope. No way. Absolutely not." She thrust them at me like they burned her fingers.

"It's already signed over. I know the taxes will be a pain. But if you take in a few renters and charge them what would be standard for here, you should be able to make it work. And the check in there should cover things for a while, along with the rest of the paperwork. How you can handle the lovely Ms. Norris next door, well, that I'll leave up to you."

"I am not taking the house!" Melody followed me down the hallway, the paperwork still in her hands as she tried to foist it off on me.

"Too late!" I laughed. Luke waited by the door and ran my things down to the trunk of his car.

"I'll call you as soon as we get settled. And be sure to turn off the lights downstairs, okay? No one needs to know we were here."

Melody sobbed for real and I couldn't keep it in check any longer. Wrapping her in a hug, we rocked on the sidewalk, my face buried in her shoulder. I got snot and salt all over her sweater, but I couldn't help it.

"The tea recipe's in there, too," I whispered, unable to speak easily around the tears that clogged my throat.

Melody's wet eyes met mine and she managed little nod, her lip caught in her teeth.

Luke stepped up behind me and wrapped his long arms around us all. "We need to get out of here or they'll detain Melody." He took my arm as we broke apart.

"Call me." Melody mimed it with her hand while she used her other sleeve to staunch her tears.

"Don't let the cops bug you!" I said. "I'll keep in touch!"

I let Luke guide me to the car and settled into the passenger's seat. He waved goodbye once more and closed his door. A grimace of pain flashed over his features as he fixed his seatbelt.

"Ready?" he asked as we waved at Melody standing in front of her house.

"I think so," I whispered. "I hope so."

As we made our way to the freeway, Luke took my hand and pressed my fingers to his lips.

"I think we have an amazing adventure ahead of us." His eyes met mine and despite the tears a smile tugged at my lips.

"I think you're right."

# 2 YEARS LATER
# EPILOGUE

**M**elody stepped off the private jet and shaded her eyes against the tropical sun. She rummaged in her purse for some giant vintage sunglasses to complete her outfit that was at least fifty years older than she was.

"Some things never change," Luke said with a laugh.

We waited until she navigated the narrow stairs down to the tarmac before I crushed her in a giant hug. Luke did the same and Melody choked back tears before she managed to speak.

"Hard life you've got going here." A giggle made its way through her sniffles and she motioned to the brilliant blue sky and warm breeze that reminded us the beach wasn't far.

"Someone's gotta do it." I grabbed one of her bags while Luke took the other.

My Range Rover waited for us and Luke took a seat in the back so

Melody could join me up front.

"Air conditioning, please!" She twisted all the vents toward her. "I'm going to melt!"

"Give it a day or two," Luke noted. "Or a few years," he added for my benefit. Neither of us had adjusted from the constant cool of San Francisco to the heat of Rio de Janeiro. The sunshine was a bonus though and both of us found ourselves outside as much as possible. Even though there were times I missed the fog and atmosphere of the Bay.

We chatted and I pointed out the sights as we drove along. Melody soaked it all in, almost pressing her nose to the glass. Her barrage of questions would have made anyone think we hadn't spoken in ages, even though we'd spent at least an hour on the phone yesterday. She'd had to call and fill me in on Laura, who had taken the upstairs apartment after she was released on parole. She and Melody had an interesting love/hate thing going on, and Melody loved to dish on what her tenant was up to. Even if it was only to discuss how late Laura had been up the night before watching reruns of Buffy.

We pulled past our gate into our courtyard and Melody laughed.

"You guys live here? It isn't some kind of hotel?"

"It's only a hotel for the next week for you," I said.

It was a pretty sweet house. We'd found it soon after arriving and within a week we'd purchased it. The vista from the glass windows overlooked the South Atlantic and miles of beaches. I spent most mornings on the sand, watching the waves, and often Luke and I walked hand-in-hand along the surf in the evenings.

"So, what are you working on now?" Melody asked soon thereafter, her stuff stowed in the guest room and a fruity drink I'd perfected in hand. We lounged on the back deck, soaking in the sun and enjoying the breeze off the water. Melody had applied three coats of sunscreen, which I didn't begrudge her. She looked pasty enough to have been living in a cave for the past few years.

Luke glanced over at me, a wary look in his eyes. We'd debated what to say about this for hours yesterday, unable to come to a firm conclusion.

But, sitting here with Melody, I realized I had to say something. She needed to know, even if she protested. After all, she knew about us she deserved the whole truth.

"I'm going to tell her," I thought at Luke.

"I know. I really hope it doesn't backfire."

"Only one way to find out."

Luke didn't really have an answer for that and I turned to Melody. "Actually, I have a feeling you're really going to like what we're working on. Personally."

She slid her sunglasses down her nose, peering over them, and I wondered if she might throw her glass at me. "What does that mean?"

"That we have plans for tonight," Luke said.

Her mouth twitched as she debated what to say. Finally, she heaved a sigh. "I don't have much of a choice, do I?"

"Oh, you have a choice. But trust us on this. You're going to want to find out."

Luke and I had already met his mark. The man was here on vacation with a couple he was playing third-wheel to, which Luke got out of him in less than one beer. He lived in San Francisco and loved to read. The trick was getting him to meet Melody, which was why we had dinner reservations tonight for the four of us. It would be the easiest coincidence ever, so long as my mark, Melody, went along with it. I'd never had the same mark more than once, but somehow it fit that Melody would end up as one of my jobs again.

"This isn't something that's going to lead to me owning a house or driving a getaway car, is it?" She shoved her glasses back up and took a long draft from her drink.

"Nope. Nothing like that!" I couldn't help the grin I wore. I had had a hard time shaking it since the first images filtered in. Luke dubbed it my "matchmaker expression."

"Am I going to like it?"

Both Luke and I laughed. "Trust me, it's going to be amazing."

Luke met my eyes across the patio, neither of us needing words to know what the other was thinking. I could only hope that Melody would be as happy as we were, and I had a strong feeling she had nothing to worry about. The universe had willed it.

# ABOUT THE AUTHOR

 Meradeth Houston has been writing since she realized the sequel to a book she loved as a kid didn't exist...and she could tell the story herself. She's the person who got in trouble for reading her under desk in school or well after her bedtime. Stories are her passion and she can't live without them. She's especially attracted to tweaks to the real world–a little magic, a little extra boost to science that already exists, a little something beyond our day to day reality. Her stories integrate these themes and female heroines who know how to get the job done.

Meradeth lives in Montana where she's also an anthropology professor and scientist. If you let her, she'll tell you more than you ever wanted to know about getting DNA out of dead bodies and old poop. She specializes in degraded DNA (translation: really old DNA that's decayed), and runs two laboratories filled with students, interns, and maybe a few shenanigans. Her research is funded by NSF and National Geographic, where she's seeking to better understand the dynamic of past migration on human populations. Her goal is to someday clone herself because that's probably the only way she'll ever get through her to-do list. Though, who knows, maybe that'll mean she's donating to someone else's soul?

Other than teaching, research, and writing, Meradeth enjoys the lakes and ski slopes of Western Montana. It's not uncommon to find her haunting the cafes of Missoula. She is also a proud dog mom and represented by Cristi Marchetti.

CPSIA information can be obtained
at www.ICGtesting.com
Printed in the USA
FSHW010225241219
65393FS